LIGHT IN THE HARBOR

DON L. SEARLE

Deseret Book Company
Salt Lake City, Utah

Library of Congress Cataloging-in-Publication Data

Searle, Don L., 1944–
Light in the Harbor / Don L. Searle.
p. cm.
Summary: Religious differences threaten to break up the relationship between Jean, a devout Christian news reporter, and Ken, a young Mormon who rescued Jean from a dangerous situation.
ISBN 0-87579-528-5 (pbk.)
[1. Mormons—Fiction. 2. Texas—Fiction.] I. Title.
PS3569.E1765R4 1991
813′.54—dc20
[Fic] 91-17827
CIP
AC

Printed in the United States of America

10 9 8 7 6 5 4 3 2 1

To Marie, whose patience
made this possible, and to Amy, Sara,
Inez, and Patrick, who helped

Contents

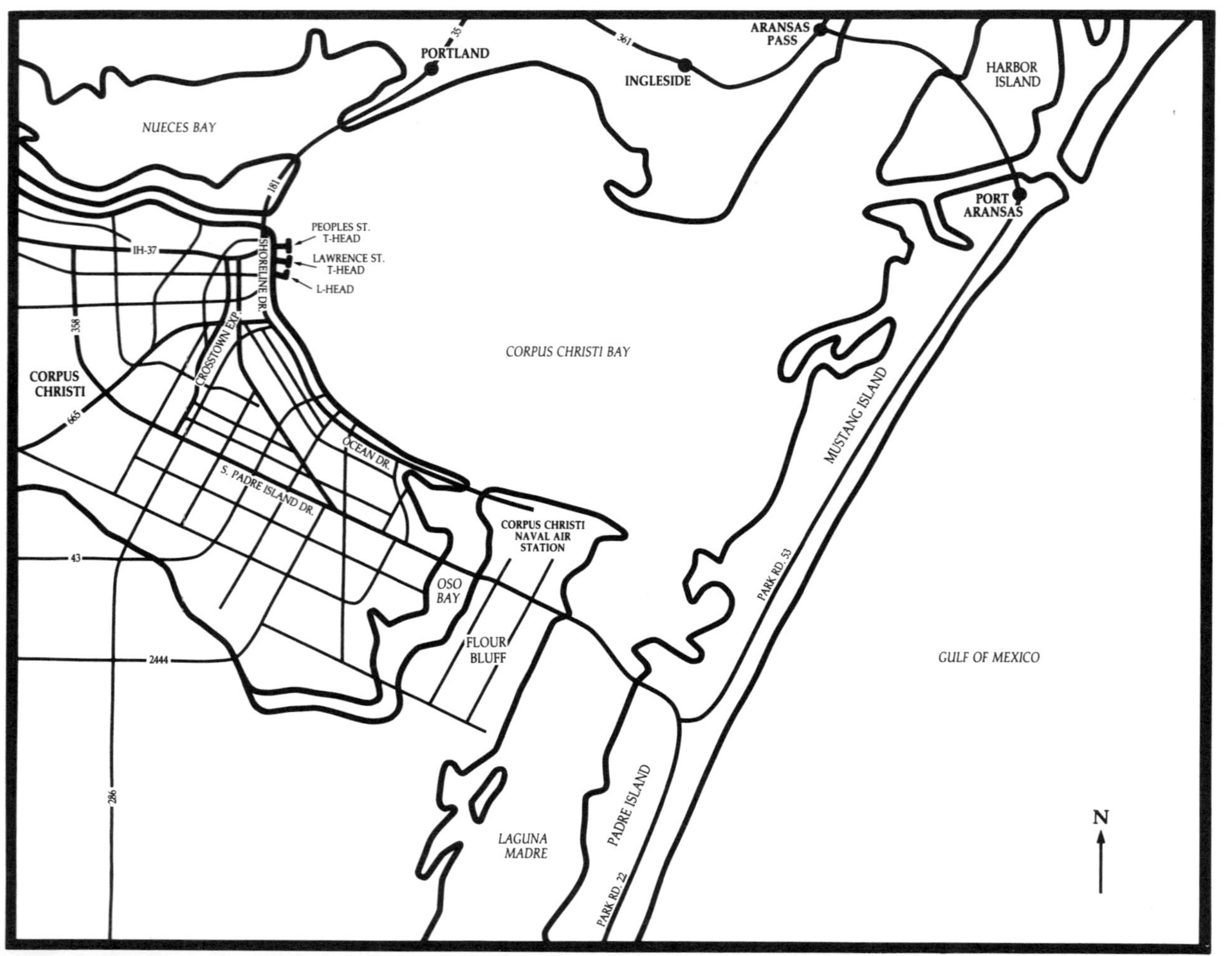
PORTLAND
35
361
ARANSAS PASS
INGLESIDE
HARBOR ISLAND
NUECES BAY
181
PORT ARANSAS
PEOPLES ST. T-HEAD
IH-37
LAWRENCE ST. T-HEAD
SHORELINE DR.
L-HEAD
358
CROSSTOWN EXP.
CORPUS CHRISTI BAY
CORPUS CHRISTI
665
MUSTANG ISLAND
OCEAN DR.
S. PADRE ISLAND DR.
CORPUS CHRISTI NAVAL AIR STATION
43
PARK RD. 53
OSO BAY
FLOUR BLUFF
2444
GULF OF MEXICO
PADRE ISLAND
286
N
LAGUNA MADRE
PARK RD. 22

1

Rescue

Three figures struggled beside the road in the glare of Ken McArthur's headlights. The tall one had his arms wrapped tightly around the woman, from behind. Her long blonde hair bobbed up and down as she struggled in the big man's bear hug; she aimed kick after kick at the smaller man, who danced around her, dodging.

Ken braked to a halt in the street, leaving the three blinded in the glare of his headlights. He shoved open the door of his Blazer and jumped to the ground.

"Let her go!" he commanded.

The smaller man backed away, leaning against the side of the woman's car, shading his eyes with one hand. The big one squinted against the lights. Then, as he made out the lone figure next to the four-wheel-drive vehicle, he slowly began to rotate toward Ken, still holding the woman.

"Let her go now!" Ken ordered, advancing toward the big man.

The man hesitated. He looked this intruder over carefully, and noted that Ken's arms hung loosely at his sides, hands empty.

The big man let out a deep chuckle. "Hitch," he said to his companion, "take care of this guy."

Hitch took two steps toward Ken, but Ken held up his right hand to stop him. "Stay where you are, little man. Your turn will come." Hitch slowed, then stopped. Ken's eyes never left the big man, but he seemed perfectly aware of Hitch's every move.

Hitch was about Ken's height, somewhat slimmer. But the big one was three or four inches taller than Ken, maybe forty pounds heavier.

"Have to hide behind a woman?" Ken challenged. "Afraid you can't take me yourself?" He kept his voice soft.

Slowly the big man's right hand went to his hip pocket. He withdrew the hand with a flip of his wrist, and the four-inch blade of his folding knife snapped open, locking in place.

Ken barely glanced at the knife. "You can put that away," he said coolly, "and I'll forget I saw it. Let her go."

The big man laughed with a deep rumble. Suddenly he flung the woman away, against her car, and lunged at Ken with the knife. He had no time to regret his decision. Before the woman could regain her balance, the man lay with the left side of his face pressed against the rear tire of her car, blood gushing from his nose. His right arm stretched out from his side, the wrist bent at an odd angle, the knuckles of his hand bloodied by the pavement.

Ken picked up the knife, which had fallen near his feet. Hitch retreated against the rear of the woman's car.

Ken motioned to the woman with his free hand. "Get into my truck," he said, keeping his eyes on the men. Quickly she climbed into the passenger side of the Blazer and slammed the door. Ken walked around the vehicle, climbed in, shut his own door, and reached across to lock hers.

"Hey!" Hitch called out, walking around to Ken's side of the

Blazer. "We saw her first." He reached into his jacket pocket and pulled out a small plastic bag full of powder. "Here, take this, and leave her with us."

Ken wanted to push Hitch's crooked, yellow teeth down his throat; the man deserved that, at least, for what the two of them probably had in mind for this woman. But there was no time; the big one was struggling to get up. The best thing to do was leave—quickly.

"Nah, she's mine now," Ken answered, grinning contemptuously. "You'd better get lost before some concerned citizen reports a kidnapping down here. The police will be looking for you two, not me."

The big man stood in the street screaming curses as Ken drove away. Ken drove two blocks south on Shoreline Boulevard, turned inland for a block, then doubled back toward the north. Four blocks up the street, he turned off the vehicle's headlights and drove down an alley that bisected the block. The alley emerged behind a small office building on Shoreline Boulevard.

Ken parked just far enough back in the alley to leave himself a view of the street, across the building's parking lot. In a few seconds, two figures made their way up Shoreline Boulevard from the direction of the woman's car. They were headed north, toward the entrance to the Port of Corpus Christi.

"Yeah, right." He chuckled. "There they go, clearing the area as fast as possible."

"Please . . . please don't hurt me," the woman murmured.

Ken turned toward her, startled. "What?"

"Please—let me go." Her voice quavered. "I won't tell anyone about this. Please don't hurt me."

He stared at her blankly. "What makes you think I want to hurt you?"

She glanced at the knife he still held in his hand.

Carefully, Ken closed the blade and dropped the knife into

his jacket pocket. "Hey, it's okay," he said, reaching out to pat the woman on the arm. Convulsively, she retreated against the far door.

"Look," he said patiently, "you're safe now. What's wrong?"

She stared at him with wide eyes. "What you said back there . . . "

"Oh—you mean that business about, 'She's mine'? You thought . . . "

Slowly she nodded.

"I'm sorry. The tough talk was on a level they could understand. I didn't mean to scare you too. I just wanted to give them something to think about so I could get you out of there safely."

She bowed her head, and her body shook with silent sobs.

"Hey, are you all right?" He hesitated. "Did they do anything to you?"

"No, you got there before they had a chance," she mumbled, rubbing her eyes with the back of her hand. In the illumination of a dim streetlight, Ken could see dark water spots on the front of the light-colored dress jacket she wore. "Thanks," she said, meeting his eyes.

"Don't mention it." He smiled at her, then turned on the headlights and eased the vehicle out of the alley.

"Where are you going?"

"Back to your car. I hope those guys were too busy getting away to go through it. Is there anything in it you need?"

"My purse and my keys," she answered, "if those two left them there."

The hood of her car was still up. "What's wrong with it?" Ken asked.

"I think it's probably just out of gas. It was low when I left for work, but I was late and didn't have time to get it filled. It turns over, and everything under the hood looks like it's connected. I was about to get back in and try it again when those two came out of the dark." She shuddered.

He tried to start her car, but couldn't. Emerging with her purse and keys, he sniffed under the hood, shut it, and returned to his own vehicle. "I think you're right about your car," he said, handing her the purse and keys.

Ken started the Blazer and drove south again until he could make a U-turn, then headed toward the high bridge spanning the entrance to the port.

"Where are you going now?"

"Police station." He turned onto the freeway approach. "We'd better report what happened."

She shuddered again.

He glanced sideways at her. In the glow of the streetlights, he could see the finely sculptured features of her face. Mascara streaked her left cheek, but she seemed composed now. "If you want me to," Ken offered, "I'll just take you home. But if we report this, it might save some other woman from the same situation."

"You're right," she said, sighing. "It's just that I'll probably have to tell some policeman everything those men said to me." She grimaced and shook her head, trying to erase the memory of the big man's words as he had held her. She brushed at her hair, trying to remove the stench of him. "I can still smell whatever he was drinking." Then she looked at Ken. "I'm sorry I fell apart on you back there. I'm not normally that emotional."

"It's understandable," he said. "What were you doing out so late?"

"I work for Channel 7. Tonight I did a live intro for one of my feature stories, and I was just going home after the newscast."

He parked in front of the police station and went around to open her door. She was out of the vehicle before he could get there. He stepped quickly ahead of her to open the door of the building.

The officer at the desk inside looked up and raised his eyebrows quizzically as they stopped in front of him. Ken waited for her to speak. She looked uncertainly at Ken.

"Her car stalled down on Shoreline Boulevard," Ken said. "While she was checking under the hood, two men grabbed her and tried to drag her off. They looked like merchant seamen."

"One of them had a knife, but he took it away," the woman added, glancing at Ken.

Grasping the knife carefully by one end, Ken withdrew it from his pocket and put it on the desk. "If there were any fingerprints on it, they're probably smudged," he said. "I think the guy I took it away from has a broken nose, and maybe a broken wrist."

The officer looked at Ken thoughtfully for several seconds and then at the woman. "Were you hurt, miss?"

"No."

"Can you describe the two men?"

"Not very well. He could do it better," she said, gesturing toward Ken.

"I'll have someone come and take your statements," the officer said, picking up the phone.

"You might have a female officer talk with her," Ken suggested. The policeman nodded.

Ken and the woman were ushered into separate rooms to make their statements. But Ken arrived back at the front desk a little before she did. "Everything okay?" Ken asked when she came back a minute later.

"Fine," she said, smiling at him.

It was the first smile he had seen from her. The dull beige walls of the room suddenly seemed brighter. If this woman's teeth were really nature's handiwork, she had the most perfect set ever grown. She wore a light gray dress jacket over a ruffled blue blouse and a pair of dark slacks. Her clothes were well-tailored but loose-fitting. Even so, there was no disguising her near-perfect shape. In the starkness of the police station, she stood out like the one perfect shell Ken had sometimes seen amid a pile of flotsam at the beach.

"Miss," the policeman at the desk said, "we'll have an officer give you a ride home."

"What about her car?" Ken inquired.

"I guess it will have to stay where it is till morning. She can pick it up tomorrow."

"If you leave *that* car there till morning, it's going to be ripped off, and you'll just have another case on your hands," Ken replied. "Do you have a gallon of gasoline around here anywhere?"

"Probably."

"Why don't you have your officer take her to her car? He can put the gas in and then follow her home."

"Thanks," she said, smiling at him again. "And thanks for being a lifesaver tonight."

"Anytime," Ken replied. It was a poor choice of words. She winced slightly, and Ken flushed. "I mean—I hope you never have to go through anything like that again. But if there's anything else I can do to help—"

"Miss," the policeman at the desk interrupted, "we have an officer waiting for you out front."

Ken followed the police car back to Shoreline Boulevard and parked behind it as the officer put gasoline into her car. She started it and was gone down the boulevard, with the police car following.

Ken drove toward one of the massive concrete jetties on the waterfront where his boat was moored with the small pleasure craft.

Since the years just before World War II, three huge concrete jetties have jutted out into Corpus Christi Bay from Shoreline Boulevard, along the downtown waterfront. From the air, the jetties look like a giant L, attached to the boulevard at its top, and two giant Ts, attached at their bases. The jetties take their names from their shapes—the "L-head" and two "T-heads."

Beyond them lies the intermittent breakwater known simply as "the Rocks." Built even before the T-heads, the Rocks are long strips of boulders laid in a broken arc in the bay. They take some of the punch out of waves rolling toward the jetties and offer limited protection from tidal waves, like the one that devastated the city's waterfront during the hurricane of 1919. Oil tankers and freighters, gliding down the channel that runs through a break in the Rocks, pass under the high, silver bridge to enter the Port of Corpus Christi. For decades, fishermen have whiled away calm mornings or afternoons out on the strips of the Rocks connected to land.

Ken's boat, an older cabin cruiser, was docked at the landward corner of the cross arm on one of the T-heads; from its berth, there was a nearly unobstructed view of the downtown skyline.

The woman was just stepping off the boat when Ken drove up and parked at the end of the pier that led to it.

"Hi," she called. "I was looking for you."

"That's the best thing anybody has told me all day long," Ken replied, walking down the short pier to meet her. He stepped onto the boat and held out his hand to help her step down again in her high heels. "Please—sit down," he invited. Cushioned benches ran along below the rail on both sides of the boat's stern; he motioned toward the one nearest her.

She sat. "Mr. McArthur—"

"It's Ken. And I didn't get your name last night."

"Jean. Jean Bradley."

"How did you find out my name and where I live?"

"I'm a reporter, remember? I checked the police report. You have an intriguing address: *Rum Runner,* Pier 18, Peoples St. T-head." She smiled. "The journalist in me is dying to know how your boat got its name."

"It's a short story, but for you I'll make it long."

Ken realized his assessment of her beauty last night had fallen short of reality. She sat with her head tilted back to look up at him. Her long golden hair cascaded off her shoulders and down over her silky tan blouse. The afternoon sun lighted her face so that it shone. She had the kind of face he really liked, oval, not too narrow and not too full.

"So, about your boat?" she asked.

"Oh—yeah. The name *Rum Runner* was my granddad's private joke on the world. He came out of the stock market crash in 1929 fairly well off by comparison with everyone else because his money was in the right places. The rumors went around town that he was doing so well because he was involved in running illegal liquor from down in Mexico. The truth is that he never touched a business deal that wasn't completely honest. But when he finally got the boat he'd always wanted, he couldn't resist winking at the legend."

"Sounds like a very interesting man. So, this is your grandfather's boat?"

"Mine, now. He left it to me when he died seven months ago. He knew it wouldn't mean as much to anyone else in the world." Ken glanced around the boat. "I must have been about six years old when I used to kneel on the cushions, right there where you're sitting, and fish. My grandfather would have to keep telling me to leave my line in the water for a while. I'd cast it out ten feet and reel it in, cast it out and reel it in."

She was watching him intently, and Ken realized that he had more than answered her original question. He laughed nervously. "And now you know a lot more than you really wanted to know."

"No, not at all. That's a touching story. You must have loved your grandfather very much."

Her relaxed manner and what seemed like genuine interest made it easy for him to tell her things that he might not have said to anyone else. She was probably very good as a journalist, he thought.

"My grandfather was as close to a real father as I had," Ken answered. "When he died, I was living in a little one-room apartment out by the refineries." He smiled broadly. "I mean, it was *so-o-o* small that I could sit up in bed and shave at the bathroom sink." Her laughter made him feel good. "Since I had to maintain the *Rum Runner* anyway, I figured I might as well live down here, where it's pleasanter. Would you like the grand tour of the boat?"

"There's more?" she said, smiling. "Of course."

"Right this way to the grand salon, miss." Stepping under the canopy that covered the wheel area, Ken held the cabin door open for her to peer in. She could see part of a narrow bunk against one wall and a set of drawers built into the bulkhead beyond it.

"I'm impressed," she said. "Do most bachelors keep house so neatly?"

"I can't speak for most bachelors. It's a habit I picked up in the Marine Corps. Always keep a shipshape bunk, ready for inspection."

"That's an interesting black-and-white print," she said, gesturing toward a large photo propped up by the bunk. "May I go see it up close?"

"Sure." He stood back to let her descend the three steps into the cabin.

Just around the corner to her left as she reached the bottom of the steps was a small ledge with a hot plate on it. On her right, the polished wood paneling of the cabin's entryway extended farther, apparently enclosing a small toilet. Portholes above the bunks on both sides of the cabin let in some daylight.

She picked up the sixteen-by-twenty print to examine it more closely. The composition was simple. Slender stalks of sea grass grew in an arc from the smooth top of a high, white dune. In the background, cottony clouds puffed up in a complementary arc against a dark sky. She studied the photo, then smiled at him. "It's beautiful."

"It's not hard if you have the right equipment," he said, watching her from the doorway.

"Don't be so modest. It also takes a very good eye."

There wasn't anything else to the cabin. She ascended the steps, and he shut the door.

"Well, I didn't see any secret stashes down there," she said. Smiling, she held an imaginary microphone in front of him. "So, Mr. McArthur, you are not, and you never have been, involved in the rum trade?"

"Never," he intoned solemnly. They both laughed.

"Thanks again for being there when I needed you last night," she said seriously. "I wanted to bring you some kind of gift to say thanks, but I was afraid you wouldn't accept it."

He frowned. "Just for doing—"

"What anyone else would have done?" she finished. "I don't think that's true. You took a big chance to protect someone you didn't even know. A lot of people would have kept on going." She paused. "Anyway, the reason I came by was to invite you to dinner at my house. I can do that much, at least."

"Thanks, but you don't owe me anything."

"Yes, I do, but that's not the only reason I'm doing it. My parents really would like to meet you."

He looked apprehensive.

"I promise, it won't get sticky. My parents are not that kind." She paused. "Except—well, we're a religious family. We say a prayer over all our meals. I hope that wouldn't bother you."

Ken looked at her oddly. "No," he said slowly, then glanced down at his faded jeans and his deck shoes, unraveling at the seams. "But, uh . . . I don't have much else to wear, and I probably look like a derelict because I took off this morning before I bothered to shave." He rubbed his palm across his chin. In the light of the late afternoon sun, the stubble of his beard was a reddish gold contrast to the sandy hair on his head.

"No problem," she replied. "We're pretty casual around our house. Mom hardly ever dresses up unless she has to go out, and Daddy is probably in his sweats already. He likes to come home from the office and unwind by working out."

Ken weighed the invitation. Anything would beat the food at the greasy spoon where he usually ate. And Jean made him feel at ease. But her parents? It was difficult enough for him to be comfortable in social situations with homey people he knew well—the kind who ate with stainless steel flatware and drank out of plastic tumblers. Everything about Jean Bradley said style and good taste. Her mother was probably the kind to set the table with linen napkins, china, and goblets.

"Please come. I'd appreciate it," Jean said, smiling invitingly.

"You're a pretty hard person to say no to."

She laughed. "Persistence is one of my good qualities. Daddy calls it stubbornness."

"Okay. Give me a couple of minutes to run a razor over my face."

"Sure. I'll go over there to the pay phone and let them know we're coming."

The city of Corpus Christi took its name from the bay on which it is situated; Spanish explorer Alonso de Pineda discovered and named the bay on the feast day of Corpus Christi in 1519. Cattle, and later oil, helped build the city into a major shipping port in the twentieth century. The huge naval air station constructed in 1940 and 1941 gave it another significant boost. And nearby beaches, particularly on Padre Island, made the city a popular vacation destination on the Texas Gulf Coast.

Two days earlier, the city had experienced what was probably the last "norther" of the year—one of those cold fronts that sweep down from the north bringing rain and rapidly dropping temperatures. It was what passed for winter in this subtropical area.

Yesterday, the bay had looked like a pale greenish slate covered by whitecap scribbling, with dirty cotton clouds overhead. But today was the kind of early March day the chamber of commerce would order to remind winter visitors why they wanted to come back next year. The bay was calmer, deep green, and the white fluff clouds were turning to orange with the dusk. Small, gentle whitecaps rolled toward shore in the fading light.

Ken followed Jean's Camaro south down the boulevard to where it turns into Ocean Drive, following the curve of the bay. They passed the "old money" mansions, and the white stucco place on the bluff above the bay where, Ken had heard, a nest of Nazi spies monitored activities at the Naval Air Station during World War II. Jean turned in at a half-circle driveway on the landward side of Ocean Drive. Her parents' home was a colonnaded, two-story, white brick house. She drove her car into a vacant space in the four-car garage. Two of the other spaces were occupied by a Mercedes sedan and a Porsche.

Ken had changed to his good pair of jeans, penny loafers, and a golf shirt before coming. It was obvious that his Sunday slacks would have been more appropriate. He parked some distance from the front of the house. Jean beckoned him toward her as she walked along the portico.

"I feel like the pizza deliveryman," he half-whispered as he met her.

"Don't worry. Come on in," she said, pushing the heavy double doors wide open for him.

Beyond a short entryway, the decor of the house lived up to its facade. On the right, a carpeted staircase swept up a mirrored wall to a second-floor balcony overlooking the huge living room. There was a formal dining room off the living room to the left, and an entrance to the kitchen at the back of the living room on the left. Through a wide doorway at the back of the living room on the right, Ken could see a room with a stereo/video entertainment center along one wall.

"Mom! Dad!" Jean called. "I have someone here I want you to meet."

Her father came down the staircase. He wore dress slacks, a white dress shirt with gold cuff links, and a conservative tie. Jean's mother came from the kitchen. The mother-daughter resemblance in face and build was unmistakable. Her ash blonde hair fell across her shoulders and over an expensive-looking knit dress that was accented by a small, jeweled pin.

The telephone rang, and Jean's father excused himself to answer it just as Jean was preparing to make the introductions.

"Mom, this is Ken McArthur. Ken, this is my mother, Carol."

Carol Bradley's handshake was firm. "Ken, I apologize for having to be a poor hostess, but I have something on the stove. If you'll let Jean and Richard entertain you for now, I'll try to make it up to you later."

"That's fine," Ken said, smiling at her. Then, as Carol Bradley retreated toward the kitchen, he whispered to Jean: "Those are your mother's casual clothes, right?"

"I told you, it's not usually like this," she said, grinning. "I forgot that she had a church auxiliary meeting this afternoon."

"Well, business intrudes on pleasure," her father said as he rejoined them. "I'll have to eat and run tonight. That was a client who's coming in at the airport later."

"Daddy, this is Ken. Take care of him for a few minutes, will you?" Jean requested. Then she called toward the kitchen, "Mom, I'll be down to help just as soon as I change," and she disappeared up the stairs.

Richard Bradley sprawled comfortably on the brocaded sectional couch. "Sit down," he invited. Ken sat carefully at the opposite end of the couch, half turned to face his host.

"My wife and I owe you a debt of gratitude. Our daughter is extremely fortunate that you happened along last night," Richard said. "A lot of people wouldn't have stopped to help. Why did you?"

"When someone is in need, you help. It's a duty." Ken paused, then added, "That's the short answer."

"What's the long answer?"

Some would have found his host's directness unsettling. Ken found it reassuring. Instinct told him that in the Marines this man would have been a major or a colonel. Ken could deal with a colonel: know what you're talking about, sound like it when you give your report, and keep it brief.

"The long answer," he replied, "is tied in with keeping the world from savagery and selfishness and with trying to promote a better way to live. We should all be looking out for each other."

Richard Bradley considered Ken's words carefully, then commented: "The world needs people who live by principles like that. But it's an interesting answer for someone who can take out a guy with a knife the way Jean says you did last night." He paused. "Weren't you taking a big risk?"

"Not really. I was sure I could handle him."

Was this self-assurance—or cockiness? Richard Bradley assessed the younger man's build. It was average, almost skinny, from the waist down. But the chest was solid under the golf shirt, and the forearms and biceps were hard, though not especially large. Ken met Richard's appraising gaze steadily. Richard chuckled. "You sound pretty confident."

"I've taken down bigger and meaner men, when I was an M.P."

"Army?"

"Marines."

"How did you happen to be driving down Shoreline at just the right time last night?"

"Sometimes I deliver valuable things for a few carefully chosen clients. Last night, I was on my way back from a delivery."

"Oh?" Richard said, his eyebrows arching.

Ken tried one of his most reassuring smiles on his host. "It's all legitimate business. Jewelry, things like that. It's just that my clients can't risk carrying valuables around personally to make a delivery on short notice. So they get a guy with a beat-up truck who looks like he just came off a shift at the refinery. I can't share the details with you, but my security precautions work very well."

As Ken spoke, Jean came down the stairs wearing faded denim pants and a plaid shirt. She entered the kitchen. A few seconds later, her mother came out and headed upstairs.

"But there's still some danger to you," Richard said.

"Some. Less than you think." Ken paused. "I carry a weapon when I'm traveling on an assignment like that. But I put it away yesterday after I got back."

"Well, you obviously can take care of yourself. But you must have done something more to inspire so much confidence in your clients."

"I got my start delivering for my grandfather. My clients were friends of his."

"Your grandfather was a diamond dealer?" Richard Bradley

asked. The probing manner was gone, but still he seemed interested.

"My grandfather had a wide variety of business interests in town," Ken replied. "You may have heard of him—Alexander McArthur."

"*You're* Alex McArthur's grandson?"

"You knew him?" Ken asked.

"I knew *of* him. I used to see him occasionally, when I had the opportunity to go to the Oil Club. But he wouldn't have known me. People either admired your grandfather, because of the honest way he did business, or they hated him—because of the honest way he did business. From the beginning with my own company, I tried to run it the way I thought an Alexander McArthur would."

"I don't think there was anyone who knew him that didn't trust him—whether they liked him or not," Ken said softly.

"I remember hearing a story about him when I was first starting out in the real estate business here," Richard reflected. "Your grandfather was well enough off when he died, but at one time he had the chance to become one of the richest men in South Texas. All he had to do was take advantage of a competitor's mistake and push him to the brink. No one could have said it was Alex McArthur's fault if the other man had toppled over the edge. But your grandfather wouldn't do it. I heard that one of his friends asked him why, and all he said was, 'This is business, not cannibalism.' He gave the other man time to recover before he poured on the competition again. I understand they became good friends."

"That would have been Jack Weissman," Ken said, smiling slightly.

"Who?"

"One of my clients."

"Well, I never knew the other man's name. I just know that I admired your grandfather."

Carol Bradley came down the stairs in a pair of denim slacks and a casual blouse. She stopped behind the couch and bent to kiss her husband lightly on the cheek. "Did you work up a good appetite prowling the jungles of commerce today, dear? I think dinner's almost ready."

Richard rolled his eyes and grinned at Ken. "Don't buy her 'you-mighty-Tarzan, I-meek-little-Jane' routine. She whips my socks off at tennis." In response, Carol neatly swung an imaginary backhand as she strolled toward the kitchen.

"Hey, do you want to see what I did today?" Jean called. She stood in the doorway to the entertainment center. "I'm on in thirty seconds, right after this commercial."

Richard and Ken walked to the doorway, where they could see the television set. Ken noted that the room was much longer than it had appeared from the living room. There was an entrance from the kitchen on one side, and at the far side of the room, to his right, an exercise center: stationary bicycle, weight bench, and rowing machine. Sliding glass doors opened on a patio and garden behind the house.

Jean's feature story was about a group of Girl Scouts who had "adopted" residents of a local homeless shelter, helping serve meals and generally being friends. Jean had handled it well, putting the girls at ease, spotlighting their work, and maintaining an authoritative on-camera presence without dominating the situation.

"Excellent, as usual, Jeanie," her father commented.

Ken lingered a moment in the doorway, waiting until she headed for the dining room. "You're really good at that," he commented. "Channel 7 is lucky to have you."

"Thanks," she said, rewarding him with one of her smiles.

As the four of them sat at the dining table, Richard Bradley looked slowly around at the other three and asked, "Why do I suddenly feel overdressed?"

Jean smiled sweetly at him. "You were too busy talking to pay attention to what was going on, Daddy. I promised Ken that we would be casual, so Mom and I changed."

"That's the way it always is," Richard said to Ken. "Out on the street, I'm a fairly successful businessman. But at home, I'm always the last to know what's going on." He glanced pointedly at Jean.

She laughed. "Poor, *poor* daddy."

Richard was serious as he turned to Ken again. "Will you join us in giving thanks to God for our food?"

Ken bowed his head with the Bradleys.

"Dear Lord," Richard prayed, "we are grateful for our daily bread. We are thankful for our daughter's deliverance at the hands of this man. For many blessings, we thank thee. Amen."

After the prayer, Richard reached for the long-necked bottle in the center of the table and poured rich, red liquid into his wife and daughter's goblets. When Richard turned toward him, Ken said, as nonchalantly as possible, "None for me, thanks."

Richard held the bottle poised in the air. "You wouldn't like a little to complement the meat? It's a good wine."

"I know. I recognize the label. But I . . . gave up wine a few years ago. Please—don't worry about me."

"Can I get you anything else?" Carol asked. "Iced tea?"

"I usually just go with water. I understand it's a vintage year for that," Ken said, smiling. The answer wasn't original; he had used it before to help break the tension in situations like this.

Carol rose and headed for the kitchen. Ken turned to Jean. "Sorry. I didn't want to inconvenience anyone."

"That's all right," Jean's father answered. "We aim to please here." He leaned back in the chair, again in his interrogation mode, and asked: "You don't like wine, or you don't drink any alcohol?"

"Daddy, don't you think that's a bit personal?" Jean interjected sharply. "Don't be so rude to our guest!"

"It's okay," Ken said, glancing at her. "No, sir," he said to Richard, "I don't drink any alcohol." Jean's father seemed to be waiting for more. "It's in connection with my religious beliefs," Ken added.

"We try to live as good Christians," Richard said, "but we don't see anything wrong in taking a little wine with our meals on special occasions." He waited for Ken to comment.

"In my faith, we believe that God has commanded us not to drink alcoholic drinks," Ken replied.

"I'll bet your beliefs made you stand out in the Marines," Richard said wryly.

"Sometimes," Ken answered, chuckling. "The guys in my unit got used to it."

Richard seemed to be on the point of saying something more, but he glanced at his daughter and thought better of it. Carol returned at that moment and poured ice water from a pitcher into Ken's goblet.

The dinner went well. Ken felt relaxed despite the china and linen napkins. Jean was lively and fun to be around, and her parents were also easy people to know. Before dinner was over, they had instructed him to call them by their first names. "When you call me 'Mrs. Bradley,' it makes me feel like a senior citizen," Carol told him.

There were only a few other people with whom Ken felt so much at ease as he did with the Bradley family this night. The truth was, he realized, that he had only a handful of friends in Corpus Christi now. The first Latter-day Saint family he had known, the ones who had introduced him to the Church years ago, had welcomed him as warmly as the Bradleys. But that family was gone from the city, along with many of his other old friends.

Except for business contacts, he had almost shut himself off from people since his grandfather's death. Living on the boat isolated him. There were many fine members in his ward, but he had only made their acquaintance, really; he never socialized with any of them. Maybe, like the Bradleys, other new friends were waiting out there somewhere, Ken thought. Maybe it was time to make an effort to rejoin society.

During dinner, Ken learned that Richard Bradley had built his own commercial and industrial real estate business into one of the leading companies on the Texas Gulf Coast. Both Richard and Carol were generous with their time and money in charitable and civic causes. They were committed members of one of the city's largest Christian churches.

Jean explained that she had finished her degree in broadcasting seven months earlier, at the end of the past summer. "My job with the station here is steady part-time work," she said. "There wasn't an opening in a bigger market in Texas when I graduated, and steady part-time here seemed like a better idea than full-time at a small station. The news director says I'll get the first full-time opening they have."

The Bradleys learned that Ken had served a four-year hitch in the Marines and had been out for a little less than a year. He explained that he was trying to establish himself as a freelance photographer. His portfolio and list of clients were growing, but not as fast as he had hoped. The special deliveries he made supplemented his income, but he also drew occasionally—more frequently than he was comfortable with, really—on a small inheritance left by his grandfather.

After Richard Bradley had excused himself to drive to the airport, Ken and Jean visited with her mother for a few minutes. Then Carol began to clear the table.

"I'd better go," Ken said, glancing at his watch. "I've got an early job in the morning."

"I'll walk you to your car," Jean said.

When they were outside, Ken told her, "I'm sorry I made it awkward at dinner."

"What? About the wine?"

"Yes."

"Don't worry about it. I'm sorry Daddy is so . . . well, blunt sometimes. But you made a very good impression on him tonight."

"Oh?" Ken asked. "How can I tell?"

"Only one other guy I've ever brought home has lasted more than three minutes in conversation with my father. Daddy's good with people; he has to be in his business. But he can slip away from them very skillfully if a conversation doesn't seem promising. I noticed that you had his undivided attention."

"Hmm. I don't think I did anything special. What was this other guy's secret?"

"Freddie Tueller, in the third grade," she recalled, smiling. "He marched up to my dad and said, 'Sir, I'm thinking about selling land for businesses when I grow up. What can you tell me about your job?' " They laughed together. "I'll be sure to try that," Ken said. Then: "Can I call you sometime?"

"Sure."

"Well, as long as I'm here, and since I don't have a phone on the boat, would you like to go snorkeling with me this Saturday?"

"I've always wanted to try snorkeling. But it's been years since I put on a mask and snorkel, and that was in a swimming pool."

"That's okay, you'll catch on fast. Maybe it will get you interested in scuba diving. I can teach you to do that too." He smiled hopefully.

Her smile was impish. “We’ll just start with the snorkeling until I find out what kind of creatures lurk in the deep.”

“There’re really not more than a half-dozen women eaters to deal with. Midmorning’s a good time to start snorkeling.”

Jean smiled as she headed toward the house. “I’ll be at the boat about ten,” she called over her shoulder.

2

Shark Bait

Ken drove out over the high bridge spanning the entrance to the port. The snorkeling gear and his rubber raft were packed into the back of the Blazer.

"Where are we going?" Jean asked.

"To the Port Aransas jetties. This looks like as good a spring day over there as we'll get for snorkeling." He grinned at her. "I forgot to ask you the other night if you can swim."

"Silly boy. I swam the two hundred freestyle and the anchor leg on the relay for my high school swim team," she answered, smiling.

"Ray High School, right?"

"Of course. Is there any other in town?"

"I went to Miller."

She winced dramatically. "And I'll bet you were . . . a football player?"

"Defensive end. All-district, two years in a row."

"Oh, no!" she said in mock horror. "A football jock from Miller High. Are you sure this whole thing isn't just an excuse to lose a Ray High girl in the ship channel?"

"I'm sure," Ken replied, laughing. "You're going to enjoy this. Diving gets into your blood. I've had the chance to dive in some of the most beautiful spots off Texas and Hawaii. Someday I'm going back to Honduras to dive at some of the beaches on the north coast."

"Did you go to Hawaii and Honduras when you were in the Marines?"

"Just Hawaii. I was a missionary in Honduras, and missionaries didn't get to dive."

"*You* were a missionary?" As soon as Jean said it, she blushed. She hadn't meant to sound incredulous. Ken showed a self-assurance that said he lived by his convictions, and he had spoken of his religious beliefs when he refused the wine at dinner with her family. But he didn't fit the missionary mold. "I'm sorry. I mean—our church helps support a missionary couple in Africa, but they're old, and I don't think they go diving or . . . well, you don't look like any missionaries I've known."

"My church sends guys out when they're nineteen," he said matter-of-factly. "I was a missionary before I went into the Marines."

"Which church do you belong to?"

"The Church of Jesus Christ of Latter-day Saints." She looked at him blankly. "Mormon," he added.

"Oh. . . . Oh, you mean like those young guys in white shirts I see around town on bicycles."

"Right."

"I can just see you on a bike." She laughed lightly.

"They called me the 'Terror of Tegucigalpa,' " he said, gripping the steering wheel tightly and putting on a wild face.

She regarded him thoughtfully for a moment. "How did you go from being a missionary to a Marine?"

He was silent for a time before he answered. "My mission was the best and most intense thing I'd ever done. There was a terrific letdown when it was all over after two years. I didn't know what I wanted to do with the rest of my life. I had four jobs in ten months. Then it sort of came to me that I had served my God, now maybe I ought to serve my country."

"You aren't like the Marines I've known, either."

"There are all kinds of people in the Marines, Jean. But for me it was a mismatch," he answered. "They did right by me. You know—'The Marine Corps builds men.' I grew up a lot, and I gave the corps my best while I was in. But I learned that it wasn't what I wanted to do with the rest of my life."

"So you know now what you really want to do?"

She truly seemed to care. Ken was surprised at her ability to draw him out. A long time had passed since he had talked to anyone about his aspirations. But talking to Jean seemed easy.

"I think so," he replied. "I saw plenty of ugliness in life when I was growing up. Over the past few years I've discovered that there's a lot of beauty in it too. If I could capture a little of that on film and share it, that's what I'd enjoy doing." He paused, then grinned. "Of course, it helps if you can make money at it."

"Well, it looks to me like you're good enough."

"Thanks. I hope I can convince a few magazine editors and art directors of that. I picked up photography through a friend, a member of my church in Hawaii. I haven't had any formal training, but I've got a small library of photography books in a drawer on the boat."

They drove in silence for a few minutes. Then he asked, "What about you? Where do you hope to go in broadcasting from here?"

"I don't know. I'm not ready to leave here yet. I really don't have a track record in this market. I need a full-time news beat to prove I'm good at what I do. I keep hoping the news director is serious about giving me a chance." She sighed. "If it doesn't happen soon, I suppose I'll have to try one of the smaller stations somewhere."

When they arrived at the jetties, Ken unloaded the raft and pumped it up. They shed their street clothes and left them in the truck. Jean wore a modest, deep green suit; he noticed how it accentuated the green of her eyes.

Ken gave her some instruction with the snorkel before rowing them out a short ways to the spot where they would dive. "I'll stay close to you," he promised.

She was awkward in the water at first, but soon using the snorkel came more easily. She lost track of time, caught up in what she was seeing beneath the surface, but Ken glanced frequently at the diver's watch he wore. He never let the two of them stray far from the anchored raft; he would lead Jean to it from time to time, telling her to hold onto the side and rest awhile. He enjoyed looking into her green eyes up close as they talked about what they had seen. Finally, he motioned her to the surface and said, "We've been diving for nearly two hours. That's enough. It's quite a workout if you haven't done it before. You'll feel this later."

"It's beautiful down there!" she said as he rowed back to shore. "I had no idea you could find coral like that around here. Why haven't you taught me to dive before now?"

"An oversight—due to lack of opportunity. You should have met me sooner."

"Well, I expect you to make up for lost time."

They stowed their gear in the Blazer, got into their street clothes, and headed back around the bay. In the truck, she settled against the door and dropped off to sleep. She didn't stir until they were almost back at his boat. It was already late afternoon.

She opened her eyes and stretched as he stopped at a traffic light. "You were right," she said. "That did take a lot out of me.

Guess I'll have to get into better shape if you're going to teach me how to dive."

Jean helped him carry the raft and snorkeling gear to the boat, then waited in the stern while he stowed them in the cabin. "I don't know about you, but I'm famished," she said when he came out. "Want to come home with me, and I'll fix us something to eat?"

"I can't," he answered. "I've got to go up to the YMCA for my nightly shower. Besides, I don't want to wear out my welcome."

"Daddy has a shower down by his exercise room. I'm sure he won't mind if you use it. And I'll break out some steaks. Mom won't care as long as I cook for her and Daddy too."

"Steak? What's that?" He smiled at her, but he didn't move.

"Come on," she said, beckoning. "It's the least I can do for the diving lesson. And you haven't even begun to wear out your welcome."

"Well, let me get a couple of things I'll need."

He came out of the cabin in a few minutes wearing his clean jeans and golf shirt and carrying a gym bag.

"Aw, you dressed up," she said with a mock scowl.

"You mentioned steak; I thought it might be a formal dinner. Anyway, after last time, I didn't want to show up at your parents' house looking like a total beach bum."

When Jean ushered him into her house this time, her mother was just coming in from the patio, in a pair of Levis and a light-colored sweatshirt. She carried a potted plant. "Oh, hi," Carol said. "Sorry you caught me at my worst. I've just been working in the garden."

"Carol, if that's your worst, other women would kill to look like it." He didn't intend it as flattery: her hair was neatly combed back, and whatever she had done in the garden, she had managed to do without touching dirt. Carol Bradley was an attractive woman, and under the right conditions she would probably have passed as Jean's older sister. Jean's easy, natural beauty had obviously been inherited.

"My goodness," Carol said, smiling at Ken. "I could stand to hear more of that kind of talk. Jean, bring this man home often."

"We worked up an appetite diving, Mom, and I promised him a steak dinner. Can I cook some for you and Daddy too?" Jean asked.

"Are you kidding? Would I turn down an offer from someone else to cook dinner?"

After her mother stepped into the kitchen with the plant, Jean grinned at Ken. "Nice work, Mr. Diplomacy. Now you're in with both my mother and my father." She pointed to a door at the far side of the exercise room. "There's the shower. I'll go clean up too, and then I'll cook dinner."

When he had showered and dressed, Ken left his gym bag in the exercise room and waited in the living room until Jean came down.

"You didn't have to wait out here," she said. "Make yourself at home. Watch TV if you want."

He followed her into the kitchen. "Maybe I can help with the dinner."

"How are you with tossed salads?" she asked as she plopped the steaks into a pan.

"I can toss as well as anyone."

"Good. You'll find lettuce, tomatoes, onions, carrots, and anything else you need in the refrigerator. There's a knife in that drawer."

When he had finished with the salad, she had him set the small table in the kitchen dining nook. "I told you it wouldn't be formal," she said.

He was just finishing when Richard and Carol came into the

kitchen. "Bradley party, table for four?" Ken said. "Right this way."

Carol laughed. "Don't you just love it," she said to her husband, "when you find one of these little, out-of-the-way places with great food and fine service too?"

She glanced over the table settings, then took four wine glasses from a cupboard and put them on the table. She filled a small carafe with ice water and put it in front of Ken's plate.

As they sat down to eat, Jean said, "Daddy, you could ask our guest to say grace tonight. Ken used to be a missionary for the Mormon church."

Carol frowned. But Richard seemed impressed. "Oh, really? Well, please, Ken, go ahead." Ken said a brief blessing on the food, and the others responded to his "amen."

After the blessing, Richard asked a couple of questions about Ken's missionary work: Where had he served? Were the people receptive? Then Carol began telling him about the missionary couple that their church was supporting in Africa. Soon the conversation drifted to other things. It was light and friendly, and Ken felt as though he had known these people for months.

"How was the diving?" Richard asked.

"Daddy, I never knew there were such beautiful things down there just under the surface," Jean answered. "I thought you had to go really deep to find them. Have you ever done any diving?"

"No, that's one of the pleasures I've missed. Maybe Ken could take me sometime."

"Glad to," Ken said.

"Did you see any sharks?" Richard asked.

Ken put his finger to his lips to indicate there was a secret he wasn't telling. "I didn't want to scare Jean," he said.

Jean was poised with her fork halfway to her mouth. "Sharks?" Had she seen large, gray shapes passing near them once or twice while they were under water today?

"Sure," Ken answered casually. "They're a constant danger. I saw one, but it was only about twelve feet long—just a little one." He looked her in the eye soberly. "It's fairly safe where I took you. They haven't attacked anyone over there in three, maybe four years."

"Is that so?" Richard asked innocently. "Do they go for novice divers?"

"Especially blondes. But they're deathly afraid of dark green swimsuits because they think those belong to the underwater park rangers, so I knew Jean was safe." Richard laughed out loud, and Ken grinned.

Jean looked from one to the other. "Oh, that was really cute. Did the two of you work that one out before I came down?"

"No," Ken said, chuckling, "your father just gave me an opening, and I couldn't resist. You really do have to watch for sharks when you're diving, but I didn't see any today."

"I owe you for that, Ken," Jean said, grinning. "I'll find a way to pay you back."

"Watch out, Ken. She means it," her father warned.

When they had finished dinner, Carol said, "Well, the least I can do is the dishes, Jean. But I think I'm going to enlist a helper."

"Oh, I don't think it's fair to ask Ken to do that," Richard said quickly. "After all, he's our guest."

"Nice try, lover," Carol responded, "but there's a dish scrubber over here with your name on it. Bring me those plates, will you?"

Richard sighed. "Did I tell you that when she beats me at tennis, she gloats?" he said to Ken.

"And did he tell you that he makes her play him for a dime a stroke in golf?" Jean said. "Come on, Ken, before he finds some way to weasel out of dish duty. It's tough to stuff those dishwashers."

They strolled out to the living room and sat on the couch to talk.

"Your parents are nice people," Ken said. "A lot of fun. You have the kind of family life I always wanted when I was younger."

"I wish you could meet my older sister Allison and her husband, Jay. Allie and I are really close, and Jay's the best male friend I've ever had. I know you'd like them."

Ken glanced around the living room. "You know, you really are blessed, Jean. You're intelligent, you're beautiful, you come from a fine family, and you live very well."

She frowned. "I suppose you're right, Ken. But I'm no idle rich girl, and I don't like it very much when people think that." There was an edge to her words. "We didn't always live this way. It was a lot different when I was younger." She looked him steadily in the eye. "While I was growing up, I realized that I couldn't always live on Daddy's money. So I earned a scholarship to the university, and then I worked while I was going to school. I bought my own car with money I saved. And I pay Mom and Dad room and board now that I'm living at home."

"Yeah, well, that's . . . uh, very *responsible* of you." Ken looked at her quizzically. He had simply mentioned a few of her blessings; why had she felt it was necessary to make the point about being able to take care of herself?

"Sorry. I didn't mean to sound like I was lecturing," Jean said. "It's just that sometimes people seem to believe everything comes easy for me."

"Not much that's worthwhile in life ever comes easy, Jean. I've had to learn a lot of valuable lessons the hard way," Ken answered. Then he smiled disarmingly. "Speaking of lessons, when do you want to try scuba diving?"

"When can you teach me?"

"Well, if you're free Tuesday afternoon, we could go to a

pool and I could show you how to use scuba gear. I think I know where I can borrow some for you."

He took her to the YMCA pool twice during the week to teach her the basics of using the scuba equipment. She was a quick learner, but he made her run through the procedures repeatedly anyway, to be sure she could handle them.

"There's a diving group I sometimes go with on Saturdays," he told her. "Come with me this weekend, and we'll run through all this again in open water."

When he picked her up on Saturday morning, she was wearing jeans and a white T-shirt with large red lettering that said: "SHARK BAIT."

"Like it?" she asked, smiling sweetly.

"I just hope you're wearing your park ranger swimming suit," he answered, returning her smile.

Her first diving experience in open water went well. When they were through, she surprised Ken by asking if he would mind being part of a feature story for the television news. "I sold the news director on a story about snorkeling. Would you help me with it?"

He agreed. On Wednesday morning, she met Ken and two couples from the diving group at a beach, where she interviewed them on camera. The station's photographer brought along a small camera in an underwater housing, but because he was not a diver, Jean asked Ken to shoot some underwater scenes. Then she invited Ken over to her house that night to watch the completed story with her parents. Jean would be in the studio at the station to do a live lead-in and wrap-up.

The story went off well. The station's news format was the kind that called for happy talk banter, so at the end, Jean held up the "SHARK BAIT" shirt and explained to the two news anchors that it had been a gift from Ken McArthur, the diver who had shot the underwater segments.

Richard Bradley looked at Ken, who sat shaking his head, and laughed. "I told you she'd find a way to pay you back."

On Thursday morning, the day after her story on snorkeling aired, a rapping on the cabin door of the *Rum Runner* woke Ken early. Stumbling to the door to open it, he found Jean and the sunshine.

"Hi, sleepyhead," she said cheerily. "Are you ready to go?"

"Are you kidding? By my watch, you're about two days early for your next diving lesson." He looked down at the rumpled sweat pants and T-shirt he wore. Then he peered warily at her car on the jetty. "Is this another set-up? Did you bring a camera crew to catch me this way?"

She laughed. "No. Are you mad at me?"

"Of course not. I can take a joke. But I have a surprise for your next dive. It will be about an hour long, and I've prepared a special tank—with thirty-five minutes of air in it."

She laughed again. "Are you working today?"

"I was planning a trip down Padre Island to shoot some pictures I think I could sell."

"Could you postpone it?"

"Well, yeah, there's nothing critical about today. Why?"

"Daddy needs a delivery made to San Antonio, and he wondered if you would do it. He said he'll pay your usual fee. The envelope needs to be in downtown San Antonio by noon."

Ken glanced at his watch. Seven-fifteen. It was possible.

"I doubt very much your dad would want to pay my usual fee. I get a small percentage of the value of the items because of the risk. Is this something that anybody would want to steal?"

"I don't think so. It's just some original papers that have to go directly into the hands of one particular person, and fax won't do."

"Well, in that case, tell him I'll do it for gas money and the price of some film. I'll stop in San Antonio after I make the delivery and shoot some photos to add to my portfolio." He paused and thought for a moment. "Tell him if he'll send his daughter along to ride shotgun, I'll do it for the gas money. How do you think that would strike him?"

"He'd probably tell you to ask his daughter if she'd like to go."

"Would you?"

"Sure. I was the one who suggested you, and I'm not working today."

"I can be ready in twenty minutes."

"Good. I'll call Daddy and tell him we'll meet him at his office."

Diving lessons had left little time for chatting about other things. The trip to San Antonio was the first time Ken and Jean had talked uninterrupted for more than a few minutes. He asked about her college career. She told him about her courses in reporting and broadcasting, and about the plays she had appeared in as a theater minor.

With a reporter's interest, she asked him about everyday life and politics in Honduras. The depth and clarity of Ken's answers told her that he had been keenly aware of life around him while he was in that country. He didn't have her educational background, but somehow Jean felt that she wouldn't be able to outdistance this man intellectually. Their conversation was stimulating, and the three-hour drive to San Antonio seemed much shorter.

After they made their delivery, Jean took Ken to lunch at a downtown restaurant her father had recommended. Richard had insisted that gasoline money wasn't enough.

"This has been easy duty, compared to most of my deliveries,"

Ken said. "I haven't done much but be your driver today. Your father could have sent you alone and saved some money."

"I wouldn't have come alone. And don't worry about Daddy. He'll still come out okay on this," Jean answered. "If it hadn't been you, he would have had to pay a courier. And I've enjoyed it."

Ken drove to one of the old Spanish missions in the southern part of the city. "Would you like to do a little sightseeing while I shoot some photos?" he asked.

"Sure."

Ken slung his Nikon, with a wide-angle lens, around his neck and carried a telephoto lens in a case that hung from his shoulder. He and Jean strolled through the mission's peaceful grounds, and she watched as he shot a variety of architectural photos, capturing both broad views and details of the buildings and plants, trying various positions to frame his shots. He had finished two rolls of film when he asked, "Would you mind if I took some photos of you?"

"No, I suppose not. What do you want to do with them?"

"Well, the first thing that comes to mind is a sixteen-by-twenty blowup to improve the decor on my boat," he said, smiling. "But I'd like to put a human figure into some of these scenes to add interest and a sense of scale."

Jean struck an exaggerated model's pose against the building. Ken laughed. "No, let me tell you what to do," he said.

She wore jeans, a simple cotton blouse, and sandals. The style fit well with the simplicity of the old buildings. He stopped at several spots to direct her. He posed her in one section of a garden while he shot wide angle photos. Soon he was concentrating on her, not architecture. Finally, he posed her in a doorway. "Lean against the door jamb," he directed, "so I can frame you against the darkness of the interior. Look at me and fold your arms across your chest. Now give me a smile. . . . Now give me a look that says you own this place. . . . That's *good*."

He kept shooting as he directed her. "You're a natural at this," he said. "Have you ever thought of supplementing your income by modeling?"

"No!" she said curtly.

"But you're good. You could—"

"I said no. It wasn't a hint."

"Okay, okay! Forget it." He busied himself with rewinding the film, then juggling the camera while he removed the cassette and inserted another.

"I'm sorry," she said quietly.

He looked up.

"I didn't mind doing that when *you* asked me," she continued. "But I've had offers before . . . not the kind I could accept."

Ken frowned. "Well, there are legitimate modeling jobs that would put you in great demand."

"Thanks, but I spent four years in college trying to prepare myself in a field that I can grow into all my life. I want to concentrate on that."

He considered her answer for a moment. "Makes sense. But would you mind if I use a couple of these shots of you in my portfolio? You make me look awfully good."

"No, of course not." She smiled and added, "As long as I don't end up on an advertisement for something, by surprise."

"Like, maybe, shark bait?" he said, grinning. She laughed. He continued, "I couldn't do that to you, Jean. Anyway, it's not legal."

They were back on the road to Corpus Christi when she asked, "Do you have many photo clients?"

His brow furrowed. "A few advertisers, one of the other TV stations—"

"Booo!"

"—a couple of businesses, and assorted others. I have some photos on file with an agent in New York, but that hasn't brought me much yet. I shoot a few weddings, bar mitzvahs, other odd jobs."

"It's hard to make a living that way, isn't it?"

"Yes. I keep trying for some kind of freelance magazine assignment that could put a little money in the bank and give me some name recognition. That could help me snare some bigger jobs. Right now, while I don't have a family and I can travel, that kind of freelancing would be ideal."

"Sounds exciting. But what will you do some day when you have a family?"

"Then they'll come first. I'll have to find a staff photographer job somewhere, or get involved in a business—maybe even set up a studio—so I can keep regular hours. After the way I grew up, I'm going to be there for my family whenever they need me."

"Well, I hope you get one of those big assignments you want," Jean said. "By the way, there was a photography exhibit in town two weeks ago. Did you see it?"

"Yes. I like to go down to the gallery sometimes and look at whatever they've got—photos, paintings, sculpture."

"Do you? I do too!" This was a side of Ken she hadn't glimpsed yet. He not only liked to shoot photos, but he liked other art for its own sake. They talked about the kinds of art they both liked, then about music, then films, then other things they found relaxing and enjoyable.

It was remarkable, Ken thought, how well she would fit in with the people he knew in the Young Single Adult group. "Jean, I've been invited to a party tomorrow night, with a singles group from my church. I think you'd like the people. Would you go with me?" he asked.

"I'd like to, Ken, but I can't." She sounded genuinely disappointed. "I already have a date tomorrow night. Ask me some other time, okay?"

"Sure."

The party was a picnic in a park, with softball, volleyball, and a watermelon bust. Ken enjoyed it thoroughly. He hadn't met some of these people before, and it was pleasant getting to know the others better. He was surprised when a couple of the new people asked if he had just arrived in town; they had been here for months and had never seen him at an activity.

Ken spent some time talking and swinging on the park swings with Becky Rollins, an attractive legal secretary who was outgoing and vivacious, just like Jean. This party could only have been better, Ken thought, if Jean could have been here—because of the missionary value of an activity like this, of course.

Jean had gone to dinner and a concert with Ron Harrison—or, as he preferred to be known now that his career as a stockbroker was taking off, R. Dean Harrison. She had dated Dean several times before. Jay, her brother-in-law, had introduced them. Dean was good company, attentive and witty, and Jean enjoyed the evening.

"Would you like to go get something to drink?" Dean asked after the concert was over.

Jean knew he would pick one of those trendy places that cater to upscale young people. He would order a good wine, and she could sip hers politely. Dean wasn't like some of the men she had dated; she didn't have to worry whether he would be able to drive home safely after they had stopped for a drink. Still, there was almost always someone—or a party of someones—who drank too much and became obnoxious, even in the nicer bars. And the din was usually oppressive.

"I don't think I'd better stay out any later tonight, Dean," she replied. "I have a scuba diving lesson first thing in the morning, and those are real workouts. I'd better get all the rest I can."

"I didn't know you took diving lessons."

"I just started a couple of weeks ago. The guy who's teaching me lives on a boat down on one of the T-heads. He's a very experienced diver."

"Beach bum type, huh?" Dean asked, grinning. There was a little too much emphasis on the words, Jean thought.

As Dean drove her home, she reflected on the contrasts between him and Ken.

Dean was settling into the profitable career he had planned, with the nice apartment and the BMW he wanted, and looking for someone to share it all. Jean knew he had been dating several women who might fit in with his aspirations and life-style. There had been hints that Jean might be his choice. Obviously Dean knew very well where he wanted to be in the next ten years—but then what? What was important to him in life besides being comfortable?

If Ken was vague about where he wanted to be in ten years, she thought, he certainly seemed to know what he wanted out of life forty years from now. The things he seemed to value were things that could really become part of him—not just things to own, or wear, or display. What would it have been like, Jean wondered, to go to a party tonight with a group of people who drank nothing stronger than root beer? Dull? Not likely. Ken was anything but dull.

Dean pulled into her driveway. Jean knew exactly what would happen next. He would park, turn in the seat to talk to her, and soon he would move toward her. . . . It bothered her to be taken for granted, and it had always bothered her to feel that she somehow had to pay for the evening out, even if it was only with a goodnight kiss.

"You can park right there by the door," she suggested to Dean.

Suddenly a floodlight mounted on the front of the house switched on, and Dean stabbed at the brakes with his toe, skidding to a halt.

"Oh, dear," Jean said, "my father must have wondered who was coming into the driveway this time of night. I'm sorry." Her timing was perfect. She opened the door and slipped out before Dean could respond. "Thanks, Dean, it was a wonderful evening. Maybe we could do it again sometime."

The expression on Dean's face showed that the evening hadn't been as wonderful as he had hoped. "Sure," he answered. "Maybe I'll call you next week . . . or sometime."

"Okay." She shut the car door and walked toward the house as Dean drove away. Once inside, she leaned back against the door and stared into the darkened living room. She felt guilty for what she had just done. A few days earlier, her father had installed an automatic floodlight to illuminate the driveway for arriving guests, and she had deliberately steered Dean into the path of its motion sensor so it would flood the driveway with light.

Why had she treated Dean so casually? There must be dozens of women in Corpus Christi who would give up their next week's lunch money to sit where she had been sitting a few seconds earlier. Maybe she would try to make it up to him, Jean thought. Maybe in a few days she would call Dean to tell him again what a wonderful evening it had been.

Maybe.

3

"Why Didn't You Give In?"

It was early Tuesday evening when Jean made her way carefully down the pier, holding a large sack. Stepping onto the boat, she heard voices coming from the half-open door of the cabin. She started to knock, but what she saw inside stopped her. A woman had Ken backed up against the bunk on one side of the cabin. It was Gloria, the girlfriend of one of the men in the diving group.

"What's the matter?" Gloria wheedled. "Don't you want the same thing I want?"

"Ah . . . look, Gloria, I never try to move in on someone else's girlfriend," Ken answered.

"But this is just between the two of us. Ray doesn't know I'm here." She toyed with the top button of Ken's shirt. He trapped her hand in his and held it away from his chest.

"Gloria, there are other reasons I can't do what you want. That comes only with a commitment I can't make to you."

"I'm not talking about long-term commitment. Neither one of us has to feel obligated."

"You're not listening, Gloria. I don't live that way."

"What's the matter, Ken?" Gloria's question was half challenge. "I can take it a little easier if I'm coming on too strong for you."

Jean stepped down into the cabin. She was flushed with anger. "Why don't you just do us all a favor and slither on out of here?"

"Oh!" Gloria stepped back quickly. She looked slowly from Jean to Ken. Then she smiled wickedly. "Oh. Now I understand. I guess this confirms some of the things I've heard from a few of the people in the diving group."

"And you'd just love to make sure they hear more, wouldn't you?" Jean said acidly. "Well, remember that two can play the game. They might like to hear what I saw too. Take off, Gloria. Your broom is double-parked outside."

Gloria shoved Jean aside as she made her way up the stairs.

"Incredible!" Jean said as she watched Gloria step up to the pier and walk away. "I've known a few women who seemed capable of that kind of behavior, but this is the first time I've watched one in action."

Ken sat back limply on the bunk. "Wow! Is it hot in here, or what?" He fanned himself with his hand. "What a barracuda! I think you just evened the score in the rescue department."

Jean blushed. "I should have left instead of eavesdropping."

"I'm glad you hung around. Your timing was great. What brought you here right now?"

Slowly she smiled at him. "I came to make sure you get a decent meal at least one night this week. You may keep house nicely, but I'll bet you don't cook."

She stepped out onto the deck and brought in the sack she had carried aboard. "I'm going to show you what you can do with this hot plate you keep in the cabin." She blew dust off the appliance and searched around its base. "Where do you plug this thing in?"

"Just a minute." Ken opened the stowage compartment at

the head of the bunks and brought out a rolled-up extension cord. "Hold this," he said, handing her the outlet end. Then he headed out of the cabin, paying out cord as he went.

Seconds later, the cord went slack in her hand, and there was a splash outside. She peered out the door. He was standing on the pier empty-handed, and the kinked coil of cord lay in a heap on the deck of the boat; the plug end of the cord dangled over the stern.

"It slipped out of my hand," Ken said ruefully.

Jean laughed. "I don't believe this! No wonder you don't cook very often."

"Patience," he said. "It took Edison a long time to develop electricity, and—"

"Edison didn't develop electricity, silly!"

"And where would we all be if Mrs. Edison had been standing in the kitchen all the time, saying, 'Tom, will you hurry up so I can plug in the stove?' "

Ken stepped onto the stern, fished the cord out of the water, dried the plug off with the tail of his shirt, then blew on the plug for good measure. "I don't want to short out all the power on the T-heads when I plug this in," he said. Waving the plug in the air to be sure it was dry, he climbed back onto the pier and connected the power cord to an outlet on a light pole on the jetty.

"Think of my life-style as camping out at the waterfront," he said, grinning, as he stepped back onto the boat.

"How do you get lights in here?" she asked.

"Right now, batteries. That's why they're so dim—and why I usually go to bed early."

With the hot plate heating up, she began pulling things out of the paper sack she had brought. She diced up some vegetables and canned meat into a skillet. "Observe," she said dramatically, "that these are all common products, available in any store. Watch closely so you can do this at home."

In a few minutes, she spooned the final product onto two plates she produced from the sack, along with two forks. "Din-naaah is served," she said, affecting a waiter's pose and handing him one of the plates.

They sat on opposite bunks to eat. "This is delicious," he said. "You made up this recipe, didn't you?"

She tried not to smile. "What makes you think I didn't get it out of a cookbook?"

"Sure. *The Extremely Low-Budget Gourmet's Cookbook,* right there in the section labeled 'High-Class Hot-Plate Cuisine.' "

She laughed. "You can be pretty inventive when you're a college student on a tight budget."

"Well, I don't believe I really could do this. I think I missed the part where you waved your magic wand."

They ate in silence for a few minutes. Then he said apologetically, "I'm afraid Gloria will find some way to drag your name through the mud with her friends."

"I'm not worried about Gloria. I'm still mad about what she tried to do to you. But I'm sorry if this messes you up with your diving buddies."

"I'm not too popular with some of them right now anyway," Ken replied with a thin smile. "After you went home Saturday afternoon, I punched one of them out." He carefully rearranged the food on his plate. "I didn't like something he said . . . about the way you looked."

She thought for a moment. "Ray Healey?"

Ken looked up at her, surprised. "How did you know?"

"I could tell by the way he looked at me whenever he was around. Sometimes I could even feel it when my back was turned."

"I should have punched him again."

"No . . . thanks for defending me, but no. It wouldn't have changed anything." She paused. "I suppose this means no diving lesson next Saturday?"

"Not unless we can find you some diving gear somewhere. I borrowed Gloria's for you to use." Ken smiled wryly. "She was the one who invited me to join the group when I ran across them at the beach last year. She didn't do much diving herself, but it was funny how she suddenly recovered her interest and wanted her equipment back after you showed up."

"I hope this doesn't mean you're out of the group," Jean said, frowning.

"It probably does," Ken answered. "Ray organized the group, and the rest of them follow his lead." He smiled again. "But don't worry about it. I didn't fit in very well anyway. They all like to 'party hearty,' as they say, after a dive. They stopped inviting me along; said I was a wet blanket. I can't imagine why." He laughed.

Jean smiled. "Well, maybe we could just go snorkeling this week."

"Sure. I know some other nice places."

She ate in silence for a few moments. Then: "Answer a personal question for me?"

"Okay."

"Why didn't you give in?"

"What?" He looked puzzled.

"To Gloria. A lot of men I've known would have jumped at the chance. And you had every reason to believe that she was right, that no one else would ever know."

He raised his eyebrows.

"Even ministers and priests have caved in to that kind of pressure," Jean added.

Ken looked down at his plate, frowning silently.

Jean felt her face flushing. "I'm sorry. I shouldn't have asked. I didn't mean to make it embarrassing."

"No, it's all right," he said reassuringly, looking up at her. "I was just thinking. I guess there are a couple of reasons. The most important is that back when I became a missionary I made some covenants—promises to God—about the way I would live from then on. What Gloria wanted would be breaking them."

He reflected for a moment. "I had plenty of opportunities to give in that way while I was in the Marines. A few of the other guys were always wanting to teach me how to be a 'real man.' " He held up two fingers on each hand as imaginary quotation marks. "I used to take some flack because I wouldn't go with them when they hit the streets in Honolulu. But I couldn't break those promises."

Jean mentally reviewed all the men she had ever dated, wondering how many could have measured up to his standard.

"Would you like to know the other reason I didn't give in?" Ken asked.

"If you want to tell me."

"Your face came to mind. I knew you'd be disappointed in me. Men who give in to propositions like Gloria's don't deserve to have dinner with friends like you."

She smiled at him. "Thanks. Thanks for telling me that."

He looked at her thoughtfully for a few moments. "Answer one for me?"

"Sure."

"If they could look as good as you, a lot of women would flaunt it. You don't. Why not?"

It was her turn to be silent, thinking. Then she answered, "I'm really not sure what it is that makes a woman good-looking to men. If I've got it, I didn't do anything on purpose to get it. But the way some men have told me 'You're beautiful' was . . . embarrassing. It almost makes me ashamed. I guess that's another reason I wouldn't be a model. I don't want to encourage that kind of attention."

"That's smart."

"The truth is, there's more to it, Ken. I've been laughed at so much for telling people how I really feel about man-woman relationships that I've just quit explaining it. But the way you stick to your own principles, I think you'll understand."

She gazed at the wall behind him, somewhere over his head. "There was this girl in high school, when I was a sophomore. She was cute and popular. She was in some of my classes, and we got to be friends. I looked for her when I started my junior year, and somebody said, 'Oh, didn't you hear? She had to get married.' The next time I saw her, she had a little daughter that she was raising by herself because the guy ran off and left her after a year. I decided, back when I first heard about the trouble she was in, that that was never going to be me."

Jean paused, then looked him in the eye. "So there are parts of me—in my mind, in my heart, my body—that I don't share, and I never will, until I find someone who's willing to share the way my father and my mother have—starting with a lifetime commitment, in front of the minister in our church."

Ken smiled at her and held out his fist in a thumbs-up sign. "Good for you, Jean. Don't ever settle for less."

Then his smile faded, and he looked away. "I know I've told you more than once that you're beautiful. I hope that didn't make you feel—"

"Don't worry, you're not one of the men I was talking about. But some men I know can't talk to me like Jean is a real person. They make me feel like a . . . just a *body* they'd like to spend a couple of hours alone with."

"I like talking to you, and you *are* a real person, Jean. Men who don't treat you that way don't really care about anyone but themselves. Hold out for someone who cares about you."

Somewhere, Jean thought, she had heard those words before. From her father? Pastor Michaels? But hearing them from a man so near her own age was refreshing—and a bit surprising.

"So—are we on for snorkeling Saturday morning?" Ken asked.

"Okay. Or . . . how about this? My sister and her husband asked me to go to the beach with them Sunday afternoon. I'm sure they won't mind if you come, and I know you'd enjoy meeting them."

Ken hesitated for several seconds. Finally, he answered, "I'm sorry; I won't be able to go then. I'll be in church."

"Well, what time do you get out? We can't go until after our church service anyway."

"About three, but—"

"We'll pick you up then. Just tell me where."

"No, I mean I can't go to the beach at all on Sunday. I go to worship services, then I have some volunteer work to do for my church—and I just don't do recreational things that day. I'd love to go with you some other time, though."

"Is this like not drinking the wine?" Jean asked.

"Well, yes."

"I'm sorry. I didn't know. Shall we stick with the snorkeling Saturday morning?"

"I'd like that. Can you meet me here about nine?"

"Sure." She began to gather up the plates, forks, and the skillet. "I don't even want to ask you how you wash dishes here. I'll take these home and do them."

"Thanks for dinner. I didn't know how deprived I was until you came along."

"Just remember the lesson, and don't live on soup and fast-food hamburgers."

As she started out of the cabin, he asked, "When you get

up there by the pole, unplug the cord, will you, so I can reel it in?"

As he coiled up the cord, he thought about what had just happened. He had wanted to call Jean back and tell her he would go after all—but he wasn't able to do it. His hesitation when she had first asked made him ashamed. He realized that his church participation for the past several months had been as much a matter of form as anything else. True, he had been going to all of his meetings. But he had not been drinking freely of the Spirit, as in the past; often he had been impatient about having to sit through drawn-out talks or lessons.

Ken was just stowing the cord away when Jean stepped back through the open cabin door. "I phoned Jay and Allie and convinced them that we all ought to go to the beach on Saturday. That way we can make a full day of it. Will you mind passing up the snorkeling?"

"No, not at all. And—thanks. Can I bring anything?"

"No, just meet us at my house about nine." She grinned at him. "You know, you really need a telephone down here so I don't have to use the pay phone up there. Do you think you could run a phone line down to the boat without dropping it into the water?"

He stuck his tongue out at her. She laughed, and disappeared from the doorway.

Someone was playing a classical piece on the baby grand in the living room when Jean opened the door for Ken on Saturday morning.

"Come in," Jean said, "you're just in time for the concert. Allison's playing Debussy's '*Clair de lune*.' "

A woman and a man about Ken's age rose from the piano bench as Ken stepped into the living room.

"Hi, I'm Allison," the woman said. She was brunette, more

petite than Jean, and there was more of her father in her face, but, like her sister, she was beautiful.

"I'm glad to meet you. You play very well." Ken replied.

Allison smiled and nodded. Jean added, "Allie was the runner-up in the talent competition of the Miss Texas pageant four years ago."

"Spare me, Jean Ann!" Allison groaned. "When I'm a white-haired little old lady, you'll still be telling people about that."

Allison's husband had the handsomeness and the bearing of a man who would be seen on the pages of *Gentleman's Quarterly* or *Fortune*. Looking at these people, this place, Ken was beginning to feel like the pizza deliveryman again.

"Hi. I'm Jay Black—the husband of the white-haired little old lady. I won the competition as Allison's permanent page-turner four years ago. And I've been looking forward to meeting the man who almost fed Jeanie to the sharks."

Richard Bradley laughed. He stood in the doorway of the recreation room with his wife.

"Hi," Ken said. "Ready to hit the beach? Maybe I can show *you* the sharks today."

Richard chuckled. "No, thanks. I know when I'm not needed. One of the nice things about having grown children is that you don't have to sit by the pool and keep an eye on them anymore."

"Richard and I are going to spend the morning playing tennis," Carol Bradley said, slipping her arm through her husband's.

"No, golf," Richard said. "At a dime a stroke, she usually ends up owing me about a buck, and I need the money. Besides, my masculine pride couldn't stand another loss at tennis."

"Ken, I should thank you for reminding my children about honoring the Lord's day," Carol said. "We tried to teach that to them when they were younger."

Allison looked at her, puzzled. "You always told us church came first on Sunday, Mom, and then we could go to the beach."

Carol reddened. "I don't remember saying that, Allison Rae. We only gave in and took the two of you to the beach on Sunday afternoons because you begged so much." Her look at her daughter was withering.

The silence was awkward. Ken felt he was somehow involved in this electric little exchange between mother and daughter—but he didn't understand why. "Whatever you did, Carol, you obviously turned out two fine daughters," he volunteered.

"Thanks," she replied flatly and walked out of the room.

Richard glanced after her, frowning. Then he turned to the four young people. "Looks like if we play tennis today I may be in a lot of trouble," he said blandly. "Have a good time at the beach."

When the four of them were seated in Ken's Blazer, Allison leaned forward and said to Jean, "I haven't heard 'Allison Rae' in a long time. What did I say?"

"I'm not sure," Jean answered thoughtfully. Then she flashed her sister a smile. "But it's a good thing you have another place to go home to tonight."

About half an hour later, Ken was driving down the hard-packed sand of the beach, still wet from high tide, to where the beach-goers thinned out. He pulled onto the softer sand, toward the dunes, and parked when he found a spot where the nearest people were at least a hundred yards away on each side.

The women had worn their swimsuits under their clothes. But Ken walked back into the dunes to change. Just a few yards beyond the open stretch of beach that slopes down toward the water, he found an isolated spot. Standing in the depression between high dunes, he could see only sky and powdery white sand topped by arching stalks of grass.

Children cannot resist rolling, slipping, and sliding in the loose sand of these dunes. Even adults resist only with difficulty. When he had finished changing, Ken marched straight up and over the nearest dune, much as he had done when he was a boy. Small avalanches skittered down the dune's rippled surface and over his ankles as his feet sunk into the sand.

He marched up the next dune. Jay passed him at the crest, with the beach in view. "Beat you back," Jay called, and began running toward the truck. Ken took the challenge. He arrived at the Blazer only a half step behind.

Jay tossed his street clothes into the truck and pulled a Nerf football from the picnic basket Allison had prepared. "Now that we're warmed up, how about some catch?"

Ken tossed his own rolled-up clothes onto the seat and started loping toward the water. He looked back over his shoulder just in time to find a spiralling pass dropping into his hands. He stopped, planted his foot, and returned it. Jay's next toss was on target again.

"Throw one to me," Jean called. Ken tossed an easy one. She snatched it out of the air and threw a nice strike to Jay. She had a good touch on the ball.

They played three-cornered catch for a few minutes, until one of her short passes brought Jay down to Ken's area. Her next pass seemed destined to fall short between the two men, but Jay sprinted for it. Somehow Ken snatched it out of his reaching fingers. After the same thing happened for the second time a few minutes later, Jay exclaimed, "Hey! I remember you! McArthur. You kept us from winning the district title my senior year in high school. You took a pass away from our best receiver on the six-yard line with thirty-five seconds to go."

Ken smiled broadly. "Next-to-last game of my senior year. Broke my shoulder on the play. That was the end of my football career."

"I see you've recovered," Jay said wryly. He draped an arm

around Ken's shoulders. "If we ever choose up sides for anything, I want you on my team this time."

The South Texas sun can be searing on a beach without shade, even in April, so after their morning swim, they erected a beach awning next to Ken's truck. The four of them ate their lunch, talked of high school days, and napped until the afternoon sun crept under the awning from the west. Then they went in swimming again.

There is an exhilaration in riding over the crest of breakers as they form before hitting the beach, in trying to ride them toward shore, in throwing the body against the more powerful ones as they rush to land. That is what they were doing when Jean waited for a particularly big one and pushed Ken into it just as it broke. She was already retreating toward shore, laughing, when he came up sputtering.

By the time he chased her down, they were nearly a quarter mile from the truck. He was faster, but she dodged and weaved and would not quit. Finally he scooped her up in his arms and carried her into the surf to throw her into a big breaker. "No! Don't you dare!" she screamed. She clung tightly to his neck, and he tumbled into the surf with her.

"Truce! Truce!" she called as they came up. "I give up."

"Until the next time?"

As Ken and Jean strolled back up the beach, Jay tossed her the Frisbee. She tossed it back, trying to make it harder for him to reach, and he returned it the same way. Quickly, the two of them were engaged in competition.

Ken walked up to the truck to rummage in the ice chest for a soft drink. Allison had retreated to the shade of the awning next to the truck.

"Can you find something in there you like?" Allison asked. "There's no beer. Jean said you don't drink it."

"Uh . . . no. But you could have brought some, and it

wouldn't have bothered me. I'm used to having friends who don't believe the same things I do."

She wrinkled her nose. "It's okay. I don't really like beer, and Jay only has one occasionally with his friends, to be sociable. We didn't mind passing it up. Toss me a creme soda, will you?"

He opened one and handed it to her.

"Jean said you used to be a Mormon missionary. Have you been preaching to her?" Allison asked.

The question took him by surprise. Obviously the tendency to be direct ran in this family. "No," Ken answered. "Why?"

"I thought maybe I knew what was bothering my mother earlier," Allison answered. "If you were preaching to Jean about your church, that would do it. Mother serves on the outreach board at our church. She kept wanting us to preach to our friends when we were in high school, but we wouldn't. Jeanie always told Mom that faith was too personal to be pushed on anyone else." Allison smiled at him. "So you probably wouldn't get anywhere with Jean if you tried."

"You and Jean are pretty close, aren't you?"

"As close as sisters can be." She laughed. "But it wasn't always that way. We used to fight a lot when we were younger. Right after we moved into the house where Mom and Dad live now—when I was sixteen and Jeanie was thirteen—we fought so much that Mom made us spend a week without seeing each other. I had to stay in my bedroom when Jeanie was out of hers, and vice versa."

She smiled at the memory. "I said that was fine with me, and Jean said she could stay in her bedroom until I got married if she had to. But about the middle of the week we began to miss each other. On Friday I found a note under my door from Jeanie. It said, 'I love you, Allie. Let's be best friends.' And we have been ever since."

Ken frowned thoughtfully. "I hope I didn't do something to

make your mother mad. Your mother and father have been very nice to me. So have you and Jay. Do the Bradleys always welcome people so warmly?"

"Always. It's a family tradition," Allison said. "Especially when my sister is fascinated by them."

Ken looked at her strangely. "Jean's a good person to have for a friend. I'm glad I met her."

"Yes. Jeanie says the same thing about you. She talks about you a lot." Allison smiled knowingly.

Ken groped for a way to explain that he and Jean were developing a fine friendship, and nothing more. "Jean is a wonderful person," he began, "but—"

"Hey!" Jean called from the water's edge. "You two stop sitting around in the shade. We need two more down here for some serious Frisbee competition."

"You were saying?" Allison asked, looking up at him expectantly.

Ken wasn't really sure what he had been saying. He put his empty soft drink can down on top of the cooler. "I think I need to go show Jean who's the Frisbee flash here," he answered.

4

Bad News on Channel 7

Ken was examining some color slides in the light from the open cabin door when Jean stomped down the stairs and plopped on the bunk opposite him.

"You want to tell me why men are so treacherous?" she challenged.

"Whoa," he said, leaning back against the wall behind him. "I don't think I can bear the guilt for the entire male half of the world's population."

"Well, okay, you're not that way, but *most* men—"

"Your father—and Jay?"

"Why are *some* men such treacherous slimeballs?"

"Want to tell me what happened?"

"I lost my job."

He waited, but Jean sat slumped on the bunk, chin on her chest. "That *is* bad news, but what's it have to do with men?" he asked.

"Suddenly there's no work at the station for me anymore. It seems there's no money in the budget."

"Why?"

"Because I wouldn't play pat-a-cake with Gordon, the news director."

"Is this the guy who's been telling you he'd get you on full-time as soon as there was an opening?"

"Yes."

"Tell me about it."

"I was in the dressing room checking my makeup. Gordon walked in, shut the door, and told me he was sure he could get me on full-time now—if I wanted to work closely with him. Then he grabbed me in a bear hug and tried to kiss me."

Ken leaned forward tensely. "What did you do?"

"I got away from him by using a little move that Jay taught me once. I left Gordon hanging over a chair trying to breathe. The last thing he told me when I walked out was 'You're through here. We can't afford you anymore.' "

"Can you tell me where to find this guy?" Ken was staring at some point in the distance behind her. His face was expressionless, as though a veil had been drawn behind his eyes. She could read nothing in them. Jean had seen this expression once before, and she remembered what happened to the big man who had imprisoned her in his bear hug the night Ken had rescued her.

"No—I mean, yes, of course I can tell you where to find him, but you can't do anything to help the situation now," she answered.

"Did you say anything about this to anyone at the station?"

"No. It would have been my word against his, and he's a good friend of the station manager."

"So he's going to get away with it! That—"

"Ken! I can't waste time worrying about *him*. What am I going to do? I needed that job."

There was a note of pleading in her voice. Ken came back from wherever he had been in his mind and focused on her.

"Jean, I know this looks tough right now. But you won't have to worry about getting a job. You're good at what you do. You'll be able to find work somewhere else." He smiled reassuringly. It was the wrong thing to do at the moment.

"Have you ever been thrown out of a job?" she asked, her voice rising.

"Yes. It wasn't the end of the world. I found another one. And you're a lot better prepared than I was. Channel 7 isn't the only place you can find work."

"Oh, sure! Thanks for the sympathy. San Antonio and Houston and Dallas-Fort Worth are all pretty competitive markets. I don't have a lot to show for working here, and I sure can't count on a recommendation from the news director. Maybe I'll be able to find a job in some place like Odessa or Laredo—if I'm lucky."

"Stop that! Don't sell yourself short. You're a good television journalist."

"How would you know?"

"What—you mean a mere high school graduate and ex-Marine?"

"No—no. I'm sorry. I was just being rude and surly. I didn't mean it the way you thought. Please don't ever believe that. You're one of the most intelligent men I know. But you're not in the business."

"Look," he said, crossing to sit by her, "I guess I didn't sound very sympathetic. I'm sorry about that. Sometimes in the M.P.s I was detailed to help escort VIP parties. I've seen professional news people at work up close, and as far as I'm concerned, you're as good as any of the others. You just haven't been used properly where you've been working. You've got to believe that."

"Do you really believe that, Ken? Or are you just trying to make me feel better?" She looked at him as though trying to read his thoughts.

He took her hand and held it softly between his. "Jean, I'll bet you were one of the top students in journalism at your school, weren't you?"

"Yes."

"And aren't there people at the school who would give you good recommendations?"

"Yes."

"I believe you have what it takes to be in network news, if that's what you want to do some day."

"Now you're just flattering me," Jean said.

"No, I'm not. I mean it. I like you too much to lie to you." He smiled suddenly. "But I wouldn't encourage you to try for the big time just yet. Go after something locally first. I'd miss you if you left here."

She squeezed his hand and smiled tentatively. "That's what I want, for now—to work in my hometown. But I'm afraid there aren't any openings here at the moment."

"Have you thought about working for some kind of video production company?"

She considered it for a few seconds. "That might be fun—if the job had a creative challenge to it. But I don't know of anything like that around here."

"You could check it out. You'd be a natural for it, with your interest in theater." He paused. "I know you can find a way to make a living in your field. And really—would Odessa be so bad, if you had to go there for the time being?"

She sighed. "No, I suppose not. It could be whatever I make it. But that would be disappointing because I had my sights set higher."

"Be honest with yourself, Jean—deep inside, do you believe that you have what it takes to work in Dallas or Houston?"

She thought again for several seconds before answering. "Yes . . . of course I do. I guess if I didn't believe that, I shouldn't be in this business. But I don't have the experience yet that a station in a major market would want to see. And if they wanted to contact my last employer—well, Gordon would certainly blow my chances for me."

Ken gazed off into space again. "How often has some guy tried that kind of move on you?"

"Not as often as I made it seem. I've really known a lot of nice guys." She laughed a short, bitter laugh. "Somehow, you've been around when the worst ones have come along." Then the hardness in her eyes went away again. "Thanks for caring enough to help."

"I hate to think of men like that backing you into a corner. We need to get you some kind of protection you could carry in your purse."

"You mean a weapon?" She shook her head vigorously. "No, thanks. It would be dangerous. They'd probably just take it away from me and use it against me."

He thought about her answer for a moment. "Okay. You're right. It was a bad idea. Maybe there's still too much training for combat left in me. But there must be something we can do to help you protect yourself."

"A weapon wouldn't have done me any good today anyway. Gordon was between me and my purse." She sighed. "I suppose I need to ask Jay to give me a quick course in defending myself."

"Does he know a lot about it?"

"Yes. He works out at it every day. Jay is some kind of . . . I think he's a black belt. When he and Allie were in high school, he made her learn enough to defend herself—she could take a mugger apart if she had to. So, maybe I'll ask him to teach me how to do it."

"That might not be a bad idea. There are some things I could teach you too. And maybe you ought to let me screen your next employer."

"I can handle that myself," she said testily.

"Sorry. I didn't mean you couldn't. I'm just worried that your ex-news director might not be the last guy like this you meet. And I still think you ought to report him. If you don't, he may tell people he fired you because your work wasn't good enough."

"He would say that anyway. And with just my word against his, I don't want to take chances on a lawsuit—unless he goes out of his way to bad-mouth me professionally."

"Well—it's up to you. Are you feeling any better now?"

She sat up straight on the edge of the bunk. "I'm still upset, Ken. I have no idea what I'm going to do for work. I suppose I'll have to start sending out audition tapes and resumes tomorrow. But I'll be all right—I think. Thanks for the encouragement."

She rose to leave. "I'm sorry you had to take the brunt of this. Usually, I go home to cry on Mom or Dad's shoulder when something goes wrong. But you came to mind first, and you were closer, so . . . anyway, thanks for listening."

"For you, the doctor is in anytime," Ken said, smiling. "Remember, don't sell yourself short."

"Okay. But I'll probably have a lot of time on my hands until I find another job. Come and see me?"

"Count on it."

Two days later, Ken knocked on the door of the Bradley home.

Carol Bradley answered. "Ken—it's good to see you. Come in. I'll get Jean." She walked into the recreation room. A few seconds later, the sound of the exercise bike stopped, and Jean came out in a pair of shorts and a sweat-stained T-shirt.

"I wish you had let me know you were coming," Jean said. "I would have cleaned up first. I'm getting in shape for the big job hunt."

"You haven't done any hunting in Corpus Christi yet, have you?"

Jean frowned. "No. I sent out a couple of resumes and tapes yesterday, but I haven't done any looking here. Why?"

"I just came from Channel 9. They're going to have an opening in the news department in a couple of weeks. I asked if they had heard from you, but the news director said no. You'd better jump on it."

She looked at him strangely. Out of the corner of his eye, Ken could see Carol watching them from the kitchen doorway.

"I don't know whether to thank you, or get mad at you for meddling in my life," Jean said. He could see the sharply etched line of her jawbone.

"You can thank me—after you have the job. The news director would like to see you tomorrow morning at nine. Here's his card."

"I know who he is—Mark Hillyard," she said curtly. "Did you think to ask me if I wanted to apply there?"

"Well, no, but I thought you'd want to know—"

"I don't like it very much when people start thinking for me."

"Yeah, well . . . look, I was over there to drop off some promotional photos I made for them. When I heard about the opening, I thought you'd want a shot at it," he explained patiently. "Mark said he knows your work, and if he'd known you were looking for a job, he would have called you."

"Oh, really." The words were icy.

"Yes, really," he said sharply. "So I did a dumb thing—I set up this appointment without asking you. Will you keep it?"

"I'll think about it. Right now I've got to go clean up." She dropped the news director's card on an end table as she headed for the stairs.

Ken stared after her. Carol crossed the room from the kitchen.

"I couldn't help overhearing," she said. "Thanks for trying

to look out for Jean. I'm sorry she was so rude. Losing her job the way she did—well, she's been mad at everybody."

"Right. And I guess I wasn't exactly a diplomat about this, was I?"

Carol smiled indulgently at him.

"Can you encourage her to keep that appointment anyway?" Ken urged. "It's important."

"She'll go—if I have to take her just like I did when she was starting school. Will you stay for dinner? Jean will be all right in a little while, as soon as she gets over her snit."

"Thanks, but I have to make a run to Houston right now. I'll probably stay overnight and stop to take some pictures tomorrow morning on the way back. I'll find out what happened when I get back."

Lying flat on his back and reaching up from underneath, Ken tried to unscrew the oil filter carefully, but it slipped loose suddenly. He bobbled it in one hand and writhed away from the oil streaming into the pail he had placed beneath the engine. The filter slipped from his fingers and rolled away, out from under the truck.

The toe of a high-heeled shoe stopped it and pushed it back. "You lost something," Jean called.

"Hi. Come down here where I can see you."

"I can't. It wouldn't be very ladylike in this skirt, and I'd ruin my nylons. Come out here where I can talk to you."

Ken wriggled out from under the truck and got to his feet. She looked at his face and giggled. "You've got oil spots all over. You look like you've got black freckles."

He wiped two fingers across his face. They came away black.

"Here," she said, handing him the dry rag he had left on the fender of his Blazer.

He rubbed the rag over his face. "So—don't keep me in suspense. Tell me about the interview."

"I got the job," she said excitedly. "I'm starting immediately—this afternoon. He said he wanted to be sure Channel 9 hired me before someone else could make me an offer."

She took the rag from him and dabbed at the oil he had smudged over his forehead. Then she stopped to look into his eyes. "I'm sorry I was so mean to you yesterday. After I left you at the door, I felt bad about what I said. I felt even worse when I came back to apologize and you were gone."

"I'm just glad you went for the interview."

Jean laughed. "I'm stubborn, not stupid." She stood back to study his face. "You're really decorated. It's going to take more than a dry rag to get that off."

He took the rag from her and walked over to wet it under the water faucet on the edge of the jetty; he wiped his face again and looked her way. She giggled again. "That just smeared it worse. You look like you're made up for the big battle-in-the-jungle scene in a war movie."

Ken casually reached down and capped the flow of the faucet with his finger, sending a stream squirting in her direction. "No!" she cried, retreating behind his truck. "I have to be on camera in an hour."

"What are you covering?" he asked as he strolled back toward the vehicle.

"They're giving me the arts beat," she said, coming out of hiding. "It fits. I'll get some good from my theater minor after all."

"What's going on in the theater this afternoon?"

"There's a hearing at three-thirty on county funding for the arts. They're sending me to cover it."

"See? I told you you're the kind of talent any station would be glad to have."

She smiled at him. "Thanks for having so much confidence in me—and for pushing me."

He smiled back. "Even if I was meddling in your life? You were right about that. I think I was looking out for my own interests as well as yours. I didn't want you to leave town yet . . . just when we were becoming good friends."

"Listen, at least I owe you dinner. I think I can be back here about seven if you can be ready."

"Great. I'll fire up the hot plate."

"No, I mean the real thing. I'm taking you out to a restaurant." She looked at the speckles on his face again and grinned. "Will you have enough time to get out of your jungle-fighter camouflage?"

"No, but I know a great place down by the docks where no one will care. You'll be a bit overdressed, though."

"Seven-thirty, then? I want to take you someplace nice."

"I'll be ready at seven. I suppose it wouldn't do any good to say that you don't have to do this just because I did something to help you?"

"What do you think? See you later."

He was standing in the stern of the *Rum Runner,* looking at the city skyline lighted against the gathering dusk when she drove up. He wore a dress shirt and tie, and his sport coat was slung over his shoulder. Already, in mid-April, it was beginning to be too warm in South Texas to put on a dress coat, except in air-conditioned buildings or cars.

"Sorry I'm late," she called as she walked toward the pier.

He stepped up to meet her and made a show of checking the time. "Seven-thirty, you said. Hmm. I've been waiting for more than half an hour."

"Is that why your hair's still wet?" she asked, flicking water from the strands on his forehead. "Shall I feel the hood of your truck to see if the engine's still warm?"

He laughed. "Okay, I just got back ten minutes ago. I'm glad I didn't miss you."

"You look very nice," she said.

"Thanks. I thought I'd better dress up if we're going someplace civilized."

"Do you like fish?"

"Love it."

"How about the Golden Net?"

"The new place out on Ayers? Sure."

He held the door of his Blazer open for her. She hesitated before the high step up into the four-wheel-drive vehicle, then turned to look at him. "You have to be acrobatic to get in and out of one of these in a fitted skirt and heels. Do you mind if we take my car?"

"No, that's fine."

She rummaged in her purse for her car keys and handed them to him.

He opened the passenger door for her, and she slid into the seat. "Are you sure you want me to drive?" he asked. "The last time I drove one of these, I stacked it up against a building."

"Just drive as if it were your father's car," she replied.

"That one *was* my father's car."

"Do you want me to drive?" she asked sweetly.

He chuckled. "No, no, I'll drive as carefully as the family chauffeur."

"In that case, Kenneth, please step on it. I'm hungry."

After he had maneuvered into the traffic on Shoreline Boulevard, she said, "Ken, I think tonight is the first time I've ever heard you mention your father. I assumed . . . well, is he still living?"

"Yes. In Houston."

"And your mother?"

"She died when I was eleven, but they were divorced a couple of years before that." He sighed. "My father and I never got along after the divorce. I couldn't forgive him for walking out on my mother, and he never seemed satisfied with anything about me."

"That must have been hard for you."

"It was. I lived with him for a while after my mother died, but when I was thirteen, he and my grandparents agreed that I would be better off with them. As far as straightening out my life, it was the best thing that could have happened to me."

"It sounds like growing up was rough for you."

"Granddad and Grandma helped me get through it. My grandmother died a few years ago, but by that time the two of them had shown me the difference love can make in a life."

"And the car wreck?" Jean asked. Then she quickly added, "I'm sorry. It's none of my business. I was just caught up in what you were telling me."

"That's okay." He paused briefly; she thought he gripped the wheel tighter. "The accident was my fault. Sometimes my father would drop into my life to do something generous for his son—as if he felt it was his duty. One night when I was sixteen, he let me take his car—his pride and joy—out to pick up some friends."

"And you couldn't resist showing it off for them?"

He smiled grimly. "I never had the chance. On the way to pick them up, I punched the accelerator too much in a turn and slid into the side of a building."

Ken pulled to a stop at a traffic light. He stared straight ahead. "I was lucky to come out alive. And my father—he came steaming into my hospital room and chewed me out about the car. I deserved it. But he didn't even ask about me first." The light changed, and he pulled away slowly.

"I'm sorry I made you rake that up. I can tell it's painful."

"Don't worry. I've learned to live with it. My father is what he is, and I am what I am. We don't see each other very much, and when we do, it's 'Hi, how've you been? How's business?' "

"Well—forgive me. I feel like a fool."

He glanced at her, surprised. "Why?"

"I was just remembering when you told me how blessed I am to come from the family that I do. As I recall, I lectured you about how things haven't always come easy for me." She looked away. "I didn't understand what you were really saying. I'm sorry."

"Forget it. You didn't know." He pulled into the restaurant parking lot, parked, and turned to smile at her. "I hope you have an in with the maître d' so we can find out what's good today."

"Better than that. I know the owner. And wait till you taste the red snapper."

At the entrance to the restaurant, they stood back to let another couple exit. "Why, hello, Brother McArthur," the woman said.

"Hello, Sister Steiner," Ken replied. "Let me introduce you to a friend of mine. Jean Bradley," he said, turning to Jean, "I'd like you to meet Irene and Joe Steiner."

"I'm pleased to meet you," the woman said, extending her hand to shake Jean's. "I believe I know your mother. Aren't you Carol's daughter?"

"Yes," Jean said. "And I believe I've seen you before—in a newspaper photo?"

"Carol and I are on the board of Drug-Free Youth together. Please tell her I said hello."

Inside the restaurant, after the waiter had seated them in a booth, Jean looked at Ken inquiringly. "*Brother* McArthur?"

"Joe and Irene are members of my church. Everybody there is 'Brother' or 'Sister.' Irene is president of the Young Women—the organization for girls between twelve and eighteen."

"From what my mother says, Mrs. Steiner is involved in a lot of other things in the community too. She must be a very busy woman."

"I suppose she is. She's a very caring person. She has a lot to offer."

The waiter had taken their orders and they were waiting for dinner when a short, slim Asian woman in a dark skirt and white blouse approached their table.

"Hello, Vonnie," Jean said, smiling.

"It's good to see you again, Jean. You don't come around often enough."

"I can't eat out all the time, Vonnie. And you're never home to visit. I know, because I've called."

Vonnie laughed. "You know us—hard-working immigrants making good on the American dream. I keep telling Steve this place is doing well enough now for me to stay home sometimes."

"Vonnie, this is Ken McArthur," Jean said. "Ken, Vonnie is one of my best friends."

"Obviously, this is a man of good taste," Vonnie said to Jean, looking at Ken out of the corner of her eye. "He knows a classy lady when he sees one. Ken, come back often—and bring Jean with you. I owe her a lot, and I only get to pay her back when she comes here."

"No freebies tonight, Vonnie," Jean replied. "We're celebrating my new job, and I'm buying, because Ken helped me get it."

"Really? Where?"

"Channel 9—full-time."

"All right! I'll be able to say I knew the famous Jean Bradley when she was my tutor." Vonnie glanced toward the cash register, where a customer was waiting. "Oops. I'll see you later."

"Tutor?" Ken asked after Vonnie walked away.

"When she came into our school in the eighth grade, she

hardly spoke any English. A lot of the girls wouldn't have anything to do with her, but I liked to talk to her," Jean explained matter-of-factly. "I ended up helping her learn the language. In fact, that's how my mother got interested in the charity work she does with Asian families."

"You mean you were a friend to Vonnie when nobody else wanted to be."

Jean frowned. "Well, yes, I guess so. But it wasn't like I made her a project of some kind. I just didn't want her to be left out. Allie helped me include her in some parties and other things. Vonnie and I became good friends. A lot of my other friends learned to like her too."

Jean and her family seemed to do naturally many of the things that Jesus had taught, Ken reflected. He wondered how his own life measured up; there was definitely room for improvement in reaching out to others.

The meal was leisurely and delicious. Vonnie stopped by their table to talk twice more, and when they left, she invited them back for a free dinner some other time.

Ken drove slowly back toward the T-head. "Vonnie doesn't talk like someone who's been in the country for only ten years or so," he said.

"She's a quick learner. She knows a lot more about the culture and language in this country than I know about hers. 'Vonnie' is only close to a part of her whole name. I can't begin to say it right." She laughed. "And 'Steve' isn't even close to her husband's name. He's a refugee too. One of our teachers couldn't pronounce his name, so he just called him Steve."

"Your mother is involved in so many charity activities. I've never known anyone like that."

"I think she feels blessed, the way you said I am. She feels like she ought to give something back."

"Did your mother get Irene Steiner involved in Drug-Free Youth?"

Jean thought for a moment. "No, I believe it was the other way around. It surprises me to learn that Irene is a member of your church. I didn't think I knew any other Mormons."

She was lost in thought for a while. "Ken," she said finally, "you've changed some of my perceptions about missionaries, and about Marines, and now about Mormons. Somehow I always thought of Mormons as people who dress like the Amish and live quietly somewhere back in the mountains."

He chuckled. "Farming the land with horses and walking into town for Sunday services?"

"Yes, something like that."

Ken was silent for a moment, then he glanced over at her. There would never be a better opportunity to ask, he thought. "Would you like to come to church with me on Sunday to see what Mormons are really like?"

"Sure, if I can do it after I go to church with my family. What time?"

"Noon."

"That will work. We get out a little after eleven. Our church is up on the bluff, not far from the T-heads. I'll drive down and meet you at the boat."

Ken was elated. He had begun to feel an urgency about introducing Jean to the gospel. And maybe Allison had been wrong. Maybe when Jean knew more about his church, she would be willing to listen to missionaries.

He parked her car by the *Rum Runner*'s pier. She came around to the driver's seat, and they said goodnight. As he watched her drive away, he felt that he had left something undone. But it was a dumb idea, he decided. People who were just good friends didn't kiss each other goodnight.

5

The Captain and the Crew

Ken was waiting on the jetty when Jean drove up. She came around to the passenger side of her car and let him open the door for her. "You drive," she said. "You know where we're going."

He said nothing for several blocks, though he seemed on the point of speaking two or three times. Finally he ventured: "I probably ought to tell you what happens in a Mormon church service, so you'll know what to expect."

"Okay."

"Well, we sing. There will be several songs. Uh—there won't be a minister to preach—all the talking is done by members. Maybe there'll be some kids who give talks. Maybe the ward choir will sing. A ward is a local congregation—did I tell you that? And . . . ah . . . the bishop will conduct the meeting. A Mormon bishop is the leader of the ward, but he's not like a Catholic bishop—"

"Ken?"

"What?"

"Are you nervous about having me visit your church?"

He exhaled slowly. "Yes, I guess I am."

"Why? I'm not going there to do an investigative report. I'm just going to see what ordinary, garden-variety Mormons are like, remember?"

He was silent for a few moments. Then he shrugged. "Sorry. It's just that I know it won't be what you're used to seeing. In our church, members get involved in the worship services and in all the gospel teaching that goes on. Some people seem to think that's strange."

She smiled at him. "You seem pretty normal to me. Why don't you just let me experience it, and if I have any questions, I'll ask you later."

"Okay."

The sacrament meeting was about to begin when they arrived. They found seats near the back. As the meeting progressed, she observed attentively. He sang the opening and sacrament hymns in his creditable bass while she followed the words in the hymnal. As the bread tray came down their row, he leaned over and whispered, "There's no need for you to take any of this. It has a special meaning for members."

Ken squirmed as two young people read from collections of stories for their "talks." Then a couple who had recently moved to Corpus Christi from Kansas spoke about how they had been converted to the church and what it meant in their lives. Occasionally Ken glanced at Jean out of the corner of his eye; she gave no hint of her reaction to the talks.

The closing hymn was "How Great Thou Art." As Ken opened the book to the proper page, Jean leaned over and whispered, "I know this one!" When the congregation reached the chorus, Ken could see members of the ward choir four or five rows ahead of them turning to search for the source of Jean's clear, soaring soprano. He stopped to listen in awe. She sang as though she had been professionally trained.

"You have a beautiful voice!" he told her after the benediction.

She shrugged. "Mom and Dad saw that Allie and I both had music training. Allie preferred the piano, but I chose voice lessons. I don't get to do much singing now. I suppose all that training just contributes to the lovely, golden tones that I project on the air." She laughed.

Ken and Jean found themselves face-to-face with the bishop as they made their way through the crowd in the foyer, so Ken made a brief introduction. The bishop responded warmly and shook Jean's hand. Then Ken withdrew a gray envelope from his pocket and handed it to Bishop Williamson.

After the bishop had walked away, Jean looked at Ken questioningly. "You have to write notes to your . . . "

"Bishop?"

"Yes."

Ken smiled. "No. That was an offering."

They attended the Gospel Essentials class. After it was over, Ken steered her toward the foyer. "The meetings break up into separate sessions for men and women now, and I don't want to send you off alone, so we'd probably better leave."

As they drove away, he waited for her to say something. Finally he asked: "Any questions?"

"Yes, a couple. Is the bread and water that those boys passed around some kind of communion?"

"There's a similarity. The bread and water are symbols of the body and the blood of Christ. When we're baptized, we make promises to live the way he taught. Every week when we take the sacrament—the bread and water—it helps us remember our promises."

"Those boys who brought the bread and water—do they have any kind of special training?"

"Probably not the kind you're thinking of. They start when

they're twelve. Before then, they're supposed to have been taught at home and in church classes what the sacrament means and how sacred it is."

She sat in silence for a minute or so.

"Any other questions?" he asked.

"Yes, but I'm not quite sure how to ask it. That man that they talked about during the Sunday School class—did I understand that you believe he's a *prophet?*"

"Yes."

"He looked like any older man in a suit—like some of the men my father deals with in his business. I expected something different."

"You mean someone like Charlton Heston as Moses, coming down off the mountain with the stone tablets?"

"Not exactly. Well . . . I don't know what I'd expect a prophet to be like. But it seems to me he would look different."

"I think Moses was probably a man of his own times, don't you?"

"I suppose." She thought for a moment. "Do you mean you believe that the man in that picture goes up on a mountain and talks to the Lord?"

"I don't think it happens just that way, but we believe he's the Lord's spokesman on earth. When our Heavenly Father has something he wants to share with his children today, he teaches it through his living prophet."

"It must be comforting to believe that."

"It's true."

Jean turned in her seat to look at him intently. "How can you be so sure?"

"Anyone can be sure of it, the same way people were when Peter and Paul preached to them after Jesus was gone. The Holy Ghost can testify of it in your heart."

She watched him for several seconds as he drove. Then she

turned to stare straight ahead without speaking. He glanced sideways. The pleasant natural expression she usually wore told him nothing. She might be simply thinking about what he had said, or she might have been offended. "So," he said tentatively after they had driven several blocks, "would you like to come to church with me again next Sunday?"

"Yes," she said, turning to smile at him. "And would you come with me to my church on Sunday morning before we go to yours? Then maybe you could come to my house for dinner later."

"Sure. I'd like that." Inwardly he relaxed. "But Sunday is a long way away. Maybe I could drop by your house tomorrow and polish the door knocker, or walk your poodle, or something, so I could see you sooner."

She laughed. "We don't have a poodle, silly."

"I'll bring you one. Every house with a four-car garage ought to have its own poodle. I understand there's a good supply at the pound."

"Down, boy. I have to work all day tomorrow. I'll drop by the boat after I'm through."

But it was Wednesday before they saw each other again. She knocked on the door of the *Rum Runner*'s cabin just after eight-thirty in the morning.

"It's unlocked," Ken called from inside. She pushed open the door and descended the stairs. He was sitting on the spare bunk reading a paperback. Two granola bar wrappers and a one-pint milk container with a straw sticking out of it sat on the bunk beside him.

"Ah, a little light reading over breakfast," she said. "Mike Hammer?"

He held up a copy of *A Stillness at Appomattox,* by Bruce Catton.

"Excuse me," she said. "Nourishing the mind as well as the body. I didn't know you were a Civil War buff."

"I'm not, really, but I enjoy history."

"You enjoy learning in general, don't you?"

"I think I owe that partly to Mrs. McGillis. They surprised her and me and everyone else when they put me in her advanced English class my senior year. But she taught me to love reading."

"Well," Jean said lightly, "you overlooked your private library when you gave me the tour of your boat."

Ken opened the back of the book to show her the public library checkout slip. "As long as I have a library card, the world is mine. I've paid so many overdue fines at the library that I feel like one of the owners." He smiled thinly.

He seemed a bit distant—almost sullen, Jean thought. "You don't seem very happy to see me this morning." It was half statement, half question.

"I missed you Monday. And again yesterday."

Jean looked puzzled. "Didn't you get my note?"

"No. Did you leave a note?"

"I wedged it in the door of the cabin. I had to work late Monday because someone was out sick. When I came by to see you yesterday morning on my way to work, you were gone already, so I left the note. I came as early as I could today."

Ken seemed to relax. "I had to make a delivery out of town yesterday," he said, rising from the bunk. "Your note must have blown away." He fished a small key from his jeans pocket and handed it to her.

"What's this?"

"A spare key to the cabin so you can use my message center when I'm not here."

He crossed to where a large barometer hung on the wall at the foot of the other bunk. The barometer was set into a round, decorative metal frame shaped like a ship's wheel with spokes.

Holding it by two of the spokes, Ken took it down from its place. Behind it was the door of a small wall safe. "I don't know what Granddad used this for, but this is where people who are important in my life leave messages. Only you and my three steady delivery clients know about it."

"Oh. So now I could clean out your treasure hoard and take off for Mexico?" She smiled impishly.

He grinned at her and quickly worked the combination of the safe to open it, showing that it was empty. "Did you see how I did that?"

"Yes, you twirled the dial and whispered, 'Open, sesame,' and it opened."

"Come here. I'm going to teach you how to do it so you can leave notes for me inside. I always check it when I come back at the end of the day."

After she had opened the safe twice in a row to prove she could do it, he hung the barometer back in place.

"I have the day off today. What are you doing?" Jean asked.

"Rats! I'm working. It's my day in the darkroom space I rent. What are you doing tonight?"

"Fixing you dinner, if you'll come out to the house."

"I have a better idea. Have you ever seen the sunset from out there?" He pointed in the direction of the bay.

"No. Is it nice?"

"It's beautiful. Why don't we make a party of it? See if Jay and Allie can come."

"Okay. I'll bring a picnic supper. What time?"

"Meet me here about five-thirty."

She was sitting on one of the cushioned seats in the stern, reading, knees drawn up under her chin, when he drove up. "I borrowed your paperback," she said, waving the library book at him. "It *is* interesting. I can't wait to see who won the Civil War."

He carried his stack of prints down into the cabin and re-emerged.

"I thought you always checked your message center," she said. Her sly smile told him he ought to do as she suggested. He disappeared into the cabin again, but in two minutes he was back. In his hands he held a dark-blue baseball cap and an envelope. There was phony gold braid around the bill of the cap; in gold lettering on the front was the word "CAPTAIN."

"You have to be properly attired for this cruise," Jean said, taking the cap from his hands. She placed it on his sandy hair and adjusted it to the proper angle. "There. Now you'll look official when Jay and Allie come." Jean snapped to attention and saluted him smartly.

He returned the salute in the relaxed style of a senior officer. "Great. Does this mean that out there beyond the three-mile limit, whatever I say goes? Can I make people walk the plank if they get out of line?"

"Anybody but the cook."

Ken held the letter-size envelope up to the light, then carefully tore off one end.

"Was that in the safe too?" Jean asked. "I didn't leave it there, but there was an older man who came by about half an hour ago, while I was reading. He had a key, and he went into the cabin, and then came out a couple of minutes later."

Ken unfolded the note he took from the envelope and glanced at it, then looked up at Jean. "Thin man, white hair, a little shorter than me, in his seventies?"

"That's him."

"Jack Weissman. My best delivery client—and a good friend. He has a small job for me in the morning. I'll be able to take care of it and get back for a photo assignment tomorrow night."

"He seemed surprised to see anyone else here. I introduced myself and told him that I'm a friend of yours. He shook my hand—"

"Wait—let me guess," Ken interrupted. He grasped Jean's right hand in a handshake and covered it softly with his left. " 'And I'm J. V. Weissman—Jack to my friends,' " he quoted.

Jean laughed. "That's it, exactly. And then he said, 'Tell Kenneth I'm glad to meet one of his young friends at last.' "

Ken chuckled. "You made Jack's day."

"Why?"

"He's been telling me for months that I need to have a social life instead of living like a hermit on this boat. I'm sure he was glad to see some progress."

Ken and Jean sat in the stern, watching seagulls glide across the bay on the breeze, until Allison and Jay arrived on the jetty a few minutes later.

As Allison stepped aboard the boat, she glanced at the cap Ken wore and saluted. Jay, right behind her, followed suit.

In answer, Ken cupped his hands around his mouth like a megaphone and boomed authoritatively, "Take your positions for this voyage." He pointed first to one stern seat, then to the other. "I'll get your oars."

Allison looked at her husband in mock horror. "I told you not to book the economy cruise!"

Sunset was still almost two hours away, so when the boat cleared the Rocks, Ken turned south for some sightseeing along the shoreline. The two women managed to pick out their parents' home and a number of other local landmarks. Jean brought out the picnic supper, and the four of them munched as they rode along on the bay; Ken coaxed Jean into steering for a time while he devoured some of her fried chicken and potato salad.

Sunset was approaching when he stepped up behind her and reached around to put his hands on top of hers on the wheel.

"Okay, it's time to turn back toward downtown," he said, moving her hands to spin the wheel to the left. The boat went into a long, looping curve outward toward the bay. When the prow came around to the north, he stepped away to let her steer again.

"Where are you going?" she asked as he disappeared into the cabin.

"Don't get nervous. I'll be right back." He came out in a couple of minutes with a telephoto lens mounted on his camera. "Hold the boat steady, helmsman . . . helmsperson—sailor," he instructed. Jean saluted.

The sun played peek-a-boo behind low clouds, silhouetting them and turning their edges silver, then emerging to drop quickly to the horizon. It turned deep orange as it sank behind the city's skyline. In the deepening dusk, fluorescent lights punctuated the darkness of the tall, black shadows that were downtown buildings. Ken shot pictures as long as the fading light permitted.

"Am I going to run into anything in the dark?" Jean asked him apprehensively.

"No, but I'll take over if you want to put the camera in the cabin for me."

He steered the boat far out into the dark bay, then turned it around. From that vantage point, on either side of the boat, city lights curved around the bay like a jeweled necklace, with downtown—the gaudy pendant—dead ahead.

As they neared the opening in the Rocks on the return trip, Ken said, "Okay, Jean, take the wheel and guide the boat right down the channel. Watch the marker buoys." He stood beside her and occasionally corrected her steering. "You're doing great," he commented. "I'll make a boater out of you in no time."

Jean glanced over her shoulder, toward where Jay and Allison were sitting. "We want to remind you about the rules on our Love Boat cruise," she intoned loudly. "Please remember that kissing is prohibited in public areas in order to avoid embarrassing our captain and crew."

"Keep your eyes on the road up there!" Jay called back.

Once they were inside the breakwater, Ken steered the boat to the pier, and Jean helped him tie it up.

Jay and Allison said their good-byes, then paused for a moment on the pier, talking. "Ken," Jay called down, "we owe you one. How would you like to come to our place for dinner Saturday night—and bring your crew?"

Ken looked at Jean. "What do you say, crew?"

"Love to," she said. "Is seven okay, Allie? I can be off by then."

"Fine. Hope you like Chinese, Ken."

"She cooks, and I play wok music," Jay added.

Ken winced, and Jean groaned. Allison took her husband by the shirt front and led him toward their car. "Come along, lover, chop chop."

When they were gone, Jean gathered up the picnic things she had brought. "Thanks for suggesting the boat ride," she said. "It's a beautiful view from out there. You really have an eye for lovely things."

"Yes," he said, leaning slowly toward her. Half a second more and his lips would have touched hers—but the bill of the cap he wore struck her just above the eye.

"Ow!" Instinctively, she ducked away.

"Did I hurt your eye?"

"No, it's okay," she said, blinking and juggling the sack of picnic things.

"Are you sure?"

"It's okay. I'm sure. The hat didn't hit my eye. See?"

She stood looking at him wide-eyed and smiled. He took off the captain's cap and sailed it toward the cabin door. He took the sack from her arms and put it down on the nearest seat. Then he put his arms around her and kissed her.

She kissed back.

After several seconds, he let her go. "I've been wanting for a long time to do that."

"I've been hoping you would," Jean said.

Ken pulled her toward him gently and kissed her again. When he let her go, she put her fingertips to her own lips, then touched them to his and held them there for a few seconds. "I really do have to go now," she said, gathering up the picnic things.

"Saturday night is three nights away. Will I see you before then?"

"I have to cover a dance concert Friday night. It'll be late when I'm through, so it would be nice if you could meet me at the auditorium and escort me home."

Ken stopped by Jean's house at fifteen till six on Thursday evening. Carol answered the door.

"Hi. Is Jean home from work?" Ken asked. "I was just passing by on my way to shoot some photos for a client, and I thought maybe I could talk to her for a few minutes."

"Oh, dear. She called from work to say that she won't be home until after seven."

Ken frowned. "Well, I'm sorry to bother you, Carol. Please tell her I'll be out of touch all day tomorrow, but I'll meet her tomorrow night as we planned."

Carol smiled broadly. "You're no bother, Ken. You know that by now." She paused for a moment. "As long as you're here, could you help me with something?"

"Sure. What do you need?"

"I have two fifty-pound bags of plant food in the trunk of my car. I need to get them out and take one around back where I'm working in the flower beds."

Ken hefted one bag easily, depositing it in the garage where Carol showed him, then went back for the other. It was the first time he had seen the flower beds in back of the house, except through a window. They were colorful, and immaculately groomed.

"Do you like flowers?" Carol asked. "Jean told me you like to photograph beautiful things."

"Yes." He laughed. "But I hardly know one flower from another. I wouldn't know a snapdragon unless it bit me."

"God is kind to give us so much beauty, don't you think?" She surveyed her garden and reached out to caress a rose that grew a bit higher than the others on one of her bushes. In the deep shade of the late afternoon, it was a cool pink. It seemed almost translucent. Tiny red veins stood out in its petals. Ken grasped the stem of the flower, carefully avoiding its thorns, and drew it toward him to sniff its perfume.

Carol seemed to be appraising him, Ken thought.

"You're the first man Jean has ever gone with who has shown any inclination toward religion on his own," she said finally. Then she smiled. "She tells me you're going to church with us on Sunday. I think you'll be impressed by Pastor Michaels."

"Probably," Ken said, trying to keep his answer noncommittal. He decided to give the conversation another direction. "Jean told me you're working with some Asian families—helping them get used to our culture and life-style. How many of them are there?"

"Personally, I work with three. Our church committee has a group of twenty we're helping." Carol described some of the families and her committee's approach to aiding them. Apparently she had been instrumental in helping a number of refugees find jobs, schooling, places to live—and confidence in themselves. "The best part is watching them learn that they can make it on their own here. And I've found some wonderful friends, working with people one-on-one," she said.

"Like Vonnie?"

"She was Jean's success story," Carol reflected. "But I enjoyed getting to know Vonnie's mother. She's a quiet, sweet person. And yet some of these women have had to be so strong . . . " Carol stopped talking and smiled self-consciously. "You've let me go on and on. I must be boring you."

Ken shook his head.

"Richard will be home any minute, and we'd be glad to have you as our guest for dinner. Will you stay?"

Ken glanced up at the sky. "Thanks, but I can't. I have to set up for some night shots of a new building complex, and it's time to be on my way." He laughed. "Besides, Jean invited me for Sunday dinner. You're going to think I come only for the free meals."

Jean was interviewing an influential patron of the arts outside the auditorium after the dance concert when Ken arrived. As soon as the brief interview was over, she said her good-bye politely, then turned her attention to Ken. "Hi. I should have arranged for you to get into the concert."

"That's okay. Dance isn't my favorite art form."

"It has a lot to offer. Try to think of it as a kind of athletics. You can learn to appreciate it just as you would a great one-handed catch in the end zone or a good pickoff play at first base."

He grinned at her. "Right. Next time I go to a dance concert, I'll be sure to take a scorecard."

The cameraman from the station had set up his camera on a tripod in front of the auditorium so Jean could tape an introduction to her story, using the building as a backdrop. "I'm ready for a practice run-through, Jean, if you want one," he said.

Ken stood behind the cameraman to watch as Jean practiced her introduction.

The cameraman's baseball cap, bearing the station's logo, had been in the way while the man sighted through his viewfinder, so he had taken the cap off and put it down on the sidewalk behind him. It lay at Ken's feet. As Jean started her practice report, Ken scooped up the cap and put it on his own head backwards. Then he leaned forward as though peering intently over the cameraman's shoulder. Ken could see a smile playing around Jean's lips. Suddenly he thrust his hand up in an exaggerated umpire's strike sign and then gave the standard "You're out!" motion with his thumb.

Jean burst out laughing. "Stop that, you idiot!" she yelled.

Before the cameraman could react, Ken snatched the cap off his own head; when the man turned to look at him, Ken was standing innocently with his hands behind his back. "I just love to watch a professional at work," he said sociably. The cameraman looked him over skeptically, then turned to face Jean again. Ken placed the cap back in its spot on the ground.

He stood still and watched while Jean tried another practice run. She got through it with no trouble, although Ken thought he saw a smile playing around her lips once or twice as she looked at him. He walked away so he wouldn't be a distraction while she was taping what she had practiced. She went through it flawlessly. The cameraman gave her a big smile and an enthusiastic "okay" sign.

"Thanks, Brad," she said, handing him her microphone. "See you tomorrow." She took Ken by the arm. "As for you," she said with deliberate sweetness, "you can walk me to my car. I have a spot reserved for you—right in front of it!"

"Don't blame *me* for what happened—you're the one who brought up sports."

She laughed. "I like your style, McArthur. You have everything—wit, charm, your own private yacht, a touch of lunacy . . . "

"Everything but money," he said.

"Mom told me you came by yesterday. I'm sorry I missed you."

"I was just going that way, and I thought it was worth a chance that you might be home. Where do you want me to meet you tomorrow night?"

"Why don't you pick me up at work? You could even come watch the six o'clock news broadcast—*if* you can behave."

"Maybe I'll show up in the afternoon and just watch you work."

She laughed lightly. "No good. I'd be paying too much attention to you and not enough to my work."

They had reached her car. Jean wasn't eager to say goodbye, but she couldn't think of a way to prolong the conversation. She handed Ken her keys, and he opened the door for her. She leaned over and kissed him lightly on the cheek. "I'll be wishing for the day to pass quickly tomorrow," she said.

Ken followed her down Ocean Drive to her house, to be sure she arrived safely.

Something about the teamwork involved in her reporting that night had stuck in his mind, and he thought about it as he drove back to the boat. Maybe there was a business opportunity in it for him.

Jean was surprised when he showed up in the newsroom early the next afternoon, carrying his camera bag. "What are you doing here already?" she asked, her brow furrowing.

"Watching you work last night gave me a promotional idea for the station. I called the news director and sold him on letting me try it. I need to do a lot of self-marketing to keep money coming in from freelancing," he explained. "But don't worry—I'll stay out of your way while you're busy."

For the rest of the afternoon, he shot pictures around the newsroom as the staff worked, focusing mostly on the weekend anchor team. Once, he left the station with a reporter and cameraman who had been sent out to investigate an accident report. During the evening broadcast, Ken was behind the cameras, out of the range of the microphones, shooting more photos. He shot several while Jean did a live report.

As they left the station after the broadcast, Jean asked, "What is this promo idea of yours?"

Ken explained the concept he had sold to the news director: "Our teams are on your side." He envisioned every on-the-scene reporter and cameraman as part of a four-person team, along with the news anchors in the studio; that gave the station a number of experienced, mobile teams, each working to serve the viewers' needs.

"Hmm. Sounds good," Jean said. "The slogan might take some refining. How are you going to illustrate it with photos?"

He explained his plans, and Jean offered several suggestions to make his photographs more effective. Her interest was encouraging. Ken began to feel like the project was theirs and not just his alone; Jean talked to him about it all the way to her sister and brother-in-law's apartment.

Jay and Allison made Ken feel as if he had been among their circle of friends for years. After dinner, the two couples visited in the living room for a time. Then Allison brought out a photograph album to show pictures of the two Bradley sisters as they were growing up.

Jean wrinkled her nose. "Is that the 'Miss Baby Fat' collection?"

"You *never* had any baby fat, Jean," Allison replied. She was right. Jean had been a thin little girl, obviously a tomboy as a preteen, and then an attractive young woman at thirteen or fourteen. There were pictures of Allison and Jean in a variety of activities as they grew up. Despite her own success in the Miss Texas competition, Allison had as many photos of Jean, with swim medals and in school theatrical productions, as she had of herself.

"Allie is very proud of you," Ken said as he and Jean drove back to the television studio later to pick up his truck. "She told me once—at the beach—how close you are."

"I think our relationship is unique, even for sisters," Jean said. "Allison probably understands me better than anyone else alive—including Mom and Dad."

From the studio, Ken followed Jean home because it was late again. She arrived at her house several seconds ahead of him, so he was surprised when he found her car parked far out in the driveway. She was standing by it, waiting for him.

"I didn't want to make my way through everything in the garage in this dress," she explained. "You can leave the Blazer right here. Walk me to my door?"

She took his arm and steered him straight toward the garage, and then along the portico to the front door, illuminated by two small porch lamps on either side. Jean stopped by the door but made no move to open it. Instead, she turned to face him.

Ken reached for her hands and held them in his. "Jean, we haven't been alone at all today so we could talk, and I needed to tell you"—he paused, and then the words came out in a rush—"I think I'm falling in love with you."

She smiled at him. "You *think* you're falling in love?"

"Well, I've never been there before. But I've got all the symptoms. Just being with you makes me happy. When I'm away from you, I keep thinking about the next time we can be together. I forgot breakfast this morning because I was thinking about you. I printed a picture of you to carry around in my wallet so I could see you whenever I wanted. Does that qualify?"

She took one step toward him. Ken put his arms around her

shoulders and drew her close. She slipped her arms around his back and held onto him as he kissed her.

When they broke it off, she murmured, "I'm so glad to know I'm not the only one of us who feels this way." She rested her head against his cheek, until he bent his head to kiss her again.

When the kiss was over, she continued to cling to him. But finally she backed away and glanced at her wristwatch. "In only ten and one-half hours, you can pick me up for church. We can spend the whole day together." She paused. "I love you, Ken." Then she opened the front door and stepped inside.

Ken walked out from under the portico and strode directly toward his truck, far out near the entrance to the driveway. Suddenly a floodlight illuminated the area, startling him. Then he realized that Jean had deliberately maneuvered him away from the motion sensor that would have triggered this light, bathing the front door in its glare, if he had driven up here.

Somewhere in his mind another light went on, flooding a corner he had been trying to ignore.

Nine years ago or so, when the missionaries first taught him the gospel, Ken had instantly embraced the concept of eternal families. After the disastrous home life he had experienced as a boy, he had promised himself that one day he would build a home based on an eternal partnership.

It wasn't something that seventeen-year-old males talked about often among themselves, but when he heard messages about eternal marriage—usually aimed at the young women in his ward—he inwardly nodded assent. Eternal marriage wasn't an idea Marines talked about among themselves either. But while he had been in the military, Ken had picked as friends in the local ward or branch married Latter-day Saints who were already building the kind of relationships in their families that he hoped to have someday.

And now, what had started out as friendship was turning

into love for a woman who could not share his dream. Somehow, he needed to bring Jean into the dream too. But how? Allison had told him that he probably wouldn't get very far with Jean if he tried to preach religion to her. And Jean herself had said that Allison knew her as well as anyone alive.

Jean's goodnight smile stayed with him all night long.

6

Two Grains of Sand

The Reverend William B. Michaels was a polished speaker, and the sermon was a good one. Ken found himself enjoying it. The topic was basic Christianity at its best: "And Who Is My Neighbour?" As the sermon progressed, Ken made mental notes on ideas to use in the priesthood lesson he would be teaching in a few hours.

Jean sat next to Ken in the pew. She had slipped her arm through his when they sat down; he held her hand between his.

On the other side of Jean sat Allison, Jay, Carol, and Richard. Twice as he glanced down the pew, Ken saw Carol looking at him; she smiled a satisfied kind of smile in his direction. Ken noticed that Richard Bradley's gaze frequently wandered during the sermon. But Jay seemed to pay close attention. Several times Ken saw him open a small Bible he carried, apparently to read scriptures the pastor cited.

After the service was over, Jean said their good-byes quickly, and the two of them hurried across town to the LDS chapel. It seemed plain by comparison with the imposing building they had just left. Ken's fears were realized when he looked at the program. There were high-council speakers.

But the first talk was interesting—moving, in fact. It was on getting close to the Spirit of the Lord and staying there. The speaker was not so eloquent as Pastor Michaels, but what he said touched Ken deeply. Ken hoped that Jean was feeling what he felt. He glanced sideways at her several times. She was quietly observing, just as she had during the service at her own church. It was impossible to gauge her reaction to the talk. Once, Ken squeezed her hand as he held it between his, and she responded with a smile.

The second speaker began: "The stake presidency has asked me to talk about . . . " Inwardly, Ken groaned. He knew instantly that this was going to be what one of the elders in his quorum, a transplant from Utah, called a "dry council talk."

Then two minutes into it, a toddler—a little girl with blonde curls—wandered down the aisle toward the back row, where Ken and Jean sat. The little girl paused in front of Jean and looked at her. Jean held out her hands. The little girl came to her, and Jean lifted the child up onto her lap.

Quickly the little girl found a game to play, repeatedly touching Jean's long blonde hair, then touching her hands to her own hair and giggling. Jean smoothed the little girl's curls and stroked her arms until the child fell asleep.

When the sacrament meeting was over, the mother, a young woman with an infant in a baby carrier, came to reclaim her little girl. "Thanks," she said to Jean. "You were a lifesaver. I hated to make a scene by coming to get her, and she seemed to be fascinated with you."

"She was no trouble," Jean said, smiling. The child woke, and her mother took her by one hand, juggling the baby carrier in her other, and led the little girl away to the nursery.

"Jean, we have a Sunday School class now," Ken said, "and

then I have to teach a lesson to my elders quorum—one of the men's groups. Do you want me to take you home before I do that?"

"No, that's too much trouble. I can sit out in the car while you're with the men. Or maybe I could just go in with the women's group—if you don't think they'd mind."

"Of course they wouldn't mind. I just didn't want to leave you by yourself."

In the foyer, they met Irene Steiner. She smiled at Jean. "It's good to see you again."

"Irene," Ken said, "Jean would like to go to Relief Society today while I teach the elders quorum lesson. Who will be there that she could sit with?"

Irene thought for a moment. "I'll take her with me. One of my counselors can cover things in Young Women today. I'll meet you right outside the Sunday School class when it's over."

"I wouldn't want you to go to any trouble," Jean said uncertainly.

"No trouble," Irene replied. "I haven't had a chance to meet with the women for the past two years. This will be my pleasure."

During the priesthood lesson, Ken managed to slip in a few good points from Pastor Michaels's sermon. But he also made a couple of embarrassing slips; his mind was on the Relief Society.

After the meeting, as he and Jean drove away from the building, Ken asked, "Any questions about today?"

"Yes, a few. What's visiting teaching?"

Ken looked nonplussed. "Didn't Irene explain it to you?"

"I didn't want to ask her questions during the lesson."

"Most of the women in the ward are assigned to visit several other women on a regular basis. Usually they teach a short gospel lesson in the home," Ken explained. "Is that what they talked about in Relief Society today?" He hoped there hadn't been much discussion of percentages or goals.

"That was part of it. They talked about true charity—about being loving enough to meet a need whenever you see one. Similar to what Pastor Michaels spoke on this morning. But these women talked a lot about building sisterhood. It sounded good to me."

"You take to it naturally. It's the kind of thing you were doing when you took care of that little girl in sacrament meeting."

Jean smiled reflectively. "She was beautiful, wasn't she?"

"Yes."

"Ken, do all Mormon women have four or five children right in a row after they get married?"

"No. But Mormons tend to have more children than the average. We believe families are pretty important."

"How do they dare bring so many children into today's world? I'm not sure I would want to."

"Why not?" The words were born of surprise; Jean had seemed so at ease with the little girl. Ken hoped there was no trace of criticism in his voice.

"Well, there's so much around us that's just plain evil. I hate to think of children having to grow up in all of it."

"We believe life is a gift, Jean. It's tough sometimes, but God sent us here to earth so we could receive certain blessings. When we bring children into the world, we're sharing the opportunity with them."

She looked at him questioningly. "You think of this as an *opportunity?*"

"Yes. It's an opportunity to gain blessings we couldn't get any other way. Why? What do you believe life is for?"

"I believe it's a trial—a test, to find out whether we love God."

"Maybe that's part of it. But where's the test for you? I mean, it doesn't seem like much of a trial if you believe that all we really have to do is say we accept Jesus, and then we're saved. There has to be more to it than that."

Jean's brow furrowed. It sounded as though Ken was challenging her beliefs. But she didn't want to be drawn into an argument. "You could be right," she answered evenly. "Anyway, I'm still not sure how to handle life by myself. It frightens me to think about trying to help children get through it too."

"But aren't you glad your parents decided to try?"

She glanced at him, startled. "Well . . . yes, of course."

"Jean, I'm probably not explaining this very well, piecemeal, but our Heavenly Father has given us ways . . . there are a lot of things he has given us to help us get back to him, along with our families." He took a deep breath. "I know a couple of young people who can explain all this logically, in depth. Would you like to talk to them?"

"You mean missionaries?"

"Yes."

"To teach me how to be a Mormon, so I can be baptized—like the woman who talked in your meeting last week?"

"Well, baptism is the goal. But no one would pressure you if you didn't want to."

Jean was silent for a few moments. Then she turned in the seat to face him. "I don't think I want to talk to any missionaries, Ken. I hope that doesn't hurt your feelings. I'm not interested in changing churches. I want to respect your beliefs, but I can find out anything I need to know about them from you, without talking to missionaries." She continued to watch him. "You're not mad about that, are you?"

"No, of course not," Ken answered. Actually, what he felt inside was more like a deep sadness. But she had not closed the door completely, he realized. "Would you like to come to church with me again next Sunday?" he asked.

"I'd love to, but I have to work next weekend. I'll go with

you the week after next. And you can go to church with me," she said, smiling. "That way, we can spend the whole day together again."

On Monday afternoon, Ken dropped by the television station to shoot more pictures in the newsroom. Then he followed Jean home, and they spent the evening watching *Casablanca* on video and eating popcorn.

On Tuesday evening, she stopped by the boat after work to be sure he was there. "I'll be right back, so don't go away," she said. She returned in half an hour with a fast-food meal. They sat on the cushioned seats in the stern of the *Rum Runner* while they ate, watching dusk come to the city's skyline.

On Wednesday, he had to leave town early to make a delivery. When he came back late that night, he found a note in the safe, written on a page torn from a reporter's notebook: "You were gone this morning, so I came back tonight with some things for supper. You were still gone. Did you leave town because you were afraid I'd make you hook up the hot plate again?

"Call me tomorrow. I'm off all day. If you can come by the house, I'll even cook supper. I'll use our camp stove, if it will make you feel more at home.

"Love, J."

He called her Thursday morning at eight.

"Hi. I'm sorry I was gone yesterday. One of my clients came by early in the morning and asked me to make a delivery."

"I missed you. Will you come by to see me for a while today?"

"Maybe we can do better than that. I still need to drive down Padre Island on a photo trip. Would you like to bring the stuff you bought for supper last night? We could cook it on the beach and make a day of it."

"I'd love to. I'll probably be ready by the time you can get here."

Carefully, Ken hung up the phone and picked up a manila envelope off the seat beside him. Then he stepped out of his Blazer—which was already parked in Jean's driveway—strolled over to the front door, and rang the bell.

Jean answered it. Her damp hair hung in a French braid down her back. Having her hair pulled back from her face simply emphasized the natural elegance of her features. "How did you get here so fast?" she asked. "I just hung up the telephone."

"I called you from the nearest phone booth." He gestured toward his Blazer.

She walked over and peered in the window. "Wow! A yacht, a four-wheel drive, and now a mobile telephone. I feel like I'm in fast company."

He glanced significantly at the porticoed front of her house. "Yeah."

"Well, even Daddy doesn't have a mobile phone. Where did you get it?"

"My client found he didn't have enough cash on hand to pay me. This is a used phone he was replacing, so I took it in part payment."

"Nice. Now I can call you."

"Better yet, I can call you. We can chat on the phone like a couple of teenagers for hours at a time. Until a few weeks ago, there wasn't anybody I ever wanted to call." He glanced at the telephone. "Besides, if I'm really going to be serious about running a photo business, I've got to have a way for other people to call me."

"What's in there?" she asked, pointing at the envelope he held in his hands.

"That's for your mother."

"Can I peek?"

He held it just out of her reach and smiled. "Nope. You'll just have to wait until she opens it."

"Well, then, come in. I'm curious."

The envelope contained two photos of Jean. One was an informal portrait he had made at the old Spanish mission in San Antonio, and the other showed her busy in the newsroom, pencil poised over her notepad, talking on the telephone. Carol smiled fondly at the pictures of her daughter. "Thank you, Ken. How kind!"

"For your family album," Ken replied.

Jean studied the pictures with interest. "Will you make copies for me sometime?"

"Sure. I'll give you the copies I made for me, then I'll make more. I thought you might not want them, after the way you reacted to Allison's album."

"Oh, that. I was just embarrassed about having you see those old pictures of me. But you've made me look really good in these."

"It was easy. I just take beauty where I find it."

Carol laughed. "Ken, if you could bottle your way with words, you'd be a rich man."

Ken looked at her seriously. "I meant it. When there are good things to say about people, I believe in telling them the truth."

"That's part of your innate charm," Jean said. "Flattering us and then convincing us it's the truth. Come on. I'll show you where the camp stove is, and then I'll get the food."

By the time they were ready to leave her house, it was nearly nine. They drove out past the naval base, crossed the Padre Island causeway, then passed the luxury homes on the northern end of the island. From Bob Hall Pier—a narrow fisherman's platform that extends more than a quarter of a mile out into the surf—they traveled for miles down the beach.

"Look, Ken! Look at that man-of-war," Jean said suddenly. "It's a big one. It might make an interesting picture."

A Portuguese man-of-war jellyfish lay above the waterline

on the sand, beached after high tide. The gas-filled iridescent float portion of the jellyfish—looking like some misshapen balloon—was red, or blue, with touches of other colors of the rainbow, depending on the angle of view.

Ken stopped the truck and got out, taking his camera. He walked all around the jellyfish, careful to avoid the tentacles that trailed on the sand. He shot a few photos, knelt, and shot a few closeups. Then he walked back to the truck.

"No good?" Jean asked.

"Just fair. It would have been much better by early morning light."

Ken drove down to where there were no other vehicle tracks in the sand, then parked the Blazer well above the water line. "I want to shoot along the water's edge, so if you don't mind, I'd like to go first, before there are any footprints."

He kicked off his deck shoes and moved down the beach, shooting closeups of small shells in the foam at the water line, where the continually rushing breakers push a thin layer of water landward, then leave a mirrored sheet of sand each time they recede. Ken photographed large, intact conch shells, then lingered over small, unbroken shells, arranging them carefully in the sand and letting the water wash away the marks of his work before he took pictures.

Once, as Jean was wading and picking over shells not far from his truck, she glanced down the beach to see him photographing her and her reflection. Finally, he walked back toward her. "I'm going out into the dunes to shoot. Want to come?"

"No, I think I'll stay here."

She watched as he climbed the first dune, the wind billowing his shirt out like a sail. He disappeared down the other side, and she was alone on the beach. She undid her French braid and let the breeze play with her hair. She continued wading, examining the wide variety of perfect shells and sand dollars scattered on the sand. They reminded her of the ones she had taken home as treasures when she was a little girl. Jean smiled at the memory; somewhere in a bureau drawer, she still had a small box of those shells.

Perhaps an hour after she had last seen Ken, Jean was writing in the sand with her toe when she looked up to find him a short distance away, shooting pictures of her. He walked over to look at what she had been writing. She scratched through it hastily with her foot, but she was unable to obliterate it before he saw it.

"J—e—a—n M—c—A—r," he read. "Hmmm."

She blushed a deep red. "I feel like a schoolgirl whose love note has just been read to the whole class."

"Well, I like the thought." Ken didn't dare to say how much he liked it. "Want to go steady?" he asked casually.

"Aren't we?" she answered, smiling.

"I certainly hope so." He leaned over to kiss her on the cheek. "Now—are you as hungry as I am?"

"Yes. Let's see how good a camp cook you are. Break out the stove."

"You may be sorry."

She grinned. "All you have to do is boil some weiners and warm up some chili for my famous chili dogs. How much damage can you do to weiners?"

He opened the back of the Blazer and pulled out the stove. She rummaged through the sack she had brought.

"I guess I'll have to put the stove down here on the sand," he said, snapping it open. "Did you bring the propane bottle?"

"No. Didn't you? Wasn't there one with it?"

"No," he said. He snapped the stove shut again and put it back in the vehicle.

Jean examined the contents of the sack. "Maybe we could

at least have some cold chili . . . except that I forgot to bring the can opener." Both of them burst out laughing.

"Hmmm. Well, as the designated hunter-gatherer of this expedition—" Ken began.

"Who designated *you?*"

"As the self-designated hunter-gatherer of this expedition, let me see what I can provide using my wits and superior strength." He withdrew the bag of corn chips from the sack she was holding. Biting down on its top, he jerked on the bag. It slipped out of his teeth unopened. "Ow!" he said, "I think I may have chipped a tooth."

She took the bag from him and tore it open with her hands.

Peeking into the food sack, he withdrew two apples. He polished one on the front of his shirt and handed it to her.

"Nice. Very shiny," she said.

"Told you I could cook."

They sat on the sand in a small area of shade beside the truck, munching apples and corn chips as the foamy water's edge crept closer to them with the incoming tide.

Jean stared out over the breakers that sprung out of the sea by themselves and seemed to march toward the shore forever. Extending her foot, she stirred the loose sand with her toe. "Ken, do you ever feel like one of these little grains of sand? Like we're all clumped together on the beach, too small to mean anything by ourselves but part of some huge, important mass?"

"No. I don't believe that."

"What do you believe?"

He stared out at the waves too. "I believe we're all important as individuals, to a real Father in Heaven. He can see the mass, but he can also see every grain of sand. It isn't just a chance wind that blows us from this dune to that one. When we come here to earth, he carefully puts us where we can do the most good for others and for ourselves—if we have the will to try."

"I wish I could believe that."

He turned to look her in the eye. "Believe it, Jean. It's true. I've felt his power in my life."

"Have you? How?"

He thought for a moment. "Well, for an example close to home, there's the night I met you," he said, reaching for her hand. "That night I was planning to turn the way I usually go from the freeway—down Water Street to drop off a note at my client's office. But suddenly I felt like I should take Shoreline instead. If I hadn't paid attention to that feeling, I would never have seen you—and the two guys who were trying to haul you away. I wouldn't have been there to help you."

"Do you realize what it means if you believe that, Ken? It means God had to manage your whole trip so you would be in exactly the right place at exactly the right time. Do you believe he does that somehow, every time something happens to someone on this planet?"

"Jean, I don't know how closely God affects what happens to us. I think he must leave us on our own a lot of the time to do the things we already know are right. Probably sometimes he leaves us alone because we insist on doing things we know are wrong."

Ken was silent for a moment. "I can't tell you why good things don't always come to us when we want them, or why he doesn't stop bad things from happening to us sometimes. I can't tell you why my mother died when I needed her most. Maybe someday I'll know the reason. But even if I don't understand it now, I've learned that God still loves me—*me*, Kenneth Alexander McArthur. And I know that he often has a hand in what happens to every one of us here."

"I've never had anything like that happen in my life," Jean said.

"Yes, you have, Jean. Think about the night I met you. It

was you our Heavenly Father was watching over. I was just somebody he was able to use."

Jean sat in silence. How, she wondered, could intelligent people turn what was probably coincidence into the will of God in their minds? How could they believe that the God who was occupied with the unfolding of the entire universe had time for the concerns of one small individual?

"Jean—" Ken began.

"Oh, look!" she interrupted. Two gulls hovered nearly overhead. Jean stood up suddenly, reached into the bag she held, and flung one of the corn chips into the air. The nearest gull swooped low and caught it, with the other one close behind. Then both of them hovered lower on the wind.

Jean laughed. "I love to watch them do that." She jogged down the beach a short ways and threw another chip into the air. The gulls followed her, and again one caught the morsel of food before it could touch the ground. Laughing, she ran back and forth on the beach, flinging chips into the air, trying to give the slower gull a chance to get a full share of the bounty. Jean's long hair streamed out behind her as she ran.

At first, Ken just watched, but soon he retrieved his camera from the truck and took photos of Jean playing with the gulls. His favorite was a shot with Jean and the gulls silhouetted by the afternoon sun.

Later, he walked back into the dunes to shoot photos by afternoon light.

By the time Ken and Jean started back up the beach in the Blazer, it was after four. He drove a ways, then suddenly slowed and pulled over toward the water's edge.

"What is it?" Jean asked.

"The jellyfish. Look at it now."

With the rise in the tide, the man-of-war they had seen earlier lay just within reach of the water. A small pool had formed at the base of the jellyfish's iridescent float, mirroring the sky. The late afternoon sun seemed to deepen the jellyfish's colors; a lengthening shadow added drama and perspective to the composition.

"Look what happens when the light strikes it just right," Ken said. "The right light brings out facets of things that we never dreamed were there."

He reached for his camera and got out of the truck. He shot photos as he walked around the jellyfish, then as he crouched by it, and finally as he stretched out on his belly in the wet sand for a closeup view. Jean stood behind him, watching him absorbed in his work. When he finally finished and stood up, he was covered with wet muck from his chest to his ankles.

Jean burst out laughing. Holding an imaginary microphone in front of her face, she adopted her authoritative on-air voice. "This is Jean Bradley with a live report from the scene of an aborigine mud bath ritual that has just ended. We hope to have an interview . . . " Ken stuck out his arms, Frankenstein-style, and began walking toward her stiffly. "No. No!" she said, dodging away as he approached. She grabbed the camera, dangling by its strap from his fist. "Here, give me that before you get it muddy. Go scrape all that stuff off before you get back in the truck. You'll make a horrible mess."

When he climbed back into the Blazer, she told him, "I still owe you a real meal. If you'll drive to your boat and pick up some clothes, then we can go to my house and you can shower while I fix the chili dogs."

"Okay. By the way, did you bring anything to drink? All those chips made me thirsty."

"No. I forgot that too." She smiled. "It's a good thing we weren't a couple of your Mormon pioneers starting off on a trek across the great American desert."

Ken lowered the timbre of his voice to his deepest bass. "Did you fill the water barrels, Sal?" Then he switched to a falsetto. "Why, no, Heber. I thought you did that."

Jean laughed. "Just stop at the first drive-in store you see along the trail, and we'll get a couple of drinks. But you better let me go in."

After their stop, Jean sipped her drink in silence for a while. They were headed up South Padre Island Drive toward the city when she asked: "Would you do me a big favor?"

"Sure. What?"

She pushed the ice around in her cup with the tip of her straw. "Would you go with me to talk to Pastor Michaels?"

"About what?"

"Religion."

"I don't think—" He stopped. From the corner of his eye he could see that she was staring glumly into the cup. "Well—yes, if you want me to. But why? Something tells me he's not interested in learning about my church."

"Mom asked me to ask you. She's heard some things about Mormons from people at our church. She wants me and you to hear what the pastor has to say—together."

"This was on your mind a little while ago when you asked me what I believe, wasn't it?"

"Yes." She frowned. "Ken, it's awfully awkward for me to ask you this, after I told you I didn't want to listen to your missionaries. If you don't want to go, it's okay."

"Let's see if I understand what's happening here. Since you and I have been going together so much, and since I've taken you to my church a couple of times, your mother would like the pastor to set me straight on some of my weird beliefs, right?"

"No, it's not . . . well, okay, maybe it is something like that. Look," Jean said, her voice rising, "I'm sorry I brought this up. It's embarrassing. I've already had an argument with my mother about it. I told her I didn't want to ask you. I'll just tell her you said no."

He drove in silence for a ways. Then he said softly, "I'm sorry, Jean. I didn't mean to sound like I was picking a fight. I just wondered if your mother thinks I'm trying to suck you into something bad. I could never do that to you."

"I know," she said, reaching over to touch his hand. "And I don't think Mom believes anything bad about you. I think she truly is puzzled. You don't fit the image of the Mormons she's been hearing about."

"Well, I want Carol to feel good about having her daughter go out with me. I really won't mind talking to your pastor—especially if it's important to you. When do you want to go see him?"

"Since I have to work this weekend, I'm off all day tomorrow too. Could we go see him in the morning?"

7

Pastor Michaels

The building where Jean's family went to church was huge compared to LDS meetinghouses. Its tower and steeple stood out as a landmark on the Corpus Christi skyline. The chapel could seat more than five hundred people, and it had been nearly full last Sunday. Ken guessed that membership in the congregation might number in the thousands.

He and Jean sat on brocaded chairs, waiting in the paneled hallway outside the pastor's office.

"Nice building," Ken whispered.

"Yes," Jean replied, also in a whisper. "I've never been to Pastor Michaels's office before."

Ken grinned at her. "You mean to tell me you were never naughty in Sunday School and had to come talk to the pastor?"

"I never got caught," she whispered, grinning back.

Both of them jumped as the door to the pastor's office suddenly swung wide open. "Sorry I had to keep you waiting," Pastor Michaels boomed. "Come in, come in." His voice seemed to echo off the walls.

The pastor was a large, ruddy man with a full head of brown

hair, graying at the temples. He was two or three inches taller than Ken, and his biceps filled out the arms of the suit coat that strained across his barrel chest. The minister could easily have been a football player in his younger years, Ken decided; if so, he would have been the kind to be avoided by defensive ends.

"Sit down," Pastor Michaels invited, motioning them toward the leather sofa. He sat back in the plush chair behind his large, hardwood desk. "Jean, I wish we could have had this chat much sooner. I haven't had the opportunity of meeting your friend."

"Pastor Michaels, this is Ken McArthur," Jean recited dutifully.

"I'm pleased to meet you, pastor," Ken said.

"Call me Bill," the minister replied affably. "And you're the grandson of Alexander McArthur?"

"Yes."

"A fine gentleman. A fine Christian. Did you know he was a major contributor when this building was constructed?"

"No," Ken replied. "But I know that he was very generous in what he considered good causes."

"So he was. There's a wing of the hospital down the road that should have been named for him, but he wouldn't let them do it. It's a pleasure to meet his grandson." The pastor paused briefly. "I'm told you're a Mormon."

"Yes, I am."

"And I understand you've been taking Jean to church with you recently."

"Yes, a couple of times. Last Sunday, we came here and then went to services at my church."

"Your grandfather was a man known for his great integrity and honesty." The pastor leaned forward slowly and rested his forearms on his desk. "I'd like to know if you've been totally honest with Jean. Have you told her that your church does not practice the Christian religion? Does she understand that it's a non-Christian cult?"

Jean sucked in her breath sharply. She groped for a response, but Ken spoke first.

"I think I can trust Jean to judge that for herself," he said evenly. "She's seen us worshipping in the name of Christ and teaching his gospel in our meetings."

"You teach what your *prophets*"—he spat out the word—"have told you to teach. But it's not the same gospel of Jesus Christ taught in the Bible. Paul wrote in his epistle to the Galatians that some people would pervert the gospel of Christ. Are you familiar with what he wrote about someone who would do that? '*Let him be accursed*.' " The pastor's voice was taking on its pulpit timbre.

Ken replied patiently. "Paul went on to say that he taught what he had received by revelation. We do teach the same gospel that Paul taught. And we also teach what we have received by modern revelation."

Jean became a silent witness to a debate. She had been surprised by the suddenness and the force of Pastor Michaels's attack on Ken's religion. It was obviously well-planned. One by one, the pastor selected a book or pamphlet from the stack on his desk, expounding on a doctrine or historical fact about the Mormon church; all of the sources took an anti-Mormon position. Jean was incensed at the duplicity of what had happened; this was supposed to have been a friendly discussion.

The two men traded biblical references back and forth. The minister would cite one, and Ken would offer another that seemed to contradict Pastor Michaels's contention. Several times the clergyman made damning accusations against Mormon doctrine, and Ken protested that they were inaccurate. Once he told the pastor forcefully, "Now hold on! I think you're out of line treating that so lightly. I consider it sacred." Twice Ken indicated that he could not answer the minister's question fully, but he offered to study Latter-day Saint sources and bring back an answer if Pastor Michaels wanted to hear it.

Jean noticed small beads of sweat glistening in the short hair on the back of Ken's neck. But Ken remained calm and never raised his voice. A streak of sweat ran down in front of Pastor Michaels's ear, and his face became more florid as the discussion progressed. Once he slammed his palm down on the desk to make a point. He began repeating the same objections to Mormon doctrine, and his frustration seemed to grow as Ken did not give ground. Jean was surprised that Ken could hold his own despite the minister's advanced education and years of experience.

More than once, Ken seemed to be trying politely to end the wrangling. But the two men had been talking for nearly forty-five minutes when the pastor suddenly decided to terminate the discussion. "Jean," he said, turning to her for the first time since she had introduced Ken, "I'd advise you to be very careful about attending this man's church again. What they're teaching over there is pernicious and un-Christian. Don't let yourself be deceived."

He stood, walked around the desk, and held the door open for them. "Now, if you'll excuse me, I'm expecting someone else very shortly."

Jean walked past without looking at him. Ken extended his hand. "I'm sorry our discussion couldn't have been more pleasant, pastor." The minister shook hands perfunctorily and turned back to his desk.

Outside the building, Ken stripped off his sport coat in the May sunshine. The pastor's office had been air conditioned, but Ken's shirt was stained with sweat under the arms and down the back.

Jean was waiting for him on the sidewalk. She bit her lip

nervously. "Ken, I'm so sorry. I had no idea he was planning to do that. Please believe me."

"Jean, you're too honest to set anybody up that way," he said, smiling at her and taking her hand. "Don't worry about it. I've dealt with worse. There was a Catholic priest in Honduras . . . " He looked down at the sidewalk and thought for a moment, then shook his head. "I shouldn't have let that go on so long. No one wins when you argue about the scriptures. Jesus tried to teach his disciples that it isn't his way."

She slipped her arm through his as they started for her car, about a block away. "But that was so dishonest! How could he do that? I mean, he started out like it was just going to be a nice little chat . . . and then he had that ambush all planned. I feel so . . . so *used*. I don't understand. He was all kindness and comfort for our family when my grandmother died. He was like a different man today." Her face was flushed but not from the heat.

"Don't be too hard on him, Jean. He probably thought he was doing it for your own good."

"I can watch out for my own good, thank you very much! And how can you speak up for him after what he just did to you?"

Ken stopped walking to face her. "What I'm saying is, don't judge a man by one incident in his life. He's undoubtedly done a lot of fine things for a lot of people. The priest I told you about in Honduras really let me have it one day about proselyting in his parish—told me we were dead wrong, and we were leading people away to hell. But when my missionary companion got sick, and the town doctor didn't want to treat him because he was a Mormon, the priest talked him into it. He said it was the only Christian thing to do."

"Okay, Ken. Maybe you're right. But I still don't think I can come back here to church and listen to Pastor Michaels preach about Christian love. I'd be sitting there thinking, 'Hypocrite!' "

"Jean, the Mormon missionary in me wants to say, 'Sure, come to my church, *we'll* be good to you.' But you could find people there who might offend you too. You have to look for the good and overlook the faults in people anywhere. Usually, you're very good at that."

She looked puzzled. "Ken, I don't understand why you're trying so hard to defend Pastor Michaels."

"I'm not, really. I'm more concerned about you. I've never seen you so mad at anyone before. It's not like you."

She reached out to touch his cheek. "I think it's because he attacked someone I care about."

Ken took her hand and held it. "Don't worry about me. I can take care of myself."

She smiled. "You certainly did in there. I think he was shocked."

"So—we'll give the man another chance," Ken said. "Next week, if you're free on Sunday, we'll come to church here again, just like we planned, and then we'll go to my church again. Okay?"

"Okay." She smiled and squeezed his arm to her side as they resumed walking toward her car. "What are you doing for the rest of the day?"

"I have some darkroom time. I have to finish printing the photos I shot for your station."

"Darn it! I hoped we could spend the afternoon together."

"Are you doing anything tomorrow night after work?"

"No. What do you want to do?"

"I don't know yet. But I'll think of something. Pencil me into your appointment book."

"I will. Saturday, Sunday, Monday, Tuesday, . . . "

Jean was silent as he drove her car back to the boat and

parked by his pier. "Do you have time for a little walk?" she asked as he opened the passenger door to let her out.

"Sure."

She slipped her hand into his, and they walked slowly to the corner of the T-head looking out over the bay. She stopped by the barrier cable at the edge of the jetty and stared silently at the water. The sea breeze tugged at her hair and dress.

Finally, he spoke. "Something's on your mind."

She turned to face him. "Were any of those things Pastor Michaels read about your church true?"

"Some. Most were distorted to make them sound as bad as possible."

"Answer some questions for me?"

He leaned back against the barrier cable and crossed his arms on his chest. "Sure. What bothered you?"

"Polygamy. Was it . . . well, why did they do it?"

Inwardly, Ken blanched. He had seen elders quorums lost in this subject for an hour without finding their way out. "You studied American history in school. Did you learn anything about it there?" he asked.

"Not really. I've only heard about it."

This was no time for a doctrinal or historical exposition. And after the unpleasantness with the minister, Ken wanted to avoid argument at any cost. How to explain this without getting in too deep?

"Polygamy ended a hundred years ago," he said. Then he shrugged. "But it's part of our church's history. For those who lived it, it was a matter of faith—just like it was for Abraham and Sarah in the Bible. The Mormon pioneers received it as a commandment from God, through his prophet."

She seemed to be digesting the answer. He waited for her to speak again.

"Does your church really teach that Mormon wives have to be completely subservient to their husbands?" she asked.

"No," he answered, grateful for a question on any other topic—even this one. "We believe God gave men and women different roles in an equal partnership. Anyone who tries to make marriage work some other way isn't doing it the way God intended."

There was another pause while she thought. Then: "Is it true that you don't believe the grace of Christ is sufficient to save you?" The minister had made a big point of this one and had not given Ken a chance to reply.

"No. We believe that's the *only* way we can be saved. Without him, we have no hope. But we don't believe we can ignore the good works he taught us to do. And if we choose to go on disobeying his teachings, and then hope for grace to save us at the last anyway, well . . . " Ken searched for more to say; he wanted to make the point more emphatically. But she spoke first.

"Is it really true that Mormons believe you have the power to make yourselves gods?"

"No, it isn't. But we believe that God wants us to live the same kind of life he lives and do the same things he does. Eventually, with his help, we can. *He* will make it possible for us, if we follow his direction."

What more, Ken thought, could he say about this right now without overloading her? The cold spot where the breeze blew against his back told him that he was sweating again. He prayed silently that nothing he had said would turn her away from the gospel—that she might even want to learn more. He waited, but she was silent. "No more questions?" he asked finally.

Jean brushed back the hair that had blown across her face. "I don't think so," she answered. "Not right now." Everything Ken had said was new to her. Some of it was a bit strange. It seemed to make sense, however, in its own framework. The

Mormons simply looked at many things from a different viewpoint, but there was nothing to be gained by arguing over matters of opinion. "Thanks for explaining those things to me," she added.

"You're welcome. But I didn't explain very much," Ken said. He wanted to tell her more, much more. As a missionary, though, he had seen investigators' eyes glaze over when eager new elders delved too deeply into the mysteries of the gospel.

"Those are tough questions, and the answers are really more complex," he said. "You could spend a long time studying them and still be just a beginner—like me."

"Well, I'm still working on loving my neighbor."

"Me too."

"Let's go, neighbor," she said, taking him by the arm and kissing him on the cheek. "I guess you've got a date with a darkroom."

Ken was dicing meat into a skillet on the hot plate, which Jean had finally convinced him to use, when he heard voices out on the pier, then footfalls in the stern. Jean leaned through the open door of the cabin. "Hi. Can we come in?"

"We? You're bringing a party? Sure."

She descended the stairs into the cabin, followed by her mother. "See?" Jean said to Carol. "I told you if we followed that cord we'd find him cooking."

"I'm sorry you have to go through the galley to reach the dining area," Ken said. "But dinner will be served shortly." He gestured toward his portable radio, laying on the spare bunk. "And the orchestra will be playing later in the grand salon."

Carol examined the conglomeration in Ken's skillet. Her expression was a mixture of curiosity and apprehension. "What is this?" she asked politely.

"Something your daughter used to make in college. She showed me how to do it. I call it: 'Jean's Surprise.' "

"No wonder you never wanted me to visit you at school," Carol said to her daughter.

Jean laughed. "I still have to teach him how to make 'Jean's Delight,' and 'Jean's Inscrutable Oriental Mystery.' "

"There'll be plenty if the two of you want to stay," Ken invited. "I hope this tastes good. I have extra paper plates."

Carol's fingers twisted the small gold chain she wore around her neck. "Ken, I really came to apologize. Jean told me what happened today. I'm terribly embarrassed about it."

Ken stopped stirring to face her. "Thanks for telling me, Carol. What happened didn't seem like something you would have wanted."

"No. Pastor Michaels's wife asked me about you last Sunday after you came to church with Jean. That night I had a call from him. He told me there were some things I ought to know about your church." Carol glanced at Jean. "I understand that what he told me was wrong."

"I'm not trying to involve your daughter in some non-Christian cult group," Ken replied.

Carol glanced at her daughter again. "Jean made that plain. She also told me about your church meetings. Frankly, Ken, I have some . . . uh, reservations about your beliefs. I should have talked to you about them myself, instead of letting Bill Michaels do it. I'm sorry." There was a flash of fire in her eyes as she added, "But I'd do anything to protect my daughter from something that might be bad for her."

"We can talk about my beliefs anytime you like, Carol, so you can find out for yourself whether they're good or bad." He smiled disarmingly. "Right now, will you stay for dinner? I think this really is better than it looks."

"It won't be if you don't stir it some more," Jean said.

"Don't be a backseat chef. Just look at the photos," Ken answered, nodding toward the stack of sixteen-by-twenty prints on the bunk.

Using Ken's photos, Jean gave her mother a guided tour of the television newsroom and studio. Carol seemed delighted to learn more about her daughter's on-the-job activities. Watching the easy relationship between them at the moment, Ken thought they might have been any two friends—or college roommates. They were dressed alike, in jeans and casual blouses. They were also alike, he reflected, in so many of their qualities—including independence of mind and will. Ken thought it was a tribute to Richard Bradley's character that he was not intimidated by the strong women in his home; in fact, Richard seemed appreciative of their strength, seemed to encourage their independent development. If only it could have been that way between his own parents.

The last print in the stack was one of Jean at the old mission in San Antonio. "That one goes over there on the stowage compartment door where I can look at it all the time," Ken said. "I told Jean I was going to use some of those photos to improve my decor."

"Well, Jean, just imagine—the place of honor in the grand salon," Carol said, smiling at her daughter. Ken had felt the tension in Carol when she had arrived; he was relieved that she seemed relaxed now.

The two women sat on the bunk opposite Ken as they ate. "Hey, this really *is* good," Carol said.

"I keep trying to convince your daughter that I can cook, but she doesn't believe me."

"How many times has that hotplate been used since I showed you how to cook this?" Jean inquired.

"Ummh—at least once a week," Ken replied. "Of course,

that figure is for this week only. Last week, it might have varied anywhere from . . . oh, say . . . one to zero."

Carol laughed. "Spoken like a true bachelor."

Jean pointed her plastic fork at Ken. "Wait a minute. I'm a reporter. I know how to handle that kind of answer." She held the fork in front of him, like a microphone. "Mr. McArthur, isn't it true that you ate out every night last week and exceeded your food budget by two hundred seventy-three percent?"

He spoke carefully into the fork. "I categorically deny that I have wasted my money on high living." Then he put his hand over the mock microphone. "Off the record, you're not going to tell them about the good-looking television journalist I've been entertaining, are you?"

"Don't try to weasel out of this with flattery," Jean said, shaking the fork at him.

"Seriously, I've been spending a lot of time in the library, trying to scout out some new magazine contacts. It hasn't left much time for cooking."

Carol smiled knowingly. Jean just shook her head.

When they had finished eating, Carol stood and said, "Jean, I've got to be getting home. I have some calling to do tonight."

"Why don't you take my car, Mom? If Ken can give me a ride later"—she glanced at Ken, and he nodded—"I'd like to stay for a while."

After Carol had gone, Jean scraped out the skillet into an empty tin can while Ken sat on the cabin steps coiling up the long extension cord.

"I'm sorry if I was too pushy about your cooking," Jean said. "I'm just trying to help you avoid starvation. You can't afford to eat out all the time when you're on a tight budget. I know what it's like."

"I didn't mind. Thanks for looking out for me. I really am learning from you." He laughed lightly. "Jack says there have been *major* improvements in my personality and my outlook over the past three months. He keeps telling me that you're good for me, and if I were smart I'd ask you—" He stopped short and slowly looked up, to see her sitting on the bunk smiling at him.

"Ask me what?" she said.

Ken hesitated. "I've thought about asking you that question at least a dozen times since yesterday at the beach, when I saw you writing 'Jean McArthur' in the sand. But I didn't know if you really . . . "

He felt his neck and face getting hot. Jean already knew that he loved her; why was it hard to talk to her about the possibility of marriage? He knew the answer—because he still had not found a way to tell her why he wouldn't consider marrying outside his church. But he couldn't think of a good way to bring up eternal marriage just now. And Jean sat there smiling at him . . . waiting. So he waffled.

"Anyway," he said, glancing around the cabin, "I'm in no position to ask anyone to marry me right now."

"Well, you wouldn't have to be well off. I mean . . . if you feel ready to ask that question sometime . . . " Jean blushed. She had said more than she had intended. But beneath her embarrassment there welled up a secret satisfaction. What he had said to her seemed to carry an assurance beyond the meaning of the words. Both of them, she felt, wanted the same thing.

"You really have been good for me," Ken said. "I was drifting along in life before I met you. I admire the way you've seen what you wanted and gone after it. I'm trying to do the same thing. I need a future and a more stable life now."

Jean understood then that Ken would not ask her to marry him unless he was sure that he could support them both. And in her heart, she knew that she needed a man confident of his own ability to provide for them—no matter how much money she might be able to make.

Ken had gone back to coiling the power cord. "I was drifting in my faith before I met you—taking it for granted. You've been helping me renew it. I'm grateful to you for that too."

Jean had always hoped to marry a man strong in faith. This one certainly was. His was no ecumenical faith, however, that would permit him to shift from one church building to another and go on worshipping as he always had. He was committed to certain beliefs and practices that she could not share, Jean realized. That would be a problem in any marriage. But she was prepared to make concessions.

"I wanted to talk to you about what happened this morning," she said. "I went home and told my mother off for sending us to Pastor Michaels—and then I had to apologize. She really didn't know what he was going to do. She made me bring her down here so she could tell you that.

"Pastor Michaels called me later to say he had made a mistake," Jean continued. "He said he was sorry about the way things turned out."

"And do you feel better about him now?" Ken asked.

"Yes. At least I believe his heart is right. He really is concerned about me."

"Good." Ken tried not to be disappointed that the problem between Jean and her pastor had been resolved so easily.

"He said he hopes I'll come talk to him when I have questions about religion. I made an appointment to go see him next week," she added.

"Sounds like a fine idea." Ken didn't look up as he finished tying the cord in a bundle.

"But I think I'd like to talk to your missionaries anyway."

"Oh?" Ken wondered if the sudden rise in the pitch of his voice had given away the eagerness he felt.

"Yes. Can you arrange it some evening next week?"

"I told you what the missionaries will want you to do."

"I still don't think I'm interested in changing churches, Ken. I just want to know more about why you believe the things you believe. Do you think the missionaries will talk to me anyway?"

"I can ask them. I think they will. But what changed your mind?"

"I've been thinking about all the things you told me. And you asked some interesting questions this morning that Pastor Michaels couldn't answer." She paused and smiled. "Besides, I need to know a lot more about the Mormons because I'm in love with a man who is one."

8

The Man in the Iron Mask

The still-unfamiliar buzzing of the portable telephone brought Ken instantly awake. Where was the thing? Somewhere down below. He groped for it over the edge of the bunk. "Hello?" He yawned.

"How can you still be asleep at this hour on Monday morning? It's already 7:45," Jean said.

"What makes you think I was asleep? I've been up since 5:30 . . . ah—chasing barnacles." He slapped the panel at the head of his bunk. "There goes one of the little devils now. You have to keep after them every minute when you live on a boat. I'm already tired."

She laughed. "You know what happens to liars, don't you?" Her tone softened. "You didn't call yesterday. I missed you."

"I tried your house. No one answered."

"Mom and Dad were gone. You could have called me at work. It's pretty slow around there on Sunday."

"I'll pick you up at the station about 5:30 this afternoon for a picnic in the park, okay? I'll bring the food."

She laughed lightly. "Are you going to cook?"

"No. I'll have it catered—by Speedi Mart."

"I'll look forward to it."

"By the way, I talked to the missionaries yesterday. They can meet with us tomorrow night about 7:00. Will that work for you?" Ken asked.

"Fine. You Mormons really jump on somebody fast, don't you?"

"What do you mean?"

"Irene Steiner called last night. She wanted me to help direct a musical your young people are doing. She said she had permission to ask me. Did you tell her to do it?"

"No. Honest. I didn't know anything about it. She probably had to ask the bishop, or maybe the stake president—that's the guy above him—because you're not a member of our church."

"Oh."

"Sounds like a great idea, though. What are they doing?"

"*The Music Man.*"

"Pretty ambitious. You'd be a big help. What did you tell Irene?"

"I told her I'd do it, if my work schedule isn't a problem. It sounds like fun. I haven't had a chance to do anything in drama or music since my junior year in college. But . . . will there be church meetings, or classes, or anything like that with the rehearsals?"

He laughed. "No. They'll probably start rehearsals with prayer. Will that bother you?"

"Of course not." She paused. "Ken, would it work to meet the missionaries on your boat with you? I don't think I'd better ask them to come to the house."

"Sure. It'll be tight in here, but we'll manage."

Sister Mikkelsen was a willowy, good-looking brunette from a small town in northern Utah. She had majored in retail management at BYU before her mission. Sister Watanabe, a convert of about three years, had been a nurse in Tokyo. From the moment Jean met the two women, she seemed to relax in the situation. She was instantly at ease with Sister Mikkelsen; they had much in common. And she took pains to draw Sister Watanabe out in talking about herself.

The four of them sat knee to knee, the two missionaries on one bunk, Ken and Jean on the other.

A friend in the elders quorum had loaned Ken a portable camp lantern to provide extra illumination in the cabin of the boat. Sister Mikkelsen joked about teaching by "borrowed light." Jean and Sister Watanabe didn't get it, so Ken tried to explain.

"The point is that we can't get along only by believing what someone else tells us about the gospel. We have to know for ourselves if it's true."

Sister Watanabe nodded gravely. "Oh, yes."

Jean seemed to be thinking it over.

At Sister Mikkelsen's request, Ken offered a prayer. He prayed that the Spirit of the Lord would be present to help the missionaries in teaching and to help Jean in understanding what would be taught.

That was the high point of the discussion; it went downhill quickly from there. Jean took it as an intellectual exercise. She asked numerous questions but only to store up information in her head, it seemed. She freely interjected her objections to what the missionaries taught.

After Sister Watanabe told her about the First Vision, Jean asked: "Doesn't it seem strange to you that God would choose a farm boy from a small village in New York to be his spokesman on earth? There must have been many people more qualified." The Japanese missionary looked at her blankly, then went on, following the discussion outline.

Later during the discussion, Jean asked Sister Mikkelsen: "If the Book of Mormon tells the history of people who lived in the Americas, why aren't all the archaeologists using it as a guidebook?" Sister Mikkelsen explained that the book was meant to be a second witness for Jesus Christ and not a history text or geographical guide. Jean seemed dubious.

Ken was touched by Sister Watanabe's sweet testimony toward the end of the discussion. Then Jean asked: "Was it difficult emotionally for you to go from a non-Christian tradition to a Christian faith?" Sister Watanabe looked puzzled and hurt. Sister Mikkelsen looked at Ken questioningly. He sat staring into space.

Jean would not promise to study the Book of Mormon, as the missionaries asked. When Sister Mikkelsen outlined the basic steps in prayer and invited her to try it, Jean said she prayed privately, but she declined to say the closing prayer: "No, one of you go ahead. I'll listen." Jean seemed untouched by Sister Watanabe's prayer that she would come to know the truth of what had been taught. The two missionaries stared at Jean strangely when she said she was looking forward to the next discussion.

After they left, Jean smiled playfully and asked Ken how many Sister Mikkelsens he had known when he was a missionary and whether he had ever dated any of them later.

He sat quietly without answering.

"What's the matter?" she asked, her brow furrowing.

"Just worn out, I guess." Ken didn't want to talk about what had just happened. He didn't understand it. Jean had seemed so willing to listen earlier. What had gone wrong?

She tenderly massaged his forehead and temples. "You need to get some rest, then. I'm going home, and I want you to go to bed right now. But don't forget to call me tomorrow."

Ken hoped the next lesson, two days later, would be the one to reach her heart. It wasn't.

Jean didn't argue about the need for salvation or faith. But she seemed to think of repentance as something needed mostly by those caught in the more deadly sins of the flesh and not by good, everyday Christians. Sister Mikkelsen tried to challenge her to be baptized. "I've already been baptized," Jean answered. "Because of my faith in Jesus, I've received the baptism of the Holy Spirit that comes in the heart of all believers." Ken heard echoes of Pastor Michaels.

Sister Mikkelsen called Ken the next day to say that she didn't think it would be productive to go on teaching Jean. Ken pleaded for the missionaries to be patient, to try again.

That night he dreamed that he and Jean were hiking a mountain trail in the jungle of Honduras when the ground started to give way beneath her. To his horror, she wouldn't reach out to him; instead, she clawed at the hillside and gradually began to slip away. Ken woke up, sweating and staring into the darkness as if into a black pit.

The next two weeks brought roller coaster highs and lows for both of them. The high times left them longing to be together constantly.

They went to each other's church meetings on Sunday and continued to see each other almost every day. He came back to the boat one evening to find a cupcake in the safe, with a brief note in her handwriting: "Missed you today. Please call." There was another note from Jack Weissman: "See her first, then call me. I have a job for you."

Ken taught Jean how to handle the boat out in the bay. The two of them spent an enjoyable Saturday introducing Jay and Allie to the basics of snorkeling. The goodnight kiss that Jean gave Ken at her door later left him feeling as if he could go for an hour's dive without oxygen.

Jean came out of her first *Music Man* rehearsal excited about the opportunity to work with Carla Warren, the director; Carla had studied drama, and Jean felt an immediate kinship with her.

Jean also found friends instantly among the young people. Ken attended one of the play's rehearsals the following week. Under Jean's tutelage, Gretchen Wilde, the young female lead, showed signs of blossoming in the part.

The low points of the two-week period, however, were the third and fourth missionary discussions. They were as disastrous as the first two.

Jean was willing to concede that there probably had been an apostasy, but she could not accept the Latter-day Saint version of the restoration of the gospel. "I believe God calls to all good Christians through more than one church," she insisted. She seemed fascinated with the idea of eternal progression, but she still refused to pray about what she had been taught or to study the Book of Mormon.

Jean felt that she was beginning to get a fair idea of the grand scheme of life, as the Mormons saw it. But she had a hard time getting them to discuss other viewpoints. They seemed unable to deviate from their programmed method of teaching.

Ken became more of a spectator during the discussions. He shared personal experiences in the gospel only when Sister Mikkelsen asked him directly about them. Jean noticed his silence. She began looking at him to see how he reacted when she answered questions, but his expressionless face told her nothing. She became more guarded in her objections to what the missionaries taught, and she deliberately found nice things to say about the Mormons. This didn't seem to draw Ken out, or to shorten the awkward pauses following some of her answers.

Still, she was surprised after the fourth discussion when Sister Mikkelsen explained tactfully that the missionaries wouldn't be scheduling another meeting with her. Jean said good-bye as warmly as she could and told them that she hoped to see them again, at church on Sunday.

After the missionaries had gone, Ken and Jean sat in the dark, opposite each other, in the stern of the boat.

"You're mad at me, aren't you?" she asked.

"No."

"Yes, you are. I can feel the cold shoulder clear over here."

"All right. I'm mad."

"Why?"

"It doesn't matter."

"It matters to me. Please?"

"Jean, you didn't even give this a chance!"

"What do you mean?"

"They asked you to pray about what they said, and you wouldn't do it. I asked you to pray, and you wouldn't. We asked you to read the Book of Mormon—even just a little of it—and you wouldn't do it. How do you expect to find out whether all of this is true if you won't give it a chance?"

"Are you mad at me because I didn't tell them I'd join your church? I don't think that's fair. I told you from the first that I didn't want to change churches, I just wanted to learn more about what *you* believe. And you said that would be okay—remember?"

"Yes."

"Then why are you mad at me?"

"Don't you even care if there's truth available that you don't have?"

"Ken, I told you I feel just fine about the way I worship God. I think I know enough for that."

"You're incredible! I've never known anyone so stubborn."

She paused before answering. "Let's not get into name-calling. What was that idea you were telling me about . . . freedom to . . . "

"Free agency?"

"Yes. Doesn't it apply to me? Can't you love me if I don't do what *you* think is best for me?"

He looked down at the deck for a time before answering. Then he looked her in the eyes. "Of course I love you, Jean. I'm sorry about what I said." He stood up and stepped across to sit beside her. "I love you too much to just turn it off. I don't think I could—even if you never agree with me. It's just that I've been trying to share a treasure with you—and I wish you could see it."

"I've already found a treasure," she said, squeezing his arm. He slipped it around her shoulders, and she leaned against him while they gazed at the lighted city skyline, reflected in colored smears on the moving waters of the bay.

Jean knew that her answer to his last comment had simply dodged the issue. She sensed that the discussion was not finished.

How long, Ken wondered, could he avoid a cruel choice if she would not seriously investigate the gospel?

Jay and Allison invited them to the beach on Saturday. Jay offered to provide the barbecue dinner if Ken would drive his truck.

The beach was crowded, but they managed to find a place where the nearest people were out of earshot. While Jay and Allison went to test the water, Ken and Jean erected the tarpaulin shelter next to his Blazer. They were just finishing when Jean playfully dumped a double handful of sand on Ken's head and down his back. He jumped up to chase her, and she darted away, out from behind the Blazer and into the packed sand roadway that ran down the beach. The driver of a pickup truck blared his horn as he was forced to brake and skid sideways to miss her.

"Stupid bimbo!" he shouted and followed it with a string of curses and threats as to what he would do next time if she didn't watch where she was going. Jean slowly backed away from the pickup. The driver, intent on her, did not see Ken approach from the rear of the vehicle.

Before the man knew what was happening, he was out of the truck, face down on the sand at Jean's feet. Ken knelt, one knee in the small of the man's back, and held him in an arm lock.

"Apologize!" Ken demanded.

"She ran out in front of me!" the man bleated. "Didn't you see her?"

"Tell her you're sorry! You don't talk to a lady that way."

"Get offa me, you—"

Ken cinched the arm lock tighter. "Tell her you're sorry."

"Ken, it's all right, let him up," Jean said. By now a group of bathers from up and down the beach had begun to gather around them.

"Tell her!" Ken insisted.

"I'm sorry, lady," the man mumbled into the sand.

"Ken, please," Jean pleaded.

"Tell her it won't happen again," Ken said to the man.

"Ken!" Jean said sharply.

Glaring up at her, he slowly moved to let the driver stand up. Ken pushed the man toward the truck, slammed the door after he climbed in, and threw the man's sand-covered cap through the open window. "Watch how you drive, before you kill somebody!" he shouted as the driver started the truck and accelerated down the beach.

Jean stood just inside the circle of spectators, her arms folded across her chest. She carefully studied the pattern she was drawing in the sand with her toe.

For the first time, Ken noticed that Jay and Allison had joined the group. Jay rested his hand on Ken's shoulder. "Everything okay?"

"Yeah," Ken said. Jean looked up at him. He looked away.

"Well, at least Jean didn't get hurt," Jay said.

"Yeah," Ken answered, glancing at her. "Scared the devil out of me, though." He pushed through the circle of people and trotted out into the surf.

For the next quarter hour, he hurled himself into the biggest incoming breakers he could find, letting them pound his body and drive him down into the sand and roll him over until he had to fight the undertow to come up for air. Finally, when it was getting harder to struggle to the surface, he gave it up and waded toward shore.

Jean was waiting for him in the knee-deep water. Small whitecaps splashed up her legs and stained the bottom half of her swimsuit a darker green.

"Hi." She held out a canned soft drink. "Thirsty?"

He took the can and held it between his hands as though studying the top carefully. "I'm sorry I embarrassed you," he said, meeting her eyes.

"It's all right."

"No, it isn't. Fine example of Christianity in action, wasn't I?" He slapped the soft drink can hard with his palm.

"Here," she said, taking it from him and punching the top open with her finger. The soda fizzed and ran over into the surf. He reached for the can and took a long swig.

"I'm really sorry, Jean. That was exactly the kind of thing my father would do, and I thought I was more mature than that."

"What do you mean?"

"He'd blow his cool and push somebody around—make them pay! I had no right to put you through that scene."

She sighed. "Well, I wish you hadn't done it—but it's over. I'll probably hear worse language before I'm old, and the whole thing was my fault anyway."

"I was just so scared—for you. And then when he talked to

you that way . . . " Ken shook his head as though to clear it. "Forgive me?"

She reached out to take hold of his hand. "Actually, it's kind of nice to know you care so much. Come on," she said, leading him toward shore. "Let's go sit in the shade."

Ken lay propped on his elbows in the shadow of the tarpaulin watching Jean and Jay throw the Frisbee down by the water. She had challenged Jay to a game.

Every male driver who passed slowed to watch her. Ken wanted to walk out there and wrap something protective around her to keep them from staring.

Undeniably, she was the best-looking woman he had ever seen. But it wasn't Jean in the swimsuit who came to mind whenever he thought about her.

It was her face. The image of her face in his mind evoked some . . . some totality that *was* Jean, something that made any day better when she came into it, and left any place dimmer when she went away. Her innate happiness was part of it. So was the way she had treated the little girl in sacrament meeting. So was her sense of humor, and the way she reached out to other people, and the way she cared about his feelings even when he had been the one to hurt her. This totality of Jean was what he wanted in his life permanently . . . if only—

"Are you in love with my sister?"

Startled, Ken turned to see Allison watching him, leaning on one elbow on her towel, a few feet away.

"Are you in love with my sister?" she repeated.

He laughed at the directness of the question. "Did anyone ever tell you that you take after your father?"

"Yes. Jay does, frequently. Are you?"

There was no dodging this. "Yes," Ken answered, returning her steady gaze.

"Are you going to marry her?"

He stifled another laugh.

"It often follows," Allison persisted. "Are you?"

How much, Ken wondered, could he safely say to Jean's sister?

Allison seemed to sense his reservation. "This is between you and me."

"I don't know the answer to your question," Ken said slowly.

"Is it because of your religion? Jean told me that she's been talking to your missionaries."

"Religion is part of it."

"You'd never find a better wife, in or out of your church."

"I know." There wasn't any way Ken could explain the eternal marriage dilemma to Allison—not when he hadn't yet talked to Jean about it. So he avoided the issue. "There are other reasons too."

"Like?"

He looked away and didn't answer for a time.

"I'm sorry, Ken. I'm not trying to pry," Allison said. "I just wondered if I could help. I want to see both of you happy, and I think I know what would make it happen for Jean."

Ken smiled. "It's okay. I was just thinking about how much I've learned since I met Jean. I've been forced to face up to the future. I have almost nothing to offer someone like her. All I can tell her is that I'd like to be able to make a living as a photographer. That's not much."

"You have everything our father had when he married our mother; you have potential. Things were tough for them for a long time before Daddy built his business into what it is now."

"Yeah—but how could I take Jean away from what she has now to what I could probably afford—some ratty apartment downtown somewhere?"

"Ken, be honest with me—would it have made any difference

to you if you had found out that Jean lived in, say, Garden Dale, and worked as a waitress?"

Ken visualized the older subdivision that Allison had mentioned. It was mostly tiny frame houses tacked together after World War II. He shook his head. "No."

"Then do you think Jean cares about whether you're rich?" Slowly Allison smiled. "Besides, it might be kind of romantic to live on your own private yacht."

Ken shook his head. "It might be impossible, if you needed space for more than three pairs of pants and one pair of shoes."

He gazed out at Jean and Jay. "It isn't just money. There's another reason too. Jean is a beautiful woman. Elegant. Sophisticated. And she could do better in a man. There are a lot of guys out there more educated and better-looking than me. I'm no Jay," he said, nodding toward Allison's husband.

Allison smiled indulgently in the direction of Jay, with his male-model good looks. "Sometimes I feel like I married every woman's heartthrob. I've seen women with dates sit and stare at him in restaurants when we go out."

She turned to look at Ken. "But don't underestimate yourself. It's too bad you haven't been around to hear Jean talk about how smart and talented you are. You may not realize it, Ken, but you're the most attractive man in the world to Jean. Would you like me to tell you one big reason why?"

He smiled. "Sure."

"Because you make her feel good about the Jean that's inside. No other man she's ever dated has done that. You have confidence in her, you want Jean to feel good about herself, and you want everyone else to know how wonderful she is. There's not much that can make a man more attractive to a woman than that."

"She is a wonderful person, Allie. She's—"

Sand splattered over the front of him as the Frisbee hit the ground a foot away. Ken brushed the sand from the fine, light-colored hair on his chest and looked toward the beach. Jean stood at the edge of the water, laughing.

He rose and snatched up the plastic disk. "All right, hot shot, grab this one," he called. He pitched the Frisbee in a low trajectory that took it directly toward her, but it suddenly rose before it reached her, sailing overhead and out over the surf. She chased it until she tumbled into the water. Ken grinned as she came up dripping.

"You did that on purpose," Allison said reprovingly.

"Me?" he replied innocently. "The old beach bum Frisbee champ?"

He lay down again facing Allison, supporting himself on one elbow so he could talk to her. "Allie, Jean is the most important person in my life. I just want her to be as happy as possible. I hope it can be with me. But if not—then her greatest happiness is still what I want."

"Thanks for letting me know that, Ken."

"She has a terrific family too. You and Jay—"

Cold, wet sand plopped on his shoulder blade and ran across his back onto his towel. He looked up to see Jean holding the dripping Frisbee. Smiling sweetly, she glanced over her shoulder to see if the road was clear and started backing away toward the beach.

Ken looked at Allison accusingly. "You let her sneak up on me."

"Me?" she replied innocently. "The protective big sister?"

Ken left Allison and chased after Jean. The chase was a short one; Jean ran straight into the surf, not trying very hard to get away. When Ken reached her, he caught her up in his arms and spun with her until he lost his balance and both of them fell into the waves, laughing. Then they walked out of the water hand in hand and sat on the beach. He stared out at the water, thinking.

Jean studied Ken's profile for a time as he looked out at the ocean. His face wouldn't be described as ruggedly masculine, but he was good-looking. His chest was well-developed. (Too many other men with a chest like that went shirtless to show it off; Jean realized that, except for swimming, she had never seen him without a shirt and full-length pants.) His chest tapered too quickly into a trunk that was almost skinny. His muscular but thin legs seemed a bit too long for his body, but they made him a strong runner. His arms also seemed too long, but they were well-developed. They helped make him a powerful swimmer. And they felt so good when he wrapped them around her.

"What are you thinking about?" she asked.

"Families." It wasn't a lie, exactly; he had been wondering if the two of them would ever have a family of their own. "You?" he queried.

"I was thinking about families just a few minutes ago—yours. Your father, really." Ken turned to look at her. "You said you hated to act like he does," Jean continued. "I can tell it upsets you just to talk about him. If you want an opportunity to be a real example of Christianity in action, there's one for you. I'm sure you'd be happier if you could forgive him."

"You don't know my father." Ken turned back toward the ocean.

"No. But I was thinking of what you said to me when I was mad at Pastor Michaels. I hate to see you carry so much anger around inside. I know it must hurt."

He didn't respond. She waited for what seemed like several minutes. Finally, she scooped up a small handful of shells from the sand and started pitching them toward the water, one by one.

"Well, I was only trying to help, but I can tell I said the wrong thing," she commented. "The Man in the Iron Mask is back."

"What?" He turned to look at her.

"The Man in the Iron Mask. It's an expression you have when you want to hide your feelings. Your face goes blank. Those brown eyes of yours just become two dark holes, and I have no idea what's going on in there. I saw it during the meetings with the missionaries, and now you're doing it again."

"Sorry. I didn't mean to shut you out. I was just thinking about my father." He turned his body so he could face her. "Has your dad ever hit your mother?"

"No! He'd never do that."

"I didn't think so."

Her eyes widened with realization. "Your father . . . ?"

"Sometimes, when he came home late, and she was half drunk. She had a bottle hidden up in the cupboard, behind the sugar. I don't know why she drank; maybe it was to forget about what he was doing. She always taught me that drinking was wrong. Anyway, he'd come in late, and she'd already be drinking. She'd preach to him about his immorality, and he'd yell at her about being a hypocrite. I could hear them, from up in my bedroom. Finally, he'd get mad and hit her."

Jean bit her lip. "Did he ever hit you?"

"Only twice. The first time I was ten. I learned to get out of the way when he was mad. The second time I was sixteen, and I decided I didn't want to get out of the way anymore." He touched his fingers to a scar, barely visible in his left eyebrow. "He has one of these too. After that happened, he never got beyond the yelling stage again."

"Oh, Ken! I'm sorry. I didn't know."

"But you're right, Jean. I've carried this anger inside for years—long enough now. I've got to get rid of it. It's only hurting me, not him."

She reached out to touch his eyebrow with her fingers.

"Jean, there's something else I've got to talk to you about," he said hesitantly.

"Go ahead." She smiled reassuringly.

"Remember when the missionaries talked to you about eternal families . . . and eternal marriage?"

"I remember a little bit of it."

"We believe that when two members of our church marry the way God wants us to, and live right, the marriage can be forever. Even after we die. What the man and woman build together doesn't ever have to end."

He took hold of her hand. "The first time I heard about it, when I was seventeen, I decided that marriage was going to be that way for me. When I get married, I want it to be a partnership that won't ever end."

"Ken, it sounds like a wonderful idea, but you know I don't believe . . . " Jean's voice trailed off as she realized what he was trying to say. She gazed quizzically at him for several seconds. "You're telling me that you can't marry outside of your faith, aren't you? At least, not if you want that dream to come true."

"That's right."

Jean disengaged her hand from his, drew her knees up under her chin, and wrapped her arms around her legs tightly. She stared out at the ocean for a time, seeming to be somewhere far away. Then she looked back at him, her chin still resting on her knees. "Why didn't you tell me about this before?" There was an edge in her voice.

"When I thought you were just a good friend, it didn't matter. Before I realized what was happening, you went from being a friend to someone I love. I guess I was afraid to say anything then; I thought you might just tell me good-bye before I could explain it. And when you were hearing the missionary discussions, I didn't want to put any emotional pressure on you."

"Well, you did. I knew I was upsetting you by not going

along with everything the missionaries said. I just couldn't figure out why. I wish you had explained this to me sooner."

"Hey!" Allison called from up near Ken's truck. "Come and get it. The steaks are on."

Jean seemed lost again in the waves she was staring at. Finally she spoke. "I love you, Ken. What you care about is important to me." She looked at him. "I'll study Mormonism with you. Just you. No missionaries this time. I don't want to hear something programmed. I just want you to talk to me."

"Okay."

"Hey, the steaks are burning," Allison called.

"And Ken—I won't promise anything. I couldn't join your church just to please you if I didn't feel it was the right thing for me to do. I couldn't live a lie, even for you."

"I couldn't stand to have you do that. All I want is for you to listen with an open mind."

"I'll try."

"Hey! I'm going to give these to the sand crabs!" Allison called.

Ken stood and extended his hand to help Jean up. "Come on, or Allie's going to send us to our rooms without supper."

9

Stalemate

Ken decided to start with the plan of salvation, since Jean had seemed more receptive to this than anything else the missionaries taught her. He reviewed all the pertinent missionary scriptures and dug out the missionary materials he had kept. He would use an illustration that had probably been passed down through generations of missionaries; it had several circles, showing a place of premortal existence, earth life, and, after a judgment, three degrees of glory.

Ken and Jean sat in the stern of the *Rum Runner* one afternoon while he explained it all to her. He was pleasantly surprised when she seemed to agree with almost everything he said.

"I believe all of that, Ken—or at least most of it," she said. "I believe we lived with God before we came here. I believe he has wonderful things in store for those who do what Jesus taught. And I believe there will be a variety of rewards or punishments for those who don't do so well. It just makes sense that way."

"What part don't you believe?"

"I can't believe God is going to surround himself only with

Mormons after we're all through here. There are a lot of other fine Christians who love him, and I think he loves them too."

"Of course he does. And people aren't going to live with him just because they wear the 'Mormon' label now. It will be people from any age or place who make covenants with him and live them. Everybody's going to have the chance."

"But what about good people who don't choose to be Mormons? My dad gives a lot of money to the same causes your grandfather did, and you know how much time my mother spends helping refugee families. Don't you think God loves people who do good like that?"

"Yes. And they'll be blessed for it."

"But you seem to believe they'll go to some lower place," she said, tapping her index finger on the circle labeled "Terrestrial" in Ken's drawing. "There's a joke I heard. Saint Peter is showing some new people around heaven, and he tiptoes quietly past one door. Someone asks him why, and he says, 'That's where we keep the Mormons. They think they're the only ones in here, and we don't want to disillusion them.' "

Ken looked off in the distance and didn't answer.

"Come on, Ken! Don't give me the Man in the Iron Mask. You wanted to talk about this."

He looked her in the eye. "It's an old joke, Jean. Did you get that from Pastor Michaels?"

She reddened. "Why don't you give me some credit for being able to think on my own? I visited Pastor Michaels only once. All he wanted to tell me was what's wrong with your church. I knew that wasn't going to teach me anything."

"Okay. I'm sorry." He reminded himself to be patient. "What do *you* think is going to happen to us after this life?"

"I really was a good girl in Sunday School, Ken. I've read the Bible. It says in the Book of John that those who keep God's commandments will abide in his love. Can anybody ask for more than that?"

"But what does it mean to abide in his love? What do you think heaven will be like, Jean?"

"How could I know?" She thought for a moment. "I believe people who get to heaven will rest from the cares of this world and be bathed in God's love all the time. We'll be able to praise him continuously, forever."

Ken was silent for a time. "Do you like Mark Twain?" he asked finally.

She looked surprised. "Yes. Why?"

"Ever read much of what he wrote?"

"*Huckleberry Finn, Tom Sawyer*."

"There's something he wrote—'Captain Stormfield's Visit to Heaven'—that I like a lot. He wrote about—"

"Twain wasn't exactly an expert on religion, was he?"

"No. A lot of the religious people of his time thought he was radical and irreverent. He was no friend of the Mormons, either. But what he wrote in that story rang true for me. The captain gets to heaven and finds it isn't what he had been led to expect. He's only good for about half a day of sitting around on a cloud playing a harp. Then he can't stand it anymore."

"What's the point?"

"In the story, the captain finds out that people don't just sit still after death. There are times to sing praises, but there's a lot more to do too. They can be moving forward all the time, learning and progressing."

"But, Ken, you Mormons sound as if you think people will be moving up to take over the work of God sometime after we're dead. How could that be? We're not perfect, and he is. And there's no need anyway. He's already created everything."

The rest of the discussion went on in the same vein. When it was over, both of them were frustrated. Ken felt as though he had taught her nothing. Jean felt as if she just been through cross-examination on the witness stand.

A few days later, when Ken tried to teach her about modern revelation and modern prophets, things went no better.

"Ken, I don't mean to be irreverent about what you believe, but I don't see why God would pick a plowboy from New York to restore his church."

"Jean, Joseph Smith didn't stay a plowboy. He became an educated man. He founded cities—"

"All right, he was an authentic American religious reformer. And he started a movement that's still going on. But that's not the point. I just don't think there was a need for him. For a prophet, I mean. The word of God was already on the earth, in the Bible."

"Don't you think we need prophets now, to give us God's word for us today?"

"No. We have men and women who feel the call of God in their hearts to preach the words that Jesus left us. We can't ask for better guidance than his words."

"But the Lord told us in the book of Amos that he wouldn't do anything without revealing it to his prophets. I know you'd be able to learn whether Joseph Smith was a prophet if you'd pray and—"

"Ken, you keep saying that. I *do* pray to God—but I don't believe he's up there for me to bother him with questions about every Tom, Dick, or Joseph who comes along. I have faith in the word he's already given us, and I believe that's all we need."

"Jean, God is your father, and he loves you. What's wrong with asking him about the truth?"

"I believe he's the father of all of us because he created us. But it seems so irreverent, Ken, the way you Mormons think of him. You treat him like some kind of . . . some associate you can take into your confidence. 'This is what I think, Lord. Please tell me I'm right.' "

"That's not the way it works, Jean. He expects you to study things out before you ask."

This discussion didn't lead anywhere either.

Ken gave her a Book of Mormon. He thought for a long time, and prayed over the testimony he carefully inscribed in the front. He showed her Moroni 10:4–5, which he had marked in the back, and tried to explain the promise in those verses to her. Jean listened politely, but by now her resistance had hardened almost into a constant. Too late, Ken knew he should have started with this book.

"I don't think I want to take it home," Jean said. "I'll read it here with you, okay?"

So during the next three evenings, they read much of First Nephi, taking turns reading chapters. By the third night, Jean's lack of enthusiasm was turning into overt disinterest.

She stretched languidly after finishing a chapter. How many times tonight, she wondered, had they read, "And it came to pass"? The reading was a blur. "I'm sorry, Ken, but this is boring," she said. "What is this book supposed to be teaching me? I don't think anyone really doubts that people from the Old World probably found their way across the ocean."

He looked at her, stunned. "Haven't you heard the things it teaches about Christ? I mean—well, all through the book . . . farther on it tells about how he came to the Americas and taught the people the same things he taught in Jerusalem. It's a second witness that Jesus really is the Son of God and that his work is divine."

"But I already believe the Bible. Why would I need another witness?"

"Jean, there's more to it than that. This book teaches the

gospel in its fullness—" Wrong approach, he realized; she would not understand the terminology.

"Ken," she said softly, "I'm sorry. I know this book is important to you. But when I'm reading it, I just don't feel what I feel in the Bible." Her brow furrowed, and she bit at her lip. She wanted to please him, but what else could she say? "You wanted me to tell you the truth about it, didn't you?" she asked.

"Yes. Always," he said half-heartedly.

Ken thought he was beginning to understand the meaning of spiritual deadness. He remembered his dream of the mountain trail in Honduras. Jean refused to reach out to him, even as she was sliding away. It seemed that somewhere inside she was resisting whatever he tried to teach her—because *he* was teaching it. The most wonderful woman he had ever known would not share the beliefs that motivated everything he tried to do in life. His heart felt leaden.

Jean was angry and apprehensive at the same time. Ken claimed he wanted her to be truthful about her feelings, but it made him unhappy when she was. What did he *really* want her to do? Would he only be pleased with her finally when she told him that he was right, and she was wrong?

She had always felt that if two people really loved each other—loved each other so much that the other's happiness was the most important thing in life—they could conquer anything together. But she was feeling a nagging fear. For Ken, it seemed to be either his church—or her. Which would he pick? There had never before been a man whose undivided love she wanted so much. But could Ken really give what she wanted?

After his failure with the Book of Mormon, Ken stopped trying to make Jean listen to planned discussions about the gospel. Their relationship continued to be a strange mixture of happiness and conflict. They took advantage of every opportunity, including

Sunday services at both their churches, to be together. But discussing their respective beliefs was often painful. More than once, when an argument about religion erupted, neither of them could be sure later how the discussion had started.

One evening in June, Ken stopped by Jean's house to pick her up. Her mother answered the door. "Come in and sit down, Ken," she said. "Jean's not ready yet."

He sat on the living room couch. Carol sat in a chair opposite him, arms folded, saying nothing. Finally, nodding in the direction of the gardens in the back yard, Ken asked, "How are the flowers?"

"The garden's looking good—especially the roses." Carol hesitated, then blurted, as though it were an accusation: "I know what you've been doing down on your boat!"

Ken raised his eyebrows. "What? What are you—"

"I know you've been teaching Jean about your church."

"I've been teaching her about the gospel. I wasn't trying to make any secret of that."

"I hate what you're doing! It's wrong, Ken. We accepted you into our home as a friend, and now you're trying to wean our daughter away from our church and into some . . . well, whatever it is you believe in."

"Carol, you have no idea what I believe in because you've never learned anything about it," Ken answered coolly. "I offered once to explain anything you wanted to know about my beliefs. Anytime—"

"Don't you try any of that Mormon missionary stuff on *me!*" Carol seemed to be struggling to keep control. Tears were ready to spill from her eyes; she blinked them back. "I'd fight you for my daughter—if I only knew what to do. But she won't listen to anything I say to her about religion anymore."

"I love your daughter, Carol. I'd like you to believe that. I'd never do anything that would be bad for her." Ken paused. "But

I don't think you've got anything to worry about. I guess Jean is even more independent than you realized. She won't listen to me about religion, either."

"Good! I'm going to encourage her to keep on being stubborn." She heard Jean's footsteps on the stairs, and said nothing more.

A few minutes later, as Ken drove up Ocean Drive, Jean asked, "What were you and Mom talking about?"

"Just a friendly little chat," Ken answered grimly.

"About?"

"You, and me . . . and religion."

"Oh." Slowly, Jean shook her head. "And what conclusion did you come to?"

"That neither of us can tell you what to think about it, that you're going to have to decide for yourself."

"Well, that's decent of the both of you!"

"Yeah. . . . Well, look, Jean, isn't the bay beautiful this evening?" He smiled in her direction, but she looked straight ahead and ignored him.

At times, Jean wanted to tell Ken and her mother simply to leave her alone. No decision she could make would please both of them. And why should she have to try to please them? Before she knew Ken, she had felt good about the way she worshipped God. If Ken loved her as much as he said, why did he want to force her to change?

She ought to be able to turn to her mother for help. Instead, her mother was keeping up pressure from the other side. Her mother seemed to be afraid of—what? That if Jean did not wholly accept her parents' beliefs, she was rejecting her family as well? "Jean, we've *always* worshipped together as a family," her mother had said this afternoon. "Could you really consider abandoning that?"

Ken had voiced a truth that he did not seem to appreciate,

Jean reflected: Any decision about how she practiced religion was up to her and no one else. She could not say she agreed with all of the things he tried to teach her, and Ken saw this as a problem. He seemed to feel some need to bring her one hundred percent around to his way of thinking.

Nor could Jean find comfort in the gospel as preached by Pastor Michaels; it seemed sketchy, as though he had only an outline, and Jean had often filled in the details with answers she had reasoned out in her own mind.

But trying to maintain an independent faith, against the opposition of two of the people she loved most, was wearing on her, making her doubt her own judgment. What was wrong with her? Jean wanted one of them to tell her. Was she somehow a sinner because she would not do what one or the other of them thought best for her?

Ken's truck began to slow down. He let it roll to a stop at the curb next to a park. He walked around to her side and opened the door. "Swing on the swings with me?"

She didn't pull away when he took her hand as they walked through the park. He stopped in the shadow of an oak tree and wrapped his arms around her. She rested her head on his shoulder. "I love you, Jean," he said softly in her ear. It was what she wanted—needed—to know at the moment. She squeezed him tightly in response. Then they walked on toward the swings, and soon they were laughing together as they tried to see who could swing highest.

They spent an enjoyable evening touring three more parks and testing the swings, then rating their favorites. They talked about her work and his growing photo client list, but they avoided speaking of anything on which they might not agree.

Late Thursday—Jean's day off—she met Ken at his boat with a picnic lunch for a photo trip to the small seaside communities on the north side of Corpus Christi Bay. In the older sections of a couple of those towns, he shot photos of the weathered buildings, then of Jean in a variety of settings, then photos of relics from the area's sea-going past, and then more of Jean. The two of them headed back to Corpus Christi as evening came, and he dropped her off at a *Music Man* rehearsal.

When he picked her up later, she seemed elated.

"It must have gone pretty well," he commented.

"It was okay. They're learning. They're great kids to work with."

"Well, you seem pretty happy about it."

She turned in the passenger seat of his truck so she could face him. "Did you know that Carla Warren's husband isn't a member of your church?"

Ken had met the musical director's husband a few times at ward activities or on elders quorum service projects. Dave Warren was a hard worker, quiet, a devoted family man. "Yeah. He's a good guy. Great with his kids," Ken answered.

"Well, he and Carla seem very happy." Jean waited expectantly.

He looked at her questioningly.

"Ken, couldn't it be that way for us? I'd never try to stop you from going to your church. If we had kids, you could take them with you; I wouldn't mind. I'd even go along, if you wanted."

Again, she waited expectantly for him to answer. He drove in silence for a ways, and slowly she settled back in her seat. "That's not enough for you, is it?" she asked bitterly.

"Carla's doing it the hard way," Ken replied. "She joined the church after she and Dave were married. She talked to me once about what it's like. Dave was off swinging the kids, at a ward picnic in the park. She watched him, and she said her greatest dream was for him to join the church too so they could be sealed in the temple as a family. Ask her about that sometime, Jean. Ask her why."

"Ken, I feel like you're just manipulating my emotions! It's always the same. I'm not good enough for you unless I join your church. Ever since I talked to your missionaries, I feel like you've been pushing me to do it your way—or else!"

He was taken back by her outburst. "Or else . . . what?"

"Or else we can never be married. You know I love you, and you say you love me—'*but* . . . ' It's that 'but' that hurts so much. Unless I'm the perfect little Mormon you always dreamed about, you don't really want me!"

"I do love you, Jean, just as you are. Have you been fighting so hard against learning the gospel because you feel like I'm trying to force you into some kind of mold? It isn't true."

"Isn't it? Then why do you keep telling me that if only I'd listen more closely to your lessons, if only I'd read the Book of Mormon, if only I'd pray about it, I'd know *you're* right. I think you've got an ego problem!"

"Speak for yourself! You're so stubborn that you're trying to turn this into some kind of power struggle between you and me. You're full of pride, Jean. I've been telling you all along to ask God for answers that only he can give, and you're too proud to ask him because you think you know all the answers already."

Ken had never spoken to her more harshly. Jean moved as far away from him as she could, tears streaming down her face. She dug in her handbag for a tissue and dabbed at her eyes.

Ken felt shame mixed with relief.

At last, he realized, they had gotten to the real difficulty: they were fighting over different things. He thought he had been trying to get Jean to listen with an open mind, to put aside disbelief. But she seemed to feel that he was trying to beat her down intellectually, to force her to acknowledge his superiority.

Perhaps there was a way to overcome the problem. First,

though, he would have to overcome the hurt his words had caused. They had been too quick, too sharp, too self-righteous. Ken believed that he was right about Jean's attitude, at least in part. But maybe she had been right about him too; maybe he had lashed out because her words really had bruised his ego. Glancing over at her, seeing the tears roll down her cheeks, he felt as though he had struck her in the face.

When he pulled up behind her car, parked next to the *Rum Runner*'s pier, Jean was out the door as soon as his truck stopped moving. But he managed to beat her to the driver's side of her car, planting himself beside the door so she couldn't open it.

"Let me get in. I want to go home," she demanded.

"I will if you want, Jean. But, please—give me a chance to apologize first."

"Why should I?" she said angrily. But she let him take her hand and lead her down the pier to a seat in the stern of the boat.

He sat close to her. She moved to the end of the bench.

"I shouldn't have spoken to you like that. It was wrong. But we've got a problem," Ken said.

"Oh? What was your clue?"

He let the sarcasm pass. "Look, let's go back to being friends."

"You mean stop loving you? Believe me, sometimes I wish I could! If only you weren't so darn good, and good to me—most of the time—and honest, and strong when I need strength. I wish it were easy to stop loving you." Tears ran down her cheeks again.

"No, that's not what I mean. I can't stop loving you either, Jean. I've never known a woman I wanted so much to share life with. You make me happier than I've ever been before." She let him put his arm around her. "What I'm trying to say is, let's stop beating up on each other. We get along well, except when we talk about religion. Let's stop."

She looked at him wide-eyed. "You'd do that? As much as it means in your life?"

"Yes. I've been selfish. I've wanted you to be a member of the church for me. But I want it even more for you, if you can understand that. I want you to have all the blessings of the gospel because I care about your eternal happiness."

"Ken, we've been over this before. I'm trying to live the gospel of Christ the best way I know how. I don't feel like God disapproves of me. But I feel like you do."

"I'm sorry if I've made it seem that way. You're really one of the best people I know. Maybe you're right. Maybe I have been trying to force you into believing what I believe."

He pulled her closer to him, holding her tightly around the shoulders. Inside, he knew he had to be willing to let her heart go, if that was what she wanted. The choice would be hers.

"I won't push you about my church anymore, Jean. If you still want to, we'll go to both our churches on Sundays; that way, we'll be together. But I won't talk to you anymore about doctrine unless you ask me. By now, you know how to find out if what I've told you is the truth."

Jean heard what Ken was leaving unsaid. There would be no compromise of his dream. He would go on hoping and praying that somehow, something would change so that she would come to believe what he believed. But that was impossible. The one true church? The lower heaven for people who didn't practice what the Mormons practice? The need to repent when she wasn't a sinner? She simply could not accept some of the things he had taught her.

She sighed. "Ken, what are we going to do?"

"I don't know."

They sat in the darkness watching the distorted reflections of the city lights in the restless bay.

"Bradley, Channel 9 News," Jean said into the telephone.

"Hi. What are you doing tonight?"

"Hi, Ken," she said, smiling and putting down her pencil. The reporter at the next desk grinned, put his hand over his heart, and made fluttering motions. Jean made a face at him and swiveled around toward the wall.

"What did you have in mind?" she said to Ken.

"Can I take you to dinner?"

"Sure. Want me to meet you at the boat about 7:00?"

"That will be fine."

He sounded a bit distant, she thought. "Is anything wrong?"

Ken hesitated. "No. I'll see you then. Bye."

Was it the same old problem, Jean wondered, or something more?

Their times together had been sweeter since they had stopped discussing religion. Their dates were fun again. They enjoyed snorkeling, walking and jogging together, or just talking—about anything but his church. On the Sundays when she was off, they went to each other's church meetings. Occasionally, she asked him questions about things she observed in his ward. He answered her, but, true to his word, he never brought up LDS beliefs on his own.

He came to her house often to see her, or called her during the day. She couldn't have asked for him to be more attentive. But always there was a reserve, some part of him that wouldn't open up to her anymore when they were together. She knew that the question of religion was an invisible barrier between them, a cloud over their future—if they had one as a couple. Several times she had wanted simply to ask a question about a matter of belief. It seemed silly for two people in love not to be able to talk about something so basic as their faith. But she couldn't bring herself to raise the subject. It could mean conflict, and pain.

Jean savored every opportunity to be with Ken. Other men had made her feel wanted, but no one had ever made her feel loved as Ken did. And she needed him. He had some kind of inner strength she had never felt in another man. He often seemed to draw on it to help her; sometimes he seemed to know her needs before she did.

She enjoyed the feeling of being important in his life. She was looking forward to dinner with him tonight—and maybe some time just to talk afterward, on the boat.

He was waiting for her at the pier when she arrived. She walked around the car to the passenger side, and he held the door open for her. "Is the Golden Net okay?" he asked.

"Sounds good. Maybe Vonnie will have something special for us tonight."

The temperature and the humidity were both still in the nineties when they reached the restaurant. It had been the kind of mid-July day in South Texas when asphalt turns soft and tar oozes out of it. Ken was trying to help Jean pick her way carefully across the parking lot in her high heels when another couple came out of the building. It was Ray and Gloria, from Ken's old diving group.

Gloria recognized them instantly and tried to steer Ray in another direction. But Ray recognized them too, through eyes already bleary from too much of his favorite drink.

"Well, if it isn't Mr. and Mrs. Perfect," he called, and followed with a string of obscenities directed at both of them. "You caught me off guard last time, McArthur, but not this time." He lurched toward them, face contorted with anger. Ken deliberately sidestepped to draw him away from Jean. She teetered on her heels momentarily, trying not to lose her balance.

Ken ducked away from two of Ray's wild swings, retreating, but Ray kept advancing. On the third swing, Ken used Ray's momentum to pin him against the side of his own pickup truck.

Then he maneuvered Ray into an arm lock; Ray's body arched outward as Ken forced his twisted arm up in back. Jean held her breath. Gloria stood by, ashen-faced.

Jean saw the flush begin to subside on the back of Ken's neck. She let out her breath slowly. Ken shifted his position so he could keep Ray under control without hurting him unnecessarily, then began talking calmly in Ray's ear. "Easy, my friend, easy. We can work this out. . . . Just calm down. . . . We can talk about it. You can have another shot at me sometime when you're in better condition."

Ray struggled suddenly to free himself. "Leggo my arm. I can take you right now!"

Ken momentarily increased the pressure of his hold until Ray subsided. "Easy. Not right now. We'll talk about it later. Gloria," he called over his shoulder, "can you drive this truck?" She stepped over by the two men.

"Ray, give me the keys. Where are the keys?" Ken asked.

"Pocket . . . Right pocket."

Gloria fished the keys out of Ray's pocket. Ken walked Ray around the truck, forced him up into the passenger seat, shut the door, and held it. "Let Gloria take you home, Ray. Go to bed. Sleep it off." Ray muttered to himself, but he made no move to get out of the truck.

Gloria settled herself in the driver's seat, then looked out the window at Jean. Her look was pleading. "I'm awfully sorry. He isn't usually like this."

"It's all right," Jean replied. "Will you be okay—with him?"

"Sure. I'll just push him through his door and point him toward the bedroom. He'll be fine in the morning."

Jean watched as the truck pulled out of the parking lot. "Poor Gloria. I hope she can handle Ray. Maybe I should call tomorrow to see how she is. Do you still have her phone number?"

Ken looked at her in wonder. "Sure . . . You know, you're

amazing, to be thinking of Gloria's feelings, after your last experience with her."

"Well, I was a little hard on her the first time we met. I shouldn't be judging people." She slipped her arm through his as they walked into the restaurant. "You didn't do too badly yourself. I was proud of you. Six weeks ago, you would have left Ray lying in the parking lot."

Ken's brow furrowed. "I wanted to punch him out for making you listen to that filth. But suddenly it didn't seem like the thing to do—if I really love my fellowman." He smiled at her. "You've been good for me, Jean. Since I met you, I've been relearning how to live the way the Lord wants me to. Before that, I think I was on the way to getting lost in myself and my own problems."

It was the closest he had come in more than two weeks to raising the subject of religion.

They made cheerful small talk over dinner. Ken asked about her day. He laughed at her description of a last-minute foul-up that left people scrambling behind the cameras while the news anchors tried to keep the show going. Vonnie stopped at their table to visit while they ate; Ken joked with her as though they were old friends.

Maybe, Jean thought, her intuition had been wrong when she talked to Ken on the telephone earlier. If there was something bothering him, it didn't come up.

When they returned to the *Rum Runner*'s pier, he asked, "Can you come down to the boat for a few minutes?"

In the cabin, his camera gear was spread out on one of the bunks, along with his suitcase, which was half-filled with clothes. She looked at him questioningly.

"I wanted to talk to you about this," he said. "I have an assignment from a German travel magazine. I sent them some stuff I shot in Hawaii. They wanted to know if I could cover

Texas the same way for an article on the state. It's a break I couldn't pass up."

"You have to go away?"

"I'll be traveling with their writer—for a month, maybe a little more."

She frowned. "When do you have to leave?"

"I'm supposed to meet the writer in Houston tomorrow afternoon. They sent me a letter three weeks ago, but I just got it yesterday. I called them this morning."

Jean sat down slowly on the unoccupied bunk. "So I won't see you for a month?"

"Probably longer than that. After I'm through with the magazine assignment, I'm going to take a few days in Houston to make some contacts—see what kind of freelance work is available there. I suppose this is the time to find out if my work will sell in a wider market."

"It will. It's good." She smiled weakly, then her smile faded. "But I'll miss you terribly while you're gone."

Ken idly rolled the strap of his camera bag into a tight curl, then unrolled it again. "I'll miss you too. I thought about turning down the assignment so I wouldn't have to leave right now. But I've been playing at part-time photography too long. I've got to know whether I can really make a living in the field and support a family someday. I've got to have a future to offer before I can . . . ask anyone to marry me."

Jean had realized weeks ago, and she was sure Ken must have realized too, that a moment like this would come. They had been drifting along in their relationship. But now—though neither of them had put the possibility into words—she feared that they were at a point where normal events would carry them in different directions. One of them would have to make a decision that would keep them together. And she could not think of losing him. She had determined what her response must be.

"Ken, I've been thinking . . . about us . . . about what you've been trying to teach me." Jean hesitated. "I could be a Mormon if you want me to be . . . after you come back. I could be comfortable going to your church. It teaches people to believe in Jesus, and it teaches them to live good lives. That's what I grew up with."

Ken looked startled. Slowly, he sat down opposite her. He spoke deliberately. "Jean, you don't know how tempting that sounds to me. It would be wonderful—for a little while, maybe. But we're talking about making covenants with God. Do you remember when you told me you couldn't live a lie?"

She looked away.

"You don't really feel my church is the Church of Jesus Christ, do you?"

She shook her head. "Not the *only* one. I've tried, Ken. I've even prayed to God to tell me that you're right."

"But nothing happened? You haven't felt anything that you thought was an answer, have you?"

How was it, Jean wondered, that he sometimes seemed to know what was going on in her mind? "No," she said. "What should I feel?"

"It's hard to describe. For me, it's like . . . like a swelling, and lightness in my chest—or like darkness is being driven away by light everywhere inside." He thought for a moment. "Remember the day I took pictures of the jellyfish down on the beach, and I showed you how the right light changes things? Well, this kind of light changes things inside of you. Even things you've known all your life will look different."

"I haven't felt anything like that."

"I know you can feel it, Jean. But there are a couple of things you'll probably have to do first."

"Like what?" she said sharply.

He picked up the Book of Mormon that lay on the bunk

where she had last left it. "I think you'll have to show the Lord you're serious about wanting to know the truth. And I think you'll need to ask him because you want to know for yourself—not for our sake, or mine."

"Why is there always something *more* I need to do?" Anger pushed the words out of her. Didn't he realize what was happening? She was telling him there was no need for him to compromise. She was offering to do whatever he wanted for the sake of their future, regardless of her own beliefs. And still it wasn't enough. Maybe he would never be satisfied with her. Maybe nothing she could do would ever be enough. "Why is it always something *I* have to do? Why do *I* have to make all the changes?"

"Jean—"

"Just answer me this: Is there any future for the two of us if I don't become the obedient Mormon you have in mind?"

"Is that where we are, Jean?" he asked softly. "Have you decided you just can't give study and prayer another try? Maybe we could talk about it more when I come back."

"I guess you've answered my question, Ken. We've already talked this to death," she said, rising. "I hope you have a good trip," she added flatly.

At the moment, Jean hated him. So why did she want to make him promise to call while he was away? Why did she want to kiss him good-bye? She didn't dare risk the kiss; it would take the anger out of her, and then the thing he asked her to do would start sounding reasonable. She turned and made her way up the stairs and out of the cabin.

"Jean—" Ken called after her. There was no answer but the tapping of her heels on the pier. He was a good sprinter; he wondered if he could catch her before she reached her Camaro. Then he heard the car door slam, the engine start, and the tires squeal on pavement.

He tossed the Book of Mormon onto the bunk. He had hoped that if he were patient, if he just kept loving her . . .

Angrily he threw his remaining clothing into the suitcase and slammed it shut. The photo assignment from the German magazine was exactly the kind of opportunity he had been wanting for months—and suddenly he wished he had never heard of it. He needed to stay here instead of leaving for several weeks. Jean was worth giving up his ambitions.

But what would be the point? He probably couldn't win her back now. He had fought for her every way he knew, and prayed for her, but she seemed to have made her choice.

At 2:15 A.M., he was still tossing in his bunk, unable to sleep. He got up, dressed, hauled his things out the cabin door, locked up the *Rum Runner,* and stowed his gear in the back of his truck. By 3:30, he was nearly in Victoria, ninety miles away.

10

"Could It Possibly Hurt Anything?"

Hi, Gorgeous. Haven't we met somewhere before?"

Jean turned to smile at her brother-in-law as he sat down on the couch beside her. She hadn't noticed as Jay had come into the recreation room from the kitchen, where Allie and her parents were still talking.

"You've been a stranger tonight," he said.

"What do you mean?"

"You've been somewhere else almost all night long, even while we were eating dinner. I've been watching you out here. You picked up that magazine and leafed through it, then you put it down, then you picked it up and looked through it again. Do you remember anything in it?"

Jean examined the rolled-up magazine in her hand. "No," she admitted, smiling ruefully. She put the magazine down on the coffee table. It uncurled suddenly when she let go of it, like a spring whose tension has been released.

"Is something wrong?" Jay asked.

"Not really."

"I know you better than that. Want to talk?"

Jean sighed. "Well, okay, but there's nothing anyone can do."

"Pessimism isn't the Jeanie I know." He smiled at her. "Try me."

She looked at him searchingly. "Well, if anyone could help, Jay, it would be you." She faced forward and stared at the opposite wall. Brushing her long hair back and letting it fall loosely off her shoulders, she massaged the back of her neck thoughtfully for a few seconds, then turned to face Jay.

"I've been watching you and Allie tonight."

"I did notice that."

"Jay, ever since Allie met you in high school, I've known you were the only man for her. Anyone could see that you adore her too. She's the first thing you look for when you walk into a room. You never sit down by her or stand by her without finding her hand to hold."

"It's that obvious, huh?" He smiled. Jean didn't. His smile quickly faded. "Okay. You're right, Jean. So—is the way Allie and I feel about each other bothering you for some reason?"

She looked away from him again. "I just want someone to want me that way."

"Oh . . . Ken?"

"Yes." She stared at the opposite wall for a few seconds, blinked, and then touched a finger to the corner of her eye to catch a tear before it could slide down her cheek. "I wish he could love me the way I love him. I wish he needed me the way you need Allie."

"I thought he did. I've seen the way he looks for you whenever he comes into a room, and the way he maneuvers so he can always be next to you."

Jean turned on him suddenly. "If he loves me so much, then

why does it have to be either his church or me!" she blazed. "Why?" Her look was defiant.

Jay looked away and rubbed his chin thoughtfully. Jean knew why he would not meet her eyes; she had seen that look before when Jay and Allie had had a fight. Karate was a matter of self-discipline and physical conditioning with him, she knew, but Jay was a peacemaker at heart. While it would be dangerous for some stranger to corner him physically, he shunned confrontation—especially with those he loved. Jean's hard jaw line softened, and she reached out to touch his shoulder lightly with her fingers.

"Oh, Jay, I'm sorry. Please forgive me. I shouldn't have let that spill over on you. It's just so frustrating! Ken says he loves me too. But I can feel him holding back, and I know it's because of his religion."

Jay looked at her again. "Did he say it that way—it was either his church or you?"

"No, but it's the same thing. He's determined to marry a Mormon. People in his church believe that if they marry outside their faith, they'll miss out on blessings God has promised to them."

"Well, why don't you just join his church? After all, I joined your family's church."

"I thought of that. I told Ken I'd be baptized into his church if it would please him—even though I couldn't believe what he believes. I said I'd do everything a good Mormon wife is supposed to do. But it isn't that easy. They expect you to have some kind of spiritual manifestation first. I couldn't tell Ken I had felt anything like that."

Jay frowned thoughtfully. "It would be tough on you to join, wouldn't it, Jeanie? You've always hated phonies. How would you feel deep inside?"

She looked at him intently for several seconds. "Are you two on some kind of telepathy network? That's almost the same thing Ken wanted to know."

"It's that old male intuition," Jay replied, grinning at her. She still didn't smile. His expression became serious again. "I'm sorry, Jeanie. I'm not taking this lightly. I just know you fairly well by now. Trying to live something you didn't believe would eat away at you. Then both of you would be unhappy."

Slowly she nodded. "You're right." She looked away, and her jaw line hardened again. "But what do they want of me? Ken, the missionaries, all the others at his church—they all expect me to be sure it's God's own religion. How can anyone be sure of something like that?"

"I don't know. What do the Mormons tell you?"

"They say, 'Pray about it.' I think that's one of their missionary slogans," Jean said sourly. "Jay, I know you believe in God. Do you ever pray to him? Privately, I mean?"

"Yes, sometimes—in my own way. It's not like Reverend Michaels does, standing up there." Jay gripped an imaginary lectern, and his voice took on a pulpit timbre. " 'Allllllmighty CreATor, we lowly mortals beseech thee . . . ' "

Jean giggled. "Perfect! Maybe you should have considered a career in the ministry."

"I'm sorry," Jay said contritely, "I didn't mean to make fun of Pastor Michaels. I'm sure he's sincere. But I learned to pray the way I saw Reverend Edwards do it in my parents' church—quietly talking to God. Whenever I pray, it's like that—me talking to the Lord, one on one. I hope he doesn't mind. It's the only way I know how."

"Do you think the Lord would have just one church on the whole earth that would be *his* church?"

"I don't know, Jeanie. I guess I've never wondered whether one church might be more right than another. A church has always been a place where I go to worship God, and a minister has always been someone to help me understand the Bible better. But it seems to me that knowing God is my own responsibility; it's not something a church can do for me."

Jean thought of Ken. Whatever reservations she might have about his beliefs, he seemed to know God better than she did. And the prayers she had heard Ken offer were the quiet, one-to-one kind Jay talked about.

Jay leaned back, hands behind his head, and stared at the ceiling. "Allie and I go to the same church as your Mother and Dad because we're comfortable there. But God has been pretty precise about everything else in the universe. Judging by logic, I'd guess he could have a single church somewhere that fits into his well-designed plan. I've never thought about how to find out which one it is."

"Well, then you see my problem. I don't know how to tell either."

"I think you have more than one problem."

She frowned. "What do you mean?"

"You talk about this as if Ken and his church are a package. Are they? I know how you feel about Ken, but I think you need to sort out how you feel about his church. You seem to be struggling with that in your own mind."

"I told you, I don't know—"

"Jeanie, why did you stop drinking wine with us at dinner?"

"Because I think it's . . . " She paused to weigh her answer for a moment; she mustn't let this sound like criticism. "Because I've come to believe that alcoholic drinks may not be good for us."

"Why?"

"Well, none of us gets roaring drunk on a little wine, Jay. But I've seen what it can do to some people when they drink a lot of it. I know what it does to me. If a lot of wine has that effect, it seems to me that even a little bit doesn't do any good."

"I don't know much about the Mormons, but they don't drink alcohol. Or at least Ken doesn't."

"No. They believe God gave a revelation that says they—well, all of us—shouldn't do it."

"See? You've got a little bit of Mormon in you already." She smiled. He laughed. "That's my Jeanie."

"I can't say they don't have some good ideas, Jay. A lot of things I've heard them preach would make anyone better."

"Carol tells me they're not Christians," Jay said tentatively.

"Well, they teach about Jesus, and most of the Mormons I've met seem to be trying to follow his word—the same way we are." Jean's brow furrowed. "I guess we could quibble about the definition of a Christian. But I've always thought it depended on what was in a person's heart. I don't know how Mom, or anyone else, could judge that. Only God would know."

Jay reflected on her answer for a moment. "Well, the Lord told his disciples, 'He that is not against us is on our part.' I've heard Pastor Michaels say we should extend the hand of fellowship to all believers."

Jean smiled wryly. "I don't think he meant the Mormons." She gazed into the distance. "They do teach some things that sound strange—compared with what you and I have always been taught."

"Like what?"

"Well, one of the big points for Ken is eternal marriage. They believe two Mormons can get married in their temple and it will be forever—even after they die."

Jay looked skeptical. "But the Bible says, 'In the resurrection, they neither marry—' "

" 'Nor are given in marriage,' " Jean finished. "Pastor Michaels tried that one on Ken. Ken's answer was another scripture, 'What God hath joined together, let no man put asunder.' He said that marriage could continue past death if it were done in this life, by someone who has authority, and that Jesus gave his apostles the authority."

Jay stared at Allison in the kitchen for several seconds before he spoke. "It would be wonderful—if it were true." He turned back to Jean. "But the apostles are gone."

"The Mormons believe they have a modern prophet, and apostles with the same authority . . . and they believe we can all be adopted children of Israel . . . and . . . oh, they believe in more than one heaven."

Jay sat looking at her quizzically.

"Oh, Jay, I was so busy thinking up arguments sometimes that I didn't listen closely to everything Ken was trying to teach me. At least I can't remember all of it now. I think I understand some of the things they believe, but I don't know how to explain them. Everything sounds so logical when *they* explain it."

"Maybe you need a refresher course." He paused, thinking, for several seconds. "Or maybe there's only one way to find out if what Ken taught you is right."

Jean shifted on the couch so she could face him squarely. "Are you seriously suggesting that I need to do what they say? Study their doctrine and pray about it?"

"Jeanie . . . I don't know. I've never tried to ask God directly what's right—at least, not about religion." He smiled slightly. "I have to admit that sometimes, when the pastor couldn't give me an answer, I've thought and reasoned about a question until I've come to my own conclusion."

Jean smiled with him. "Me too. What else is there to do?"

"Well," Jay mused, "Jesus told us, 'Ask, and it shall be given you.' He must have meant that." He studied the back of the couch as he ran his fingers over it lightly. Then he looked up at her again. "Could it possibly hurt anything, Jeanie? If you pray and get some kind of answer, one way or the other, wonderful! And if not—have you lost anything?"

"Well, no—I suppose not. I—ah . . . I tried praying about it once or twice, because Ken asked me to. But I resented doing it, because I thought he was just trying to force me to see things his way."

A smile played around the corners of Jay's mouth. "You mean you prayed something like this: 'Lord, I don't believe Ken knows what he's talking about, but if you want to give me some kind of sign . . . '?"

Jean grinned at him. "Something like that. And I suppose I could have read their book with more of an open mind."

Then she was serious again. "There's another problem, Jay. I pray to God for peace on earth, and for love among everyone, and for bread every day, the way Jesus taught. But it's hard for me to believe that God would take time out to bother with my little individual concerns. I'm one small speck in the universe, and there's a world down here full of war, and famine, and hurt—"

"You're spending too much time covering the news, Jeanie. A lot of good things happen in life too."

"Well, yes. But I'm just not sure whether God even knows about little Jeanie."

"Be sure to tell me what you find out," Jay said, smiling. "Really. I'd like to know."

Slowly she shook her head and grimaced skeptically.

Jay leaned forward and put his hand gently on her forearm. "Where's that list of questions I saw you writing in church today?"

She blushed. "I threw it away."

"I don't think you're comfortable in our church anymore, Jeanie. You seem to be blaming Ken's church for taking him away from you—and yet you see some good things in it. I think you need to find out how you really feel about the Mormon church."

"Jay, you're . . . well, that's at least partly true. I don't know if I'll be able to find out whether Ken's right about what he believes. But I don't get some of the answers I need in our church. I know Mom would be upset to hear me say that." She smiled conspiratorially and lowered her voice, "You'd probably be in a lot of trouble with her if she knew that you're encouraging me to study Mormonism."

"Right," he said, grinning. "But you're more than just Allie's sister. You're my friend. If it's really a Christian group, and if you'd be more comfortable there—well, I want to see you doing whatever will make you happy."

"Thanks, Jay. It's good to know that I can count on you, and Allie." She looked somewhere beyond him. "It's hard for me to see, though, how the Mormons can be so sure . . . "

"Jeanie, I don't think God's going to come down in a cloud and tell you, 'Yes, my child, this is the one.' I can't tell you if there's a way to know for sure which church is *his* church. But maybe you'll learn that this one is best for you right now in your life. That's your first problem—knowing how you really feel about Ken's church.

"After you find out the answer to that one, then whatever happens with Ken will happen. That's your second problem."

The accountant's logic of it was undeniable. Jean laughed delightedly. "Jay, how can anyone who's only twenty-seven be so smart?"

Then she glanced toward the piano in the living room. A small crystal vase sat on top of it—something Ken had brought her, with a flower, after one of his delivery trips had forced him to break a date. This evening, Jean had cut one of her mother's pink roses and put it in the vase. Jay glanced at it too; this was where her gaze had wandered several times during their conversation.

"I'm not sure whether Ken still feels the same way about me," Jean said. "I—uh—kind of shut the door in his face before he left. I hope I didn't ruin things between us. I wish he'd write, or call. He's been gone for two weeks, and I haven't heard a word from him. Nothing."

"Maybe you can open the door again. Has he heard from you?"

"Well—no," Jean said, "but I don't know where he is. He's traveling."

"Doesn't his father live in Houston? Maybe Ken will drop in there."

"I don't think so. Ken and his father don't get along."

"Can you find out what German magazine he's working for? Journalists are supposed to be good at tracking things down, Jeanie. Maybe it's worth a shot."

"But I wouldn't know where to start. I don't speak German, and . . . " The rest of the excuse wouldn't come out of her mouth. Somewhere in her mind, Jean could hear Ken telling her to have more confidence in her own ability. Slowly she smiled at Jay. "I guess I could give it a try." She leaned close and pecked him on the cheek. "And thanks. . . . Thanks for making me talk about this."

"Aha!" Allison accused from the doorway. "Putting some moves on my husband when you think my back is turned."

"Allie, you know there's not a woman alive who could ever steal this man's heart away from you."

Allison sat down on the couch by her husband, intertwined her fingers with his, and squeezed.

"But if you could clone him," Jean added, "I'd appreciate it."

Ken tried to concentrate on totaling his expenses for the magazine assignment thus far. But Jean wouldn't stop staring at him from the photo in his wallet, which lay open on the desk. And Ken couldn't help staring back. The thought that he might have changed her mind somehow if he had stayed in Corpus Christi—and passed up this assignment—wouldn't leave him alone.

He wanted to go to her. If he started out driving right now . . . but no. No good. Sitting in this motel in Amarillo, he was closer to Wyoming than he was to Corpus Christi. By the time he could get there tomorrow, she'd be at the studio for the evening newscast. And then she'd probably get home late, and get up early the next morning . . . to go to church with her parents.

It was crazy! He flipped his ballpoint pen across the room in disgust. It clattered against the venetian blinds and fell to the floor behind the bed. He ran his hands through his already mussed hair and looked at Jean, leaning against the wall of the old mission in San Antonio . . . telling him silently, "You're mine." She was right. Thinking about giving up this assignment was insane—yet he'd do it in a minute if he thought going back would change her mind.

It wouldn't though, would it? She had made it clear that things were over between them if he couldn't bend a little in the area of religion. She had gone as far as she was going to go in making concessions to him.

If only she would go just that one step farther, to investigate the church honestly and pray about it! He remembered his dream of Jean on the mountain trail in Honduras, slipping inexorably away because she would not reach out to him.

And then it came to him with a shock that *he* had been the one on solid ground in the dream. *He* had been the one who might have taken one step toward her . . . and then maybe another, to reach out.

What did that mean? Should he give up the idea, then, of eternal marriage? He looked into Jean's eyes in the photo in his wallet, into those clear, deep green eyes he could see in his mind, and he sighed. No. Not even for her. No matter how much it hurt. What would be the point, in the eternal balance of things, in winning Jean now, and then, in the end, losing her again . . . and himself too?

But had it really come down to this choice?

Maybe the trouble was, Ken thought, that he didn't know how to make choices with a partner, another person whose feelings and hopes and dreams were important to him. He had always been a loner. "The Man in the Iron Mask," Jean had called him on the beach that day when he had first talked to her about eternal marriage. She was right.

The iron mask had been fashioned originally to shield his feelings from his father and then from others—from peers who didn't know what it was to have an abusive father, from a few Marines who didn't think beyond the next night's shore leave. There had never before been anyone with whom he wanted to share some of the deeper things in his heart. Maybe he just didn't know how to do it. Maybe he wasn't prepared to share his deepest feelings with any woman, in or out of the church. He had had no models to learn from over time, no two people whose relationship had functioned in a way he thought would work for him and Jean.

Certainly not his mother and father. He had remembered, that day on the beach, that his father had been in the habit of telling his mother how things were going to be in their marriage, and when she did not conform, there was trouble. Ken had hated that about his father—that demanding arrogance. And yet, hadn't he himself been that way with Jean? Had he said, "This, or nothing?" That was what she seemed to feel.

Was there a successful marriage he knew that could show him how it ought to be done? There were his grandfather and grandmother. Wonderful people. But the model of their marriage could never work for him and Jean. His grandmother had been one of those women who was truly content to bask in the light of her husband's successes. It worked for them. But Jean wasn't that kind of woman, and Ken knew he would never want her to be.

Maybe no one else's model of marriage could really work for the two of them. Maybe every couple had to build their own model. And maybe he had wanted to make it too rigid. If he loved her as much as he thought, maybe he could work out a way to take one step toward Jean, and then another, without giving up on the idea of temple marriage.

He looked at her picture in his wallet . . . propped against the telephone. He wanted to tell her how much he missed her right now. He wanted to tell her that he was willing to change, to be what she needed in a partner. He wanted to hear her voice. There would be an instant after he said, "Hi, this is Ken," a fraction of a second that would tell him whether she was glad to hear his voice or not.

Ken picked up the telephone and dialed a long distance line, then 5-1-2 for the area code. His fingers increased their speed as they touched the seven digits of her home telephone number. The phone was on its fifth ring when he glanced at his watch. It was almost 11:40. The phone, he knew, was near Jean's room, because she could always answer it before it rang this many times. If he woke up Richard or Carol Bradley, what would he say to them? Quickly he hung up.

Jean must be out . . . with someone.

Well, what did he expect? She had made it plain that she didn't think their relationship was going anywhere. And he had not spoken to her in nearly three weeks, taking her last words as her final answer, without giving any thought to how he could change the situation . . . until tonight.

Dully, he looked down at the gasoline receipts sticking halfway out of his wallet. Klaus, the writer for the German magazine, wanted this expense report tomorrow. Ken stood up, walked across the room, and retrieved his pen from the floor next to the bed. But when he turned toward the desk, he couldn't face Jean in the picture again.

He flopped on the bed, turned out the lamp on the nightstand, and lay on his back in the dark, staring up at the ceiling.

11

Jack

Brushing back the hair that had blown across her eyes, Jean changed her position to be more comfortable as she read. She sat on the cushioned seat under the canopy, on the shady side of the *Rum Runner,* next to the pier. Small waves slapped at the hull, gently rocking the boat at its moorings. A curious gull perched atop one of the pilings that supported the pier, cocking its head this way and that to look at her, but she was oblivious to it.

From time to time she frowned intently, or marked her place in the book with a fingernail while she reread the preceding paragraphs. This was a strange piece of work, she thought . . . and yet there was a ring of faith to it. It really did teach of Jesus, but it began long before—

"Hello," a male voice called.

Jean turned to see Jack Weissman stepping down into the stern. But he didn't look like the conservatively dressed businessman who had exchanged greetings with her three or four times over the past few months. He wore dark, paint-spotted work pants, a frayed khaki shirt, and a shapeless old cotton cap. He carried a fishing rod and tackle box.

Jean stood and closed her book.

"Hello," he repeated, smiling at her.

"It's good to see you, Mr. Weissman," she said.

"It's Jack. Please call me Jack," he answered.

Jean glanced curiously at his fishing rod and tackle box.

He put them down on the deck. "Kenneth asked me to take care of the boat while he has to be away. He told me I could take it out fishing if I wanted," he explained.

"I'd better go, then, so I don't hold up your fishing trip. I just came down here on my day off to do some reading."

"There's no need for you to leave—unless you're ready. I won't be going anywhere for a while. I haven't even picked up any bait yet."

This was obviously a man unimpressed by his own wealth or the power he wielded in business. Each time they had met, he had gone out of his way to be friendly. He stood looking at her with his usual pleasant expression, which seemed to be constantly verging on a smile. His gaze was steady and direct but not disturbing. He always seemed pleased to see her on Ken's boat. Jean felt at ease with him.

Then he gestured toward the Book of Mormon in her hands. "Are you going to become a Mormon for him?"

Jean reddened. "I . . . I don't know. . . . I was just reading . . . I—"

"Please forgive a nosy old man, my dear. At my age, I've developed the habit of getting right to the point because I don't have any time to squander. But perhaps I had no business asking."

From anyone else, "my dear" would have been offensive to Jean. At the university, one of her English literature professors had been in the habit of looking over his half-frame glasses and addressing young women in his class as "my dear" when he wanted to emphasize the naïvete of their last question. But from this man, the words sounded sincere, as though the courtliness of an earlier era came naturally to him.

"It's okay, Mr. Weissman," she said. He frowned momentarily, and she corrected herself. "Jack, I mean. The fact is, I can't answer your question. I don't know whether I'll ever be a Mormon."

He studied her face. "Kenneth would like you to, wouldn't he?"

"Yes." She glanced down at the book in her hands. "He asked me to read this, so I'm trying to get through it." The reading was becoming difficult at home. If she did not keep to her room, there was, inevitably, conflict with her mother over this book. "I often come here to read because it's peaceful," Jean explained, "and because . . . well, I'm really not sure."

"Because you feel closer to Kenneth down here on the boat?"

She blushed for the second time in two minutes.

"Excuse me," he continued. "I didn't mean to embarrass you. Jean—may I call you Jean?"

"Of course."

"Please—won't you sit down?" He took a seat on one of the cushioned benches in the stern. She sat opposite him.

"I often come here for the same reason. On this boat, I'm close to some of the finer times of my life. I always tell myself I'm coming to take the boat out fishing, but usually I putter around here or just sit when I need a break from my business. That's why I didn't stop to buy bait today."

A smile touched the corners of his mouth. "Since Kenneth has been out of town, I've found a reason to be down here every two or three days working on something—whether there was anything that needed fixing or not." Slowly, his smile broadened, and Jean smiled with him.

Extending her blue-jeaned legs, she pushed tentatively at one sandaled foot with the toe of the other. Should she risk embarrassment yet again? He was very direct with his questions; perhaps she could be equally candid. She looked up at him. "Jack, I don't know how to ask this without sounding like a snoop. But Ken has told me so little about you, or any of his other friends. Has he told you anything about me?"

"He's never been one to talk about his personal affairs. Growing up the way he did, I suppose he felt there weren't many people who cared." Jack shifted to settle his bony frame more comfortably in the seat. "Kenneth has spoken of you once or twice—but you're the only young woman I've ever heard him speak of. I can tell by the way he talks about you that he cares for you very much."

"You said he thought no one cared about him when he was younger," Jean reflected. "I know Ken and his father didn't get along. But wasn't he close to his grandfather?"

Jack leaned back and closed his eyes momentarily. "Ah, yes. Yes, Alex saved the boy—Alex and the Mormons." He looked at her again with his steady gaze. "Alex taught the boy to believe in himself. Then his Mormon friends taught him to believe in something outside of himself."

"What do you mean, they 'saved' him?" Jean settled back in her seat to listen. Ken had talked little about his childhood and youth. She was hungry to know more, and here was someone who could fill in some of the gaps for her.

"Have you noticed that the railing you're leaning on is thinner than the one on this side?" Jack asked. Jean lifted her elbow to examine it. "Kenneth took a knife to that railing in a fit of anger when he was fourteen—carved some deep gashes in it. His life was like that for a time; sometimes he found ways to destroy things."

Jack gazed out over the water for a moment, remembering. "When Alex saw the railing, he said, 'Ken'—that was when he stopped calling him Kenny—'Ken, you're not a boy anymore. When a man makes a mess of something like this, he's responsible for fixing it up. You're going to help me make this perfect again.' Alex showed Kenneth how to do the work. He got down there on his knees and worked with the boy, and when they were through, it was perfect. Then Alex gave Kenneth all the credit."

Jean ran her hand over the smooth railing. Maybe it was Alexander McArthur who had helped Ken build the strong self-confidence that allowed him to take on anything he wanted to do in life—the same confidence Ken had often tried to build in her.

"What did the Mormons have to do with changing his life?" she asked.

"Well, you know, a boy needs friends. Kenneth didn't have many. He took pride in being tough; he was a loner. Then he found a couple of Mormon boys on the football team who could play as hard as he could and still enjoy themselves off the field, without fighting everything and everyone around them. They had something Ken wanted in his life. Fortunately, they took a liking to him too."

Jean frowned, remembering how Ken had so quickly and deliberately taken down the driver who had almost hit her on the beach. "When you say Ken was tough—well, what was it like?"

Jack's eyes widened. "Oh my, he was always fast with his fists—got into several fights his first year in high school. When he started going to church with his Mormon friends, he got in a fight over there one night. I think it wasn't entirely his fault, but Alex made him go back and apologize to their bishop and the other boys. Alex told him, '*Little* boys fight over teasing, Ken. When they want to be men, they learn to handle things in better ways.' " Jack shook his head. "Kenneth has come a very long way in the past ten years or so."

Jean sat sideways on her seat, knees drawn up under her chin. She studied the railing Ken had once refinished. She knew some of his strengths—patience, most of the time; kindness; and a gift for building up others. Those must have been hard to develop, considering his background.

Ken had weaknesses too, but he tried to recognize them and was working on them. "Daily repentance," he explained one day when he apologized for something thoughtless he had done. "I can't afford to let little things build up," he had said. He had even admitted finally that he needed to let go of his anger toward his father.

Sometimes she had seen his weaknesses all too plainly, Jean reflected. But was she doing as well at pinpointing her own? For one thing, there was the impetuous pride that had led her to walk away from him angrily. Right now, she longed to be able to talk about anything with him—even their religious differences.

It still seemed unfair to Jean that only she had been willing to offer any compromise about religion in their relationship. But she had to admit that she had made it difficult sometimes for him to talk; Ken had been more patient, more kind than she had been during their discussions—especially the last one. If only she had sent him off knowing how much she cared! Perhaps, Jean realized, as much as she loved Ken, she still had underestimated him—and what he could teach her.

"I must be boring you," Jack said.

"No, no," Jean reassured him. "I was just thinking about the things that made Ken what he is. Your friend Alexander McArthur must have been quite a man."

"Oh, indeed. If ever there was what some people call 'a fine Christian gentleman,' it was Alex. Kenneth couldn't have had a better example when he was growing up."

Jean listened attentively as Jack explained how Alex McArthur had helped shape an undisciplined grandson. Alex had taught Ken how to handle the *Rum Runner* when Ken was fifteen. As soon as the lesson was well-learned, Alex had made the care and running of the boat Ken's responsibility. There had been other lessons in responsibility as well. After Ken graduated from high school, Alex had let him earn his own money to pay for a mission; it was the grandfather's way of being sure that Ken was fully committed to his new faith and not just to his Mormon friends.

Once, Ken had been fired from a job. Curious, Alex had quietly checked on the reasons. As he suspected, the firing had been unjust. Having satisfied himself on the point, Alex simply encouraged Ken not to let a temporary setback deter him, then watched as Ken found a new job on his own.

Jean raised her eyebrows. "Ken didn't tell me all of that story."

"Kenneth doesn't know all of that story. He never knew how much his grandfather wanted to help him out of that spot. But Alex wouldn't—for Kenneth's sake.

"I'll tell you something else that Kenneth doesn't know," Jack continued. "Alex died hard—struggling against a bad heart—because he wanted to see his grandson settled in life before he went. I told Alex that just in case he didn't make it, I'd keep an eye on Kenneth."

"Looks like you're doing a good job," Jean said quietly.

"There's not much to do. He seems to be handling things very well on his own—at least these past few months." Jack paused and slowly smiled. "But I've been doing all the talking, my dear. Tell me a little about yourself, and how you came to know Kenneth."

Was this, Jean wondered, what Alexander McArthur would have wanted to know, had he been here? She told Jack about her family and her work. She told him how Ken had encouraged her to go after her new job when she had been fired. Then she briefly recounted how Ken had rescued her the night they met.

Jack nodded. "Well, now I understand why I'm losing my deliveryman."

Her eyebrows went up once more. "You mean Ken isn't going to make deliveries for you anymore?"

"No. What happened the night he met you seemed to trouble him. I think he felt that beating up the big man came too naturally. Of course, he had no other choice, but Kenneth said he didn't want to risk being forced to do that ever again."

Jean remembered Ken's restraint with Ray Healey. Obviously, Ken had found somewhere within himself the strength to handle provocation, so maybe there was another reason for giving up a significant part of his income. Maybe he was forcing himself to reach for a goal. "It sounds as if he's bent on proving he can make it in photography," she mused.

"I'm not sure what he has in mind," Jack replied. He was silent for a moment, staring out at the water. "I wasn't so close to him when he was younger. But Alex told me that when Kenneth first read that book"—he pointed to her copy of the Book of Mormon—"it gave his life some kind of direction that wasn't there before. Now it appears to me that your Kenneth may be undergoing the same kind of change again."

Jean frowned.

"Did I say something wrong?" Jack asked, puzzled.

"No. No, it was just that you called him '*your* Kenneth.' I wish I could believe that."

"One thing I'm sure of, Jean. He's not planning a future for just one person."

"I'm sure of that too, Jack. I'd just like to believe that whatever he's planning includes me. I haven't heard from him in more than three weeks now. I tried to track him down, but he seems to be lost somewhere deep in the heart of Texas, with someone named Klaus."

"Klaus?" Jack raised his eyebrows.

"That's the name of the German writer. The magazine he works for gave me their itinerary."

"And you've tried to contact Kenneth?"

"No luck. The rooms are never reserved in Ken's name. I've left messages for him in the writer's name, but Ken hasn't returned my calls."

Jack frowned. "I'm sure Kenneth would have called you, if he had received your messages."

Jean sighed. "I'd like to believe you're right." She glanced at her watch. "I have to run, Jack. It's been enjoyable talking to you. Thanks for sharing part of Ken's past with me." She stepped up to the pier and started toward her car.

"Jean?"

She turned to face him. "Yes?"

"I hope you'll still feel free to come to the boat anytime, even when I'm here. I'd enjoy the opportunity to talk with you again."

She and Jack said their hellos a couple of times over the next several days as he arrived at the boat just when she was leaving. Then one afternoon she was sitting in her favorite spot, engrossed in reading, when she heard him call, "Well, hello again."

"Hello," she answered, smiling at him. "Looks like you're planning on some serious fishing today." She nodded toward the bait bucket he carried.

He laughed as he put down his gear and showed her the empty bucket. "And it looks like you're dressed for work today."

She wore a skirt, dressy white blouse, and heels. Her suit jacket lay in her lap. "You're right. I started early, and I still have to cover a concert tonight. I'm just taking a break for a couple of hours this afternoon."

He leaned comfortably against the rail on the wheel side of the boat. "Have you heard from Kenneth yet?"

"No, I haven't. I wish he would call or write. But maybe he doesn't want to." She blushed. "We had a fight before he left. Over this," she said, holding up her book.

Jack nodded knowingly.

Jean frowned. "I was mean to him. I hope he hasn't written me off."

"I can't believe it would be so easy for him to put someone as lovely as you out of his mind." He nodded toward her Book of Mormon. "You're still reading the book. For when he comes back?"

"Yes." She crossed her fingers and smiled. "I'm hoping that will make a difference to him." She looked down at the book. "Really, Jack, it's interesting in spots. But I struggle with it in others. It's about a small group from one of the tribes of Israel who came to the Americas centuries ago. Do you think that's possible?"

"Oh, it's possible. Parts of the house of Israel have been scattered over the whole earth for thousands of years."

"Do you think they could have known about Jesus hundreds of years before he was born?"

"You're asking the wrong person, Jean. I didn't learn much about that in the synagogue when I was a boy."

She looked stricken. "Oh, Jack! What an insensitive question! Please forgive me."

"That's quite all right, my dear," he said comfortably. "I don't recall discussing my religion with you." He tilted his head back reflectively. "Actually, it's a very interesting question you ask. I've always thought that one of the weaknesses of Christianity—based on what I've learned about it from Christians—

is that it offers so little to all of the people who lived before Jesus Christ."

Jean weighed the Book of Mormon carefully in her hands. She had just been reading, in the third chapter of a book called Mosiah, about a Jesus who would make it possible for everyone to know him, and believe.

Watching her, Jack smiled. "You must understand, Jean, that questions like yours are really out of my line. I have no formal theological training."

"Do you think a person has to have formal training before God will talk to him? I mean—a lot of the prophets in the Bible didn't. But with God's word available to almost anyone today . . . well, I've always thought he would be interested only in talking to those who've studied it the most. But now—I don't know."

Jack looked down at the deck and massaged the back of his neck with his hand, thinking before he spoke. "I believe if God wanted to talk to anyone on earth, he would look for someone who's educated in here." He tapped the area over his heart. "I don't think years of studying or a string of university degrees would impress him very much."

Jean scrutinized her book thoughtfully, then looked up at Jack again and smiled. "Pretty heavy discussion for a fishing trip, isn't it?"

He chuckled. "There was a reason I didn't buy any live bait today. I was hoping you might be here for a chat."

She stood and unfolded her jacket.

"Time to go back to work?" Jack asked.

"Yes, but I'll see you tomorrow—if you'll be here."

"I'll look forward to it."

Four days later, Jean was sitting in the cabin, reading, when she heard footfalls in the stern of the boat. She peered out the door. It was Jack, with a tow-headed boy of about nine or ten.

"Hi," she said, ascending the stairs. "You weren't here the last time I came to read."

"Business," Jack replied, grimacing. "Sometimes it makes us do what we *have* to do at the expense of what we *want* to do. Today I'm doing something I want to do." He patted the boy on the shoulder. "I'm taking my grandson fishing. Jean, this is Terry. Terry, say hello to Jean."

"Hi," the boy said shyly.

"Looks like this one's for real," Jean said, gesturing toward the full bait container Terry held.

"That's right," Jack said apologetically. "I'm sorry to interrupt your studying. We're going to take the boat out to my favorite fishing spot."

"That's okay. I was reading down there in the cabin because there's no soft seat in the shade up here in the morning. I've been doing quite well." She held up the book for him to see. Her bookmark was nearly three-quarters of the way through it.

"Your station must have you covering a very unusual kind of story today," Jack said with mock seriousness as he glanced at the shirttail hanging down over her jeans.

She smiled. "Even wage slaves get a day off sometimes." Then she looked at the boy, stirring in the water beside the boat with the tip of his unrigged fishing rod. "How are you going to be both pilot and fishing coach?"

Jack grasped the wheel and feigned scanning the horizon, then glancing back over his shoulder. He alternated rapidly between the two positions several times. They both laughed.

"I have a better plan," Jean said. "If you'll maneuver the boat away from this pier, I'll take over as pilot while you devote yourself entirely to being Grandpa."

Jack looked at her dubiously. "That's very kind of you, Jean, but I wouldn't want to impose. You probably have other things planned."

"I can't think of any way I'd rather spend the next few hours."

Following his occasional directions, she steered south toward a spot along the city's shoreline, then dropped anchor. A few months ago, she reflected, before Ken's coaching, she would never have dared attempt this. Now she enjoyed it.

Jean read, off and on, while Jack and Terry fished during the next two hours. Terry's attention wandered quickly, so Jack pointed out loaded oil tankers, riding low in the water as they left the harbor; passing planes; and sights on shore. Jack and Terry caught three small trout between them. Jack put the fish in a mesh fish trap in the water, still alive.

When he could see that Terry was through with fishing, Jack put away both poles and pulled some sandwiches, oranges, and cupcakes from a sack he had brought on board. The boy took his portion of the lunch and began devouring it hungrily while he watched the planes and gulls overhead. Jack held out half of his sandwich to Jean. "Please take this. I don't eat as much anymore as Terry's mother remembers."

"Jack, how many grandchildren do you have?" Jean asked as they sat in the shade under the canopy.

"Four. Terry has a sister, and my son has two boys. But the other three are too grown-up for fishing with Grandpa now."

"I've never heard you mention their grandmother," Jean said.

"My Lois? We were together for thirty-nine years. Undoubtedly one of the all-time great love affairs." He smiled, then turned serious. "When she died a few years ago, my old friend Alex and I leaned on each other. Kenneth's grandmother had died a few months earlier. Alex and I would sit around and pretend we were fishing on this boat while we talked over the good old times when we used to cruise the coast with our wives."

"I wish I had met your wife."

"You would have liked Lois. She was like you—always trying to improve herself and me along with her. She read her Bible faithfully every day. She'd say, 'Listen to this, Jack. Pastor Evans says this applies to you too.' "

"Oh?" Jean tried not to seem startled. "She was a Christian?"

"Yes."

If she asked what she so badly wanted to know, would it offend him, Jean wondered. "Jack," she said carefully, "is it possible for an interfaith marriage to be truly successful?"

"Ours was. Or at least I thought so."

"Didn't you ever have conflicts over religion?"

"We managed not to fight about it between ourselves. But with others it was hard sometimes. In the beginning, her family was constantly after her about marrying outside her church. As for me—I'm a heathen to the rabbi because I didn't bring my children up in the faith."

"The important thing is that the two of you were happy, isn't it?"

Jack tilted his head back, closed his eyes, and smiled, remembering. "Ah, yes, my dear, we were. I don't know if two people could have been happier together." Then he opened his eyes to look at Jean. "But you must recognize that there were compromises—compromises I think you or Kenneth might not want to make."

Jean had been heartened to hear about how well Jack and Lois got along together. But she wasn't sure she wanted to hear this part. "What kind of compromises?" she asked, frowning.

"One of us had to give up the children as far as religion was concerned. In our case, it was me. I went to the synagogue every Sabbath by myself at first, but over the years, I tapered off. I still go occasionally, and I make my contributions, but I'm not what the people there would call an observant Jew."

"Then Lois gave your children all their religious training?"

"She tried." Jack glanced at Terry, absorbed in watching the gulls. "But children are smart. They knew this was something mother and father didn't agree on. By the time they were in their teens, they were plainly going to make their own choices about religion."

"What happened?"

"Well, it may seem strange, but our daughter, Ellen, chose Judaism. She wanted to know more about the faith of her father, so she began going to the synagogue. She fell in love with a boy there and converted so they could be married."

Jean thought of her own mother's feelings about Ken's church. "That must have been hard for your wife."

"It was, in one way. But it wasn't as hard for her to accept as our son's decision. I told Lois that since she was my favorite wife, and since my name is Jacob, we should name our boy after Rachel's first son. But when it came to religion, our Joseph chose—nothing. He lives a moral life, but he says he doesn't believe in God." Jack studied his well-manicured hands. "And I'm in no position now to influence his beliefs."

It doesn't have to be that way, Jean thought, if . . . but, then, how could she second-guess Jack and Lois's approach to teaching their children? What would she and Allison have done if their parents had belonged to two different churches? Choosing one faith or the other might be like trying to choose between mother and father.

"Grandpa! Look!" Terry called. He stood on one of the stern seats holding out a piece of his sandwich. Two gulls hovered close overhead, with a small flock right behind them. The boy tossed the morsel into the air and one of the gulls snatched it greedily. The others dipped closer.

Jack smiled indulgently. "Terry, I'm going to be in trouble if all of those follow us home."

He pulled their cage out of the water and released their fish.

"Terry's mother threatened me if I brought any home for her to clean," he explained to Jean.

Jack weighed anchor while Jean started the boat. "Terry," she asked, "would you like to steer?"

The boy's eyes went wide. "Yeah."

Jack had to hold Terry up so the boy could reach the wheel and see out of the window in front of him. Jean disappeared into the cabin and returned with the "CAPTAIN" cap she had bought for Ken. She put it on Terry's head. "There. It's official. You wear this hat home and tell your mother you were the captain of the boat today."

She sat in her favorite reading spot, under the canopy, as they headed in. "Jack, how did you meet Lois?" she asked, watching as he helped Terry steer.

"I was a sailor stationed here in World War II. I met her at the USO." Jack told of their correspondence after he was shipped out to the Pacific, of the *kamikaze* strike on his ship that made him determine what was most dear to him, and of coming back to court Lois after the war. He had taken her home to New York following their marriage in 1946. But she had been extremely uncomfortable in his Brooklyn neighborhood, steeped in Jewish culture, and the people in the neighborhood had been uncomfortable with her, so the two of them had returned to Corpus Christi. Among her family, he had been simply tolerated at first, but he gradually won an acceptance of sorts. He had nearly lost contact with his own family. In this community, though, where he had become successful in business and Lois had been active in civic affairs, their religious differences had not seemed to matter so much.

"Time to let me take it from here, Terry," Jack said, putting his grandson down. He glanced toward Jean as he maneuvered the boat inside the Rocks. "What about your family, my dear?"

"You mean if I became a Mormon and married Ken?"

"Yes."

"It would be fine with Daddy—I think. It helps that Ken is Alex McArthur's grandson. But my mother . . . I don't know. She likes Ken, but she doesn't like his church. She keeps telling me all the ways she thinks it's wrong." Jean sighed. "I just wish religion weren't so critical to Ken."

"And how do *you* feel about it now? Have you decided that you could never be a Mormon?"

When Jean did not reply, he glanced at her again. She seemed to be staring at the bulkhead in front of her without seeing it.

"Not exactly," she finally answered. "But I haven't decided that I *can* be one, either. I guess I could agree with some things the Mormons believe. But I don't *know*—not the way Ken wants me to know. He couldn't live with that; for him, I have to be certain."

She continued staring at the bulkhead, chin resting on her knees, and said no more until Jack brought the *Rum Runner* up to the pier. Then she got to her feet and picked up her book. "I'll tie up the bow line for you, then I've got to run to a play rehearsal. The rest of this week looks rough. I may not see you for a few days."

She stopped to adjust the captain's cap on the boy's head. "Bye, Terry. Take care of your grandpa. He's a good friend of mine."

Jean opened her eyes and looked around the cabin of the boat. The Book of Mormon lay open in front of her on the bunk where she had left it when she knelt to pray; the two verses that Ken had marked, in chapter ten of Moroni, were outlined in red.

Nothing seemed different about her surroundings. Same faded cover on the bunk, same picture of her on the wall.

Nothing seemed different inside of her, either. There had

been no special feeling, none of that flood of light Ken had talked about. Nothing. All she really felt at first was the hardwood decking gently rocking beneath her knees. Then there was fear welling up inside of her—fear because somehow something must have gone wrong.

Maybe Ken had left out a step when he told her what to do. Or maybe she hadn't asked sincerely enough. Maybe it hadn't helped that she still wondered if God could really know every little grain of sand on the beach.

Another thought nagged at her mind: perhaps Ken, and several million other Mormons, had simply deluded themselves into thinking that they felt something when they did this. But, she reflected, Ken was intellectually solid; he wasn't given to delusions. Maybe *she* was the problem. Maybe she was somehow not good enough for God to care . . . or . . . but, no—

A tapping sounded at the cabin door. She jumped, startled. Quickly, she scooped up her book and stepped over to the stairs. Jack was just turning to leave when she opened the door.

"Hi, Jack," she said, ascending from the cabin. "You certainly aren't dressed for fishing today. What a handsome man you are!" He wore a tailored charcoal suit, a dark red silk tie, and well-polished black Florsheims like her father's.

For the first time, Jean saw Jack as the handsome young groom he must have been more than forty years ago. For the first time, she thought of his bride, Lois, not as the white-haired woman in the photo Jack carried, but as a vibrant, good-looking young USO volunteer. On the day that the two of them were wed, Jean realized, the groom's very name may have brought tears to the eyes of the bride's Christian mother. Was there, Jean wondered, a pang of fear somewhere in Carol Bradley's heart whenever she heard the name of Ken McArthur?

Jean straightened the white carnation in Jack's lapel. "I love your flower."

"Lois used to pin a fresh carnation on my suit every day before she sent me off to work. I still wear one every day . . . for her."

"I'm sure she would be pleased." Jean stood back to take in the full effect of him. "But what brought you down here in the middle of the afternoon dressed like this?"

"To tell the truth, I'm not sure. I thought I had too much work to leave the office today. But I kept seeing you in my mind's eye, down here on the boat, reading. Is everything all right with you, Jean?"

She sat down on the nearest bench. "You're an angel to come down here to find out." Her brow furrowed. "Nothing's wrong, really. Except—I'm very confused."

Jack took off his suit coat, sat down on the seat opposite her, and carefully folded the jacket so it wouldn't crush his flower.

"I see you finished the book." He nodded toward the Book of Mormon in her hands; her bookmark was sandwiched between the last page and the back cover.

"Yes," she said slowly, looking down at it. "Yes, I did. I've done everything Ken asked me to do—study, prayer, everything. And I still don't feel what Ken said I would feel." She stared out toward the city skyline. "I don't know whether to think he's crazy—or there's something wrong with me."

"Judging from my experiences with Jean Bradley and Kenneth McArthur, I can't believe there's anything wrong with either of you. Maybe there's another answer."

"If there is, I'd like to find it," she said glumly.

"I've found that God doesn't always answer prayers as we expect," Jack mused. "Or as we want."

"Do you pray often? Have you had prayers answered?"

"I think every Jew believes it's his right to talk to God anytime he wants. I suppose my way is different from anyone else's. But, yes, I have had prayers answered."

She waited for him to continue.

"Did I tell you my Lois died of cancer? I asked God not to take her; I needed her." He was looking in Jean's direction but not with his usual steady gaze. In his mind, he was somewhere else. "The doctor gave her six months. But God gave her two years, most of it free of pain, so she could help me get ready." He blinked away the mist in his eyes.

First Ken, and now Jack, Jean thought. Both of them seemed so sure God had intervened in their lives at critical times. She struggled to phrase her question tactfully.

"Jack, I know it was something that you and Lois wanted very much. But diseases can go into remission for a lot of natural reasons. How could you be sure it was an answer to prayer?"

"Sometimes you can feel it when God touches your life. I knew. Lois knew. And the doctor knew. He said it had to be prayer."

Jack appeared to be weighing something carefully. Laying his jacket aside, he crossed one leg over the other and studiously straightened the crease in his trouser leg before speaking again. "Faith is a very personal question. I know you go to church. But do you really believe the Bible?"

"Yes, of course."

"What lesson does it teach you about God that you remember most?"

She thought for several seconds. A gull swooped low over the boat and drifted above the water. The undulant surface of the bay changed rhythmically as small waves rolled toward the concrete steps ascending from the water's edge to Shoreline Boulevard.

"I think it's the part about how God loves us so much that he created this beautiful world, step by step, for us to live in. That, and how he gave us the commandments to live by so we could be happy here." Out of deference to Jack's heritage, she stopped short of mentioning the life of the Savior.

Jack stared up at the pristine cotton clouds floating overhead. "If the Creator of the universe simply started his big blue-and-green top spinning here in space and gave us some guidelines to live by and then went off to do other things—well, I'd have a hard time feeling close to that kind of God." He looked at Jean again. "But I love the God who knew the heart of Hannah. She was a nobody, really. Yet he listened to the prayer in her heart. Do you believe in that God, Jean?"

"Hannah was hardly a nobody, Jack. She was the mother of one of his prophets. Of course he knew her."

Jack leaned forward. The small, untanned creases around his eyes closed up as he smiled. "You didn't mention Jesus when you talked about your favorite lessons in the Bible. Shall I tell you my favorite story about Jesus?"

Jean's eyebrows arched.

"Remember, I told you that Lois used to read to me from her Bible. We both loved the story of the widow who put her tiny offering into the treasury. Jesus knew just how large her offering was because he knew her heart. Ah, Jean, if I were to believe in Jesus as the offspring of God, it would be *that* Jesus!"

Jean frowned thoughtfully. She loved that story too. She thought it meant that people should always give their best to God and to others. She had tried to do that. Was there some aspect of the story she had missed? "What are you trying to tell me, Jack?"

"The God I pray to knows the heart of Jack, and Lois, and Jean. He cares about you and me."

"I believe he knows if we live good lives. But how could he possibly have time for"—what was it she really wondered about?—"for the day-to-day hopes and hurts of every single one of us?"

"Somehow he does. For your sake, I hope you come to know this God, my dear—no matter what church you're in."

She looked at him searchingly. He seemed so certain of what he said—just like Ken.

"I'd like that. But it doesn't seem to be happening right now—at least, not the way Ken said it would," Jean answered.

"Maybe you can ask him about that when he comes back next week."

"You've heard from him?" Her voice rose. She wondered how it was possible to feel so happy and so apprehensive at the same time.

"My secretary took a message. Ken asked if I would take care of the boat for another week or so, while he finishes some business in Houston."

Jean could feel apprehension winning out inside of her. She longed to see Ken—yet she dreaded having him find out that nothing had changed, really, while he had been away. "Jack, I'm afraid. I don't know whether there will be anything between Ken and me when he comes back—if I can't be what he wants me to be."

"Have more faith in Kenneth than that, Jean. He's a good man, and he loves you."

"I hope he still does. But he has a dream, and if I can't fit into it—well, I don't think he's going to give it up."

"I'll pray that things work out for you—for the two of you." Jack rose to leave. "Will you be all right?"

"Yes." Jean stood too and stepped forward to kiss him lightly on the cheek. "Thanks for caring enough to come down and check on me."

"Now that you've finished the book, will you stop coming to the boat?"

"Well, I won't need to come down here so often." She smiled at him. "But I don't like to lose friends once I've found them. If you'll tell me when you're going to be here, I'd like to come visit."

He smiled back at her. "I'm here whenever. You know—whenever I've had enough of business for a while." He took a card out of his wallet and handed it to her. "Come and see me in my office anytime. You can tell my secretary to interrupt me whenever you come in. I hope it will be often."

He walked up the pier to his car. Jean was still sitting on the boat, leafing through the book as he drove away. She thought about what had happened over the past three weeks or so, since her talk with Jay.

She had reviewed again everything Ken had taught her. There was nothing illogical or irrational in what he called the gospel plan; in fact, what she could remember of it seemed to make perfect sense, especially with what she had learned from the Book of Mormon. She could find no intellectual reason not to accept it.

Yet plainly, she could not accept it without giving up some of the things she had held true since childhood . . . some of the things her father and mother had taught her . . . even, perhaps, giving up her mother's love. Why risk that, if she could not get the kind of assurance Ken had told her to expect?

She looked at the book in her hands. Did it contain the answer? Parts of it had touched her deeply. Parts of it helped clarify things taught in the Bible. But she still could not say that she *knew* the book was true. She had prayed to God for that knowledge, as Ken had wanted her to do. It had not come. Why? *Why?*

And there were other unanswered questions:

The man in the business suit who lived in an apartment out in Salt Lake City—did God really speak to him?

And were there really people on the earth who had the same power as the apostles who followed Jesus?

And . . . the questions kept coming. Ken had told her the

truth; these were the kind that only God could answer. But he didn't seem to be speaking to her.

Maybe she had been right all along, Jean thought. Maybe it was too much to expect God to take note of the concerns of one ordinary mortal.

And yet—there was the widow at the treasury, with her two small coins. And there was Hannah. Where was the God who knew Hannah's heart, Jean thought, when *she* needed him?

12

Eyes in the Mirror

Jean looked up to find both of her parents watching her. She put down her fork.

"I said, do you feel well, Jeanie? You haven't eaten much," her mother repeated gently.

"I'm all right, Mother," Jean answered quietly. Her parents continued to look at her. "I'm just tired," she added.

"Do you have to go to work tomorrow?" her mother asked.

"Yes, but not until nine, because I have to stay until seven."

"Well, you shouldn't have to work this weekend—at least not Sunday. Maybe you can get some rest then."

"I doubt it." She smiled grimly.

"Will you be going to Ken's church again after ours?"

"Probably."

"Jean Ann, I wish you wouldn't do that," her mother said earnestly. "It's confusing you. You've been troubled ever since you started listening to the things Ken was trying to teach you. I wish you'd—"

"Mother, what Ken tried to teach me is only part of the

problem," Jean said sharply. "If I could have counted on you for—"

"Jean!" Her father laid his hand firmly on top of hers. "Jeanie . . . Jean, if we're going to have a *discussion* on this subject"—he glanced at his wife before continuing—"I believe we should do it respectfully."

Jean looked at him defiantly, but only for a moment. Then she lowered her eyes. She remembered a day when she was eleven and her father had washed her mouth out with soap for speaking disrespectfully to her mother. He had been right then too—and she had resented it then too. "I'm sorry, Mother," she said to Carol emotionlessly. "I shouldn't have spoken that way. Please forgive me." She rose from the table. "I think I'll go to bed now," she said and turned to walk from the dining room.

"Jean?" her father said.

She turned back to face him.

"If you want to talk . . . "

Jean purposely did not look at her mother. "Not tonight, Daddy. I'm exhausted." She walked out of the room.

Carol watched through the dining room doorway as Jean reached the top of the living room stairs and turned down the hall toward her bedroom.

"Richard, I wish you would have a talk with her," Carol pleaded. "She won't listen to me, and you can see what a hold Ken has on her. She can't get him out of her mind."

"Ummm." He gazed at the wall, in the general direction of his daughter's bedroom. "I think she has more than Ken on her mind."

"What do you mean?"

"I don't think this is just lovesickness. It's more like . . . well, when she lost her job, and she was feeling down about everything. There's some kind of pressure . . . " Richard looked back at his wife. "But, okay, I'll talk to her—in a couple of days, when this has cooled down."

Upstairs, Jean closed the door of her bedroom and leaned back against it, trying to let the anger within her drain away. She was mad at her parents because she couldn't talk to them when she needed their help. And she was mad at herself for being mad at them; in her heart, she knew it was wrong. She understood that the confident, well-known Carol Bradley who chaired civic committees and spoke for refugees and reached out to so many others was actually fearful that she was losing her own daughter. And her father had simply defended the woman he loved.

If only she could convince them that making her own choice about a church wouldn't mean giving up all the good things they had taught her. Jean sighed. It would help if she knew which choice to make. Maybe she was even mad at God because she couldn't seem to get an answer from him.

She pushed away from the door, crossed the room to her bed, and sat down on it. The Book of Mormon lay in the center of the bed where she had tossed it, irritably, after coming home from her talk with Jack on the *Rum Runner* this afternoon. She picked up the book and placed it carefully on the nightstand by her lamp. Why hadn't she received an answer to her prayer about the Book of Mormon?

She stretched out on her bed, hands behind her head, and lay looking up at the ceiling. What did she know for certain about The Church of Jesus Christ of Latter-day Saints?

The members she had met were a lot like the good people in the church she had attended all her life. There were some fine individuals in Ken's church—Irene Steiner; Carla Warren; Brother Hopkinson, the Sunday School teacher; Brother Virgil, the choir director, who had asked last Sunday if she wanted to sing with the group; Bishop Williamson, who had gone out of his way to speak to her when she attended church with Ken. But all of those nice people seemed to *know* that their church was the true church of Jesus Christ. If it was, why couldn't she know it too? Was there some secret key she didn't have?

There was Ken—level-headed, strong, sure of his convictions. He *knew*. And he had said that she already knew enough to find out for herself if his church was the church of Jesus Christ. She grimaced, thinking how she had resisted the idea that he might have some knowledge she did not. But if he really was right, she could finally admit it now. So why couldn't she get an answer?

Jean yawned and stretched.

Many of the Mormons' beliefs made sense. In her heart, she had always felt that people existed before they came to mortality and that some part of them would go on after death. If God really had set up a plan to make sure that everyone who ever lived got a chance to enjoy the same blessings—well, that seemed like what a fair God would do.

After Jack had left her on the boat this afternoon, at least one idea from their conversation had struck home: she was trying to impose her own limitations on God himself—as though he could do no more than what she could imagine. Her God had always been abstractly good and kind—but distant. For the first time, Jean let herself think about a God who could mind the affairs of the entire universe at the same time he watched over people individually. Could he really be someone who cared for her as a daughter, someone who had known and loved her for eons? Being sure of that would change the way she talked to him, the way she listened, the way she lived . . .

She woke suddenly. She had been dozing—the clock read 8:40—for ten minutes? What had she been thinking . . . oh, yes, the things she knew about the Mormons. Each new thing she learned about them seemed to raise more questions.

Maybe there were answers. If she just went to Ken's church and tried to believe, maybe she would find them. She could be baptized, and go to meetings with Ken, and do what members do . . . and then again, maybe she would never in her lifetime get farther than wondering why she could not *know,* as Ken seemed to know. Her parents and Allie and Jay would believe that she had changed churches simply to win Ken. And maybe they would be right. But maybe to God it really didn't matter. . . .

Jean realized that she was wandering once more in the same intellectual maze that had trapped her mind this afternoon on the boat. She wasn't thinking clearly. What she had said to her father as she left the dining room was true; she was exhausted—at least mentally. Rest was the thing she needed most right now.

She got up off the bed, quickly got into her nightgown, and brushed her teeth. As she reached to turn off her lamp before lying down to sleep, she had to move the Book of Mormon away from the switch.

Should she try praying once more? Jean wasn't sure she could stay awake if it took very long. But she knelt by her bed, mentally reviewing what Ken and the missionaries had taught her about prayer.

"Dear Heavenly Father, thank you for fine parents and the good life I have. Thank you for helping me learn about you from the time I was a little child. Please help me learn about you now. I can believe that Ken is right about what he has been trying to teach me. I want to be what he wants me to be. Please tell me if he is right. Amen . . . I mean, in the name of Jesus Christ, amen."

She waited on her knees for several seconds, but it was just like this afternoon on the boat—there was no response. Nothing. She climbed into bed tiredly and turned out the light.

This room that had always been a haven for her had never seemed darker. Never before in her life had Jean felt so alone, or so sad, for no particular reason. Something was wrong about tonight, something that seemed just out of reach, something she could not quite identify. . . .

She came awake with a start at 11:35, then found it difficult to go back to sleep because she had gone to bed so early. She was wide awake again at 1:19, then 2:51. The last time she looked at the clock during the night, it was 3:43. Each time she came awake, she drifted into fitful sleep again, wondering what she lacked to receive the kind of answer Ken had told her to expect.

When her alarm went off at 6:45, she pushed herself up, slowly swung her legs out of bed, and stretched. She walked over to her dresser and stood looking at the things on top of it while she tried to remember why she had come here. Mechanically, she picked up her brush and began to brush out her hair. As she stood looking at herself in the mirror, the night came back to her—all the fruitless thoughts, the tossing and turning, the returning to the beginning of the maze again, and then falling asleep each time before she got anywhere.

Jean looked into her own eyes in the mirror. Suddenly she realized what had seemed so wrong last night when she went to bed. In all of her struggling through the intellectual maze, she had overlooked something simple, something close at hand—as close as the book on her nightstand. She had become a believer.

She stopped brushing at her hair and stood gazing into her own eyes, thinking about what had happened to her. She was no longer struggling to justify Ken's beliefs in her mind, but her own. She believed what she had learned in the Book of Mormon. And at some point, without quite realizing it, she had come to accept the things Ken and the missionaries had tried to teach her. She still didn't know a lot about their church, but she believed all the basics she had learned—not because she wanted to please Ken or someone else, but because it felt right to her.

Could her conviction really go beyond belief? Well, wasn't that the promise that Ken had marked near the end of the Book of Mormon? If it was truly possible . . . after all her resistance to the idea . . . then she must *know,* now, for herself.

She leaned forward, fingertips on the dresser to support herself, bowed her head, and closed her eyes. The brush slipped from her fingers to the floor. "Dear Lord," she whispered, "I want to know the truth. I want to know it so I can be whatever *you* want me to be. I *need* to know the truth—even if I never see Ken again, or make my mother understand. If what I believe is true—and if you really want me to know that I'm one of your daughters—please . . . please tell me . . . in the name of Jesus Christ, amen."

It happened just the way Ken had described it, like light inside, starting somewhere in the center of her and spreading—bursting—outward. It seemed to light up every corner of her being. Things she saw momentarily in some of the dimly remembered, dark corners were unsettling, but embarrassment and shame over those weaknesses and past mistakes were quickly wiped away by a powerful feeling that God loved her anyway, because she was his.

She caught her breath and looked at herself in the mirror again. Tears ran down her cheeks. But she was happy, with a happiness that far surpassed her sadness last night when she had felt so alone. She laughed out loud at the sense of discovery she felt. It had been there all along, this opportunity to know. She could have done this weeks ago, if she hadn't fought it. And now, when she was willing at last to hold nothing back, to accept whatever came . . . She laughed again at the simple beauty of it.

Jean bowed her head once more. "Thank you," she breathed. Then she sat down on her bed and lay back to enjoy the warm, delicious feeling inside of her, the love that seemed to surround her.

In a few minutes, though, she felt the urge to be up and doing. There was something—what was it?—that she must do now.

She knelt and said a longer prayer of thanks, asking that the feeling of assurance she had received would stay with her. Then, by the time she had showered and dressed, she knew what she was supposed to do today. She stepped out her door, picked up the cordless telephone on the hall table, and retreated into her bedroom with it. On the back of her bookmark in the Book of Mormon was the missionaries' telephone number. She hoped they had not moved.

Jean recognized the voice that answered: "Missionaries of The Church of Jesus Christ of Latter-day Saints. Miki Watanabe speaking."

"Sister Watanabe, this is Sister Bradley—Jean Bradley, Ken McArthur's friend. I want to take the missionary lessons again. I want to be baptized as soon as possible."

"This is . . . Jean Bradley?" Sister Watanabe seemed incredulous.

Jean laughed. "Yes. Do you think we could start tonight?"

" . . . Maybe. . . . Wait." Jean could hear two voices talking animatedly, and then Sister Watanabe came back on the line. "Yes, I think so," she said. Jean made arrangements to meet them at the chapel as soon after work as she could.

She was humming to herself when she walked into her mother's kitchen a few minutes later. Her father had already gone to work, but her mother sat reading the morning paper while she finished eating a muffin.

Jean leaned over to kiss her on the cheek and hug her around the neck. "I'm sorry for the way I acted last night, Mother. I was rude. Forgive me?"

Carol looked startled. "Yes, of course." She glanced down at the table. "I saved you breakfast. Will you eat with me?"

"Umm, can't. I need to get an early start at the station after all. But I'll take one of these delicious muffins with me." Jean selected one from the basket on the table. She continued humming as she buttered it.

Her mother smiled. "You must have rested well last night."

Jean smiled back. "Not really. But I feel great. This is going to be one of my best days ever. Don't hold dinner for me. I'll be home late."

Carol looked after her daughter, puzzled, as Jean walked out of the kitchen.

Jean was also late getting home the following night, Wednesday. When Richard Bradley knocked on her door at seven A.M. Thursday, he wasn't sure she would be awake. But she opened the door almost immediately. He handed her the phone. "There's a . . . I believe he said 'Bishop' somebody calling for you."

She smiled. "Bishop Williamson?"

"Yes."

Jean closed the door. "Hello, bishop," she said into the telephone.

"Sister Bradley, we've only met a few times, but I was excited to hear that you're going to be baptized." He paused. "I wonder if you'd mind coming by my office to talk for a few minutes this evening?"

Jean frowned. "Is something wrong?"

"No, nothing," he said quickly. "I'd just like to get better acquainted."

"I'll be off work about seven-thirty. Would eight be okay?"

"That will be fine."

Several times during the day, she found herself wondering if the bishop did this every time someone was going to be baptized. Last night, after the sisters had finished the last missionary lesson with her, Jean had been interviewed by a young elder they called the district leader. He had given her some instruction about the baptismal service and told her he would look forward to baptizing her Friday night. What more needed to be done?

Wrapping up an assignment for the ten P.M. news broadcast took extra time, and Jean drove to her appointment wondering how she could apologize for being late. But the bishop was running late too. Brother Garza, the executive secretary, asked her to wait a bit, and she sat on one of the metal folding chairs in the hallway for about ten minutes before the bishop opened his door.

Bishop Williamson said good-bye to a young man Jean had seen two or three times at play rehearsals. Then: "Sister Bradley, come in, please. I hope you haven't been waiting too long."

"No, it's okay."

If she sounded uncertain, Jean thought, it was because she didn't know how to talk to a bishop. He readjusted the position of a metal folding chair near his desk and looked at her expectantly, so she sat in it. He took a seat facing her, in a similar chair at the corner of the desk.

The room seemed spartan. A picture of Jesus on the brick wall faced the bishop's desk, and pictures of three other men hung on a side wall; Jean recognized the middle photograph as the man who was the president of the church. The bishop's desk was not large and had obviously seen a lot of use. A metal filing cabinet stood in one corner, topped by a framed photograph of a family: the bishop, his wife, two young sons, and a daughter of about fifteen.

"Sandi did a good job in *The Music Man,*" Jean said, nodding toward the photo. "She's a hard worker."

"Yes." The bishop smiled indulgently. "She makes the talent she has go a long way, doesn't she?"

Jean raised her eyebrows. "She has plenty of talent. I think you've got a budding actress on your hands."

"Oh? Well, her mother and I appreciate all the effort you put in with her. Sandi thought that having you work with them was one of the highlights of the experience. Right after the rehearsals started, she came home and said, 'Do you know who's helping Carla with the play?' " He grinned. "And I said, 'You mean the Jean Bradley who does such a good job on the Channel 9 news?' "

Jean smiled. "Thanks. They were a great group."

"I admire you for sticking with those kids when you really didn't have any obligation to them. What made you do it?"

"I guess I enjoyed helping them have fun. They made it fun for me too." This man was friendly, soft-spoken, easy to talk to, Jean thought. She needn't have worried about what to say to him.

"Lyle—that's our thirteen-year-old—said you could talk the boys into doing anything and make them enjoy it."

"I'm sure it was my magnetic personality," Jean said with a straight face. Then she laughed. "Or maybe it was because they were fascinated with my car. There were a couple of them who kept wanting me to drive them home. They'd sit in the back with the windows rolled down and tell me to punch out at the lights."

The bishop laughed too. Then he was serious again. "Sandi said she wished you were a member so you'd come to our ward all the time." He paused. "The missionaries told me they've never had anybody so eager to be baptized before." He paused again and leaned forward in his chair as though waiting for her to speak.

What was she expected to say, Jean wondered. How should she explain this? "I, ah—I fought this for a long time, Bishop Williamson. When I . . . found out for myself that it's what God wants me to do, I was ready to get on with it right away."

The bishop smiled slightly. "Am I right in assuming that Brother McArthur had something to do with this?"

Jean blushed. "Yes. Ken tried to teach me about the church, but I wouldn't listen. What I saw in him made me take another look at it on my own."

"The missionaries tell me you have a strong testimony." He hesitated, as though weighing what he had to say next. "After you're baptized, what are your plans? Yours and his, I mean?"

Jean shrugged. "I don't know. I haven't seen or heard from Ken in six weeks."

The bishop seemed surprised. "Really? I know he's been gone, but I thought the two of you were very close."

"We . . . were," Jean said slowly. "I made the church into a problem between us before he left, and he hasn't written or called."

"Do you think things may work out when he comes back?"

"I'm hoping."

"And if they don't?"

She looked down at her hands in her lap. "Then . . . I suppose I'll wish him happiness." She looked up at him. "And I'll keep coming to church, if that's what you're asking."

The bishop smiled briefly. "What if things do work out the way you want them?" he asked.

Jean only smiled broadly in return.

"Have the two of you talked about marriage?"

"Yes—when we were able to do it without fighting about religion."

"*Temple* marriage?"

"Yes. I know that's what Ken wants. Now that I understand why it's so important, I do too."

"I'm glad to hear that. Were you planning to be married civilly first, or just look ahead to the temple?"

Jean was surprised. Ken hadn't mentioned any options. "You mean . . . we could do it either way?"

The bishop was surprised too. He wondered how much she really knew about temple marriage. "Yes, of course. In some places, people can't travel to a temple whenever they want, so they get married civilly. Some of them have to wait a long time before they enjoy the blessing of having their marriage sealed in the temple."

Bishop Williamson hesitated. He knew Ken as a strong individual, and everything he knew about Jean suggested that she was too. But did they each understand how they could be tempted if they had to wait a year to marry? Had she thought this through? "There are other things to consider." He tried to choose his words carefully. "Sometimes it seems advisable for a couple, when they've become very close, to be married civilly. That way, they're not tempted to be too intimate before they can be married in the temple. Do you feel like you and Ken can handle the temptation?"

"We have so far," she answered confidently.

Irene Steiner had told the bishop a bit about the Bradley family. Did this young woman understand, he wondered, that a temple marriage could exclude her parents? "Some couples decide to have a civil marriage first so their families won't be left out when they go to the temple," he said.

Jean was momentarily puzzled by his last sentence. What was he trying to tell her? Traveling to the temple shouldn't be a problem for her family—especially if it was the temple in Dallas she had heard about. They could easily afford to go there. She was beginning to feel some apprehension about this interview again. "Ken has never talked about anything but temple marriage," she said slowly. "I want what he wants."

"Well, I admire your courage and determination," the bishop answered. "Couples who decide to do what you're going to do usually set strict limits for themselves so they can avoid temptation while they're waiting a year to be married."

Jean sat up straight. "Did you say a year?"

"Yes. That's the soonest you would be able to go to the temple."

"A *year?*"

"Yes." The bishop frowned. "I thought Ken would have told you. I'm sure he must know that it's a policy of the church. Someone who's baptized has to wait a year before going to the temple."

"No! Ken never told me anything like that. He just said . . . well, I thought he wanted to get married as soon as possible, if I would just join the church. I don't think he planned to wait."

The bishop was looking at her intently. "Does this affect how you feel about being baptized?"

"Yes! . . . No. . . . I don't know." She was angry, and she felt like crying. But she would not let it out in front of this man she barely knew. "Why should we have to wait that long? Did *you* have to wait for a year to get married?"

"I've only been in the church twelve years," the bishop replied softly. "My wife and I were already—"

"Well, would you have waited a year when you were twenty-two or twenty-three?" Jean demanded.

"Sister Bradley, I don't know. And I'm not telling you that you *have* to wait. I can marry the two of you right here in this building, next week—if that's what you both want. The state will recognize it just like a marriage by any other clergyman. But after the missionaries told me last night that you wanted to be baptized, I couldn't get you out of my mind. I felt impressed to talk to you about whether you planned to be married in the temple."

"Now I'm wondering why you brought up my family. If Ken

and I get married in the temple . . . well, were you trying to tell me that my parents can't be there?"

"Yes, that's true."

"*Why?*"

"Not everyone can go to the temple, that is, inside it, not even every Latter-day Saint. Only members who are ready to make sacred covenants with God, and keep them."

"You mean baptism isn't enough? What kind of covenants?"

"They're similar to the covenants you make at baptism, only more specific, like promises of obedience and sacrifice and fidelity in marriage."

"Even if I'm willing to make those promises right now, I can't go?"

"A certain amount of growth and preparation must take place first. For new members, that usually happens the first year. That's how—"

"And if I do go to the temple, my family is shut out?"

"Well, some people find ways to involve their families. You could—"

"I don't understand this at all." She fumbled for her car keys in her purse.

"Can we talk some more? Maybe I can help."

"I don't think so." She stood up. "This church has been a problem between me and Ken almost since I met him. Why is it so hard to be a member of your church?"

The bishop stood too. "Jean," he began earnestly, then corrected himself: "Sister Bradley, sometimes there are sacrifices, but they're worth—"

"There *always* seem to be sacrifices in your church. It's the sacrifices that are eternal," Jean retorted, walking to the door.

"Will you let me know if you still want to be baptized tomorrow?" the bishop asked. "Or we could arrange something Saturday, if that would be better for you."

The door banged against a chair as she yanked it open and walked out. Jean strode to her car, unlocked it, threw her purse on the passenger seat, got in, and slammed the door. As she pulled out of the church parking lot, she pushed the accelerator down hard, and the tires squealed on pavement.

But by the time she reached the nearest stoplight, she had slowed down, lecturing herself about taking her anger out behind the wheel. By the time she reached the T-head where the *Rum Runner* was berthed—and noted with surprise that she had come here automatically—Jean had also scolded herself for behaving childishly and rudely. Whatever she decided to do about baptism, she owed Bishop Williamson an apology. He might have had something to say that could have helped her—if she had listened.

She parked at the end of the *Rum Runner*'s pier and watched the durable old cabin cruiser rise and fall slowly on the rolling swells. Jean searched in her purse for the cabin key that Ken had given her. Then, when she had found it, she put it away again. There were no answers down there on the boat. Ken wasn't there.

She sighed. Her quick temper—the temper she had inherited from her mother—and pride had gotten the better of her in the bishop's office. The scene she had created indicated that she still had many things to learn about living the way the Savior taught. Ken could help her learn about daily repentance—if he still had a mind to teach her . . . if he hadn't turned his attention to someone else by now.

Jean wished they could have talked more about marriage. Never once had he mentioned waiting.

Ken, she thought, where are you when I need you? Do I have to choose between your dream and my family? If I choose the church, will you still wait a year for me? Or is there some Mormon woman out there for you who's already a member? Maybe someone in Houston . . . right now?

Somehow her prayer for an answer about the church came to mind. She had asked for a witness of the truth, regardless of what it might mean for her and Ken. And the witness had come. Now, there was a decision to face, on her own, one that she couldn't walk away from—Ken, or no Ken.

Jean went home to bed and cried.

Allison juggled the portable mixer with one hand while she reached for the telephone with the other. "Hello?"

"Allie, this is Ken."

She said nothing as she turned off the beater and carefully laid it aside.

"This is Ken McArthur," he said.

"I know who it is. I recognized your voice."

"Oh. Well, I . . . uh . . . called to see how things are going with Jean."

"Ken, you . . . you *dumbo!* You've left my sister wondering for six weeks if you care about her at all. Why don't you call *her* and ask her how she's doing?"

"Give me a break, Allie! Before I left, she let me know that she didn't think our relationship was going anywhere. Did she tell you about that?"

"A little bit. But if you really care about her, why did you give up so easily?"

"I guess I've been wondering the same thing. I've been trying to leave her alone because I thought that's what she wanted. But I can't get her out of my mind. I called you because I need to know . . . how she is."

"If you need to know how she is, why haven't you answered her calls?"

There was a long pause. "You mean those were for real?"

"She left several messages for you, with that German writer."

Ken groaned. "Klaus is a joker, so I didn't believe him. Every day he tried to put one over on me. In Fredericksburg, he set me up with a family who owned a German restaurant. He told me they were heirs to the king of Prussia. After I spent two hours shooting pictures of them, he told me it was all a big joke"—Ken affected a German accent—" 'one of your Texas tall tales.' So when he asked about Jean's picture in my wallet and then told me she had called, I didn't believe him."

Allison hesitated, then said, "She's been missing you."

"I've missed her too." He paused. "Allie, has she been going out with . . . I mean, do I still have a chance with her?"

Allison smiled to herself. This was the real reason he had called. She wasn't going to let him off too easily. "I'm not sure. I think you might have a chance."

"Really? Because I have to make a decision that might affect her later . . . maybe."

"Hmmm." She smiled to herself again. "What kind of decision?"

He hesitated. "I think it's something I ought to share with Jean first."

"Okay. But when are you going to talk to her? You could call her here tonight, after eight-thirty. She's coming over for a late supper."

He hesitated again. "I can't. I have a photo shoot tonight and again early tomorrow morning. Friday and Saturday were the only times these jobs could be done. Allie, are you going to tell her I called?"

"Listen, I've had to watch her for six weeks while she's been wondering what happened to you. Of course I'm going to tell her you called. "

"Allie, your sister deserves better than I've given. I promise to start working on that as soon as I get back."

"You can start by calling her. Do you know when you're coming back?"

"By Monday night, at least. But I'll contact Jean before then if I can. I promise."

By late Saturday afternoon, all of his business was finished. Ken felt jubilant. He could be in Corpus Christi by ten. He wondered if he dared stop at the Bradleys unannounced, especially that late.

He was somewhere near midtown Houston on the freeway when a persistent, nagging thought surfaced again. He had been trying to suppress it for four days, but it was too strong this time. He still had unfinished business in Houston, business that had been unfinished for years.

Ken pulled off the freeway and parked on a side street while he struggled with the idea. He had realized earlier, as he looked back on his mistakes with Jean, that he needed to learn to love people without putting strings on his approval. He knew that he had to start with his father.

The woman who answered the door when he knocked was good-looking, probably in her late thirties. She wore a wedding ring on her left hand. Ken was ashamed that he did not know that his father had remarried. He and his father had spoken only briefly, about his grandfather's estate, at the funeral last year. Ken had not bothered to ask how his father's life was going.

"Is Alan McArthur at home?" he asked the woman.

"May I tell him who's here?" the woman asked politely.

"Ken McArthur—his son."

She looked him over, then smiled. "Yes, of course. The last pictures he has of you are old." She opened the door wider. "I'm Lila. Please come in. I know Alan will be glad to see you."

His father was surprised and unusally cordial. "Lila's just fixing supper," he said after greeting Ken warmly. "Stay and eat with us. We can talk."

Lila retreated to the kitchen. Alan McArthur led the way

to his small office, sat down in the swivel chair behind the desk, and motioned Ken to a seat opposite him.

"I'm, uh, embarrassed that I didn't know about Lila," Ken said.

"Mmm. Wonderful woman. I guess I should have told you when we got married. Couple of years ago. You'll like her. She's not like some of the women I used to go with."

Ken nodded, although he really wasn't sure what the women his father used to go with had been like. He had refused to know any of them because they were not his mother.

Alan pulled a blue envelope from a stack of correspondence and tossed it across the desk to Ken. "Tell me about this woman," he said.

The handwriting was unmistakably Jean's, and the letter was dated four weeks earlier. The message was short:

Dear Mr. McArthur,

Your son, Ken, has been an important part of my life over the past several months, but he has been out of town on a work assignment for two weeks, and I cannot locate him. If Ken contacts you, will you please let him know that I need to talk with him? Thanks for your help.

Yours truly,
Jean Bradley

His father looked at him expectantly. "There's a lot between the lines here."

Ken told him a bit about Jean and explained that they had parted angrily after a disagreement. But he didn't explain the reason.

Alan McArthur looked at his son expressionlessly for several seconds. Then, slowly, he leaned forward, forearms on the desk, continuing to look Ken in the eyes. "If you love her, don't let little things keep you apart from a good woman. Don't make the same mistake I did."

It was as close as Ken had ever heard his father come to admitting that he had made a mistake in his relationship with Ken's mother.

Lila called them to dinner after a few minutes. Ken's father was right; she was a delightful person. Alan seemed devoted to her. The three of them talked long after dinner was over. Lila told him how Alan and she had met, and Alan asked about Ken's work, about his Marine experiences, about his plans for the future. Ken was surprised at his interest.

Alan McArthur pontificated on some subjects, in the manner Ken had come to expect when he was younger, and several times Alan interrupted Ken to tell his son what he should have done or what he should plan to do in a particular situation. Obviously he had no more regard for his twenty-six-year-old son's agency than he had had for a sixteen-year-old's.

And yet, his father's comments didn't stir the old hot spot of anger and rebellion. Ken refused to let it happen. For the first time, it occurred to him that comments like these might actually be a sign of concern, a way his father had of showing that he cared.

Nothing really significant passed between him and his father while he was there, but something had changed. Ken's heart felt free in a way it hadn't in years.

He was thinking about that when he passed up the last Houston exit on the freeway. Well, maybe he could find an inexpensive motel room down the road in Rosenberg. He glanced at his watch; it was past ten.

Lila had commented on the fact that Ken looked and sounded like his father. It was true—and the implications were a bit frightening. Listening to him tonight, Ken had realized that some of his father's habits had affected his own thinking more than he had ever wanted to admit.

Like his father, he could be rigid in his thinking sometimes, unable to see other viewpoints well. His dream of the mountain trail in Honduras came to mind once more. He tried to imagine himself reaching out to Jean, reaching . . . Okay, it was true that he had continued trying to offer her the gospel, but he had failed to see what Jean was trying to offer him.

The night she had talked to him about Carla and Dave Warren's marriage was an example. If he had been listening closely, he would have understood that Jean was offering what she hoped was an acceptable compromise on religion. But he had refused her rather bluntly. And on the night he left town, when she had offered to leave her own faith to please him, he had pushed his all-or-nothing viewpoint at her again when he should have—what? Well, at least he could have let her know how much he loved her for what she was.

He knew he wasn't good at sharing his feelings. But worse, maybe he hadn't been very good at listening when she shared hers. He had been careful to treat Jean outwardly like the marvelous person she was, complimenting her and building her up. But in his heart had he always given her the same consideration? Ken winced as he remembered his father's blunt pronouncements on things his son ought to do, and then his own blunt advice to Jean on how she needed to reshape her thoughts.

What would he do differently if he had another chance with Jean? To begin with, he could be more tolerant of her views, and her family's. Other things would probably come to him as he thought about it.

But no matter how much he might improve his relationship with Jean, would he marry her if they couldn't marry in the temple? How much strength would he need to live with someone he loved so much, knowing that the marriage would not endure?

He was still thinking about that when he came to the Rosenberg turnoff. Ken passed it up and kept on heading southwest, skirting the gulf, toward Corpus Christi.

13

Good-bye to the *Rum Runner*

Ken was knotting his tie when he heard footsteps in the stern of the boat. He peered out of the cabin door.

It was Jean. She made the simple pastel cotton dress she was wearing look elegant. The midday sun falling on her hair framed her face in gold, and when she stepped under the canopy of the boat, she seemed to bring the light in with her.

"Hi," she said. "Ready to go to church?"

Ken stood still, hands frozen on his tie, looking up the stairway at her.

"Well?"

"Yes," he said, willing his hands to work. "I had forgotten how beautiful you are in person."

"Stay around, and you'll be able to remember what I look like," she said lightly.

He gathered up his coat from the bunk and ascended the stairs. She slipped her hand into his as he stepped up into the stern.

"Are you sure you want to go to my church?" he asked.

"Of course. I've gone for the past three weeks. Last week, Carla let me help in the nursery."

"She *let* you help?"

"Yes," Jean said, looking at him strangely. "What's wrong with that?"

"Nothing. Well . . . a lot of women don't think of it as an opportunity."

"I enjoyed it."

When they were on the jetty, she handed him the keys to her car. He opened the passenger door, and lingered for a moment, looking at her, after she was settled in her seat.

Neither of them spoke as he drove off the T-head and out into the traffic. Then Jean broke the silence. "Allie said you called her Friday night."

Ken glanced sideways at her. "Yeah. I . . . uh . . . I was just wondering how you were doing—you know, what was going on in your life."

"You could have called *me*," Jean said.

"Allie told me that too. She has a very plain way of putting things." He shook his head.

Jean smiled briefly. She could imagine what Allison might have said to him. Allison had not been able to tell her anything about Ken's plans, except to say that she was sure Jean would be hearing from him within the next few days.

"I'm sorry I never answered your calls. Did Allie tell you why?"

"Yes."

"I didn't try to call you because I thought you might not want to hear from me . . . after our last date." He frowned slightly. "I was afraid you'd be too busy going out with other guys."

"I tried it a couple of times right after you left," she said flatly. "It was no good, so I quit."

He glanced sideways at her. The corner of her eye glistened, and he suddenly found himself on the verge of tears. "What I just said was pretty lame, wasn't it?"

"Yes."

"I was dying to call you, Jean—but I was afraid of what I might find out. I did try one Friday night from a motel in Amarillo. It was late, and you didn't answer, so I was sure you were out with someone."

"That *was* you! You hung up three seconds too soon. I sat by the phone for half an hour hoping you'd try again."

"Klaus saw your picture one day and asked if you were my wife. I told him no, you were someone who used to love me. He asked me why I was still carrying your picture if I thought you didn't love me anymore." Ken swallowed hard, then cleared his throat before going on. His knuckles were turning a bloodless white where he was gripping the steering wheel.

"You were on my mind constantly." He exhaled slowly and loosened his grip on the steering wheel. "Every time I thought that you were . . . maybe with somebody else . . . I ached."

"I was aching too," Jean murmured, scarcely audible.

Ken took his foot off the accelerator and let the car roll till it was coasting slowly beside the road. Then he stopped it, turned off the engine, and sat staring straight ahead. "I've handled things badly, haven't I?"

"Don't be so noble. We both did, really."

He turned to face her. "The worst part is that I hurt you. That's the last thing in the world I wanted to do."

"It's okay," she answered, smiling slightly.

"No, it's not." He put his arm around her shoulders and gently pulled her toward him. She moved to meet him. Their kiss was tentative—but only for the first second or so.

He broke it off finally and gazed at her. "Can I make it up to you?"

"Like that? Let's see, you were gone for six weeks, so it should take about—"

He kissed her again, longer. It ended when they were interrupted by a tapping on the driver's window. Ken turned to see brass buttons and a badge on a uniform shirt. He rolled down the window.

The face of a policeman wearing mirrored sunglasses came down to Ken's level. "This lane is for emergency stopping only, sir. Do you have an emergency here?"

"Well, ah—maybe . . . in a way." The expression on the officer's face didn't change. Ken heard Jean stifling a giggle. "No, sir," he said, reaching for the ignition key.

He glanced at his watch as they drove toward the meetinghouse. "We'll have to hurry."

"Ken, I need to talk to you—about the church," Jean said. "There's something I need to tell you, and I have some questions you can help me with."

She sounded . . . what? Concerned? He glanced warily at her. "Okay. There are some important things I need to talk to you about too. But they'll take some time. Shall we talk right now?"

"No . . . I suppose it can wait until after church." She smiled and reached to take hold of his arm. "But I want you to spend the rest of the day with me. Promise?"

"Sure. How's your calendar for the rest of the week?"

"Oh, I could squeeze you in once or twice—every day."

The congregation was already singing the opening hymn when Ken and Jean slipped into the chapel and sat down on the back bench. Ken held a hymnbook in front of them. After a few seconds, he stopped singing to enjoy listening to her. Jean looked at him inquiringly. He leaned over to whisper in her ear: "You'd make a great addition to the ward choir." She smiled and pointed to the bass line. He resumed singing.

After the opening prayer, Brother Sillsby, the first counselor in the bishopric, stepped to the pulpit. "We have no ward business today," he announced, "except to welcome Sister Jean Ann Bradley as a member of the church. Sister Bradley was baptized and confirmed Friday night. Sister Bradley, would you stand, please, so that everyone will know who you are?"

Ken gaped at her as she stood. When she sat down, she whispered, "Close your mouth, silly. People are staring at you." Then she took his hand and held it between hers.

For the first time, as the sacrament trays came, Jean took the bread and water proffered by the deacon.

Afterward, Ken did not let her hand free from his for the rest of the meeting. The testimonies that were borne went past him. He was thinking back on all the discussions about religion that had ended in wrangling between him and Jean. She had been so adamant about her beliefs before he went away. What could possibly have changed them? He was stunned. As soon as the closing prayer ended, he turned to her.

"You said . . . questions . . . How did this happen?"

"Well, I just went down into the water, and—"

"Jean! I'm so happy for you!" Gretchen Wilde, the young lead from the cast of the musical, nearly fell into Ken's lap as she wrapped her arms tightly around Jean's neck and hugged her. Gretchen was followed by Sandi Williamson and two more members of the cast. Ken stood by as Jean accepted their good wishes and complimented them on their performances a few nights earlier. She eased the group out of the chapel, drawing Ken along by the hand. In the foyer, they were met by Irene Steiner, Carla Warren, and others who wanted to welcome her into the church.

"I was going to tell you in the car, but there was too much to tell and not enough time," Jean whispered to Ken when she could. "I guess we'll have to wait till after the meetings."

Even after Relief Society and priesthood, there were more

well-wishers in the foyer. But finally Ken and Jean stepped out into the early September sunshine. He grabbed her in an exuberant bear hug and swung her in circles on the sidewalk. "Now, tell me about it," he demanded as he put her down.

She took his hand and drew him toward her car. "I'll tell you on the way. Mom and Dad are expecting us for dinner. Jay and Allie are coming too. I told them I was going to find you today and drag you back home."

"How did you know I'd be down there on the boat this morning?"

"I didn't—for sure. I just felt . . . and hoped. You can't imagine what my heart did when I saw your Blazer."

"Probably the same thing mine did when I looked out the cabin door and saw you."

As they pulled away from the meetinghouse, he waited for her to speak.

"Ken, there's still so much I need to know about being a Mormon. I'll have to study a lot and work at it, won't I?"

The reply sounded vaguely like her intellectual approach to the gospel again. Ken tried to shut out doubt about her change of heart toward the church. He wanted to accept it unreservedly, as a blessing in both of their lives. Still, he remembered the night she had offered to be baptized for the sake of their relationship.

"I'll help you all I can, Jean," he said slowly. "But there's only so much that study can do."

Frowning, she turned in the seat so she could scrutinize his face. "That was a very carefully worded answer. You're wondering if I did this just for you, aren't you?"

"Did what?"

"You know what I mean—got baptized. And the answer is no. I did it for me. When I made the commitment to be baptized last week, I still didn't know if our relationship was over. But I had to do it, because I found out for myself, just the way you told me, that it was the right thing to do."

There was no hardness in her voice; there was a serenity Ken had never heard before when they had discussed religion. He glanced at her uncertainly. He could see the familiar, firm line in her jaw that meant she was sure of her decision. "Jean, I— okay, I admit I'm surprised. Shocked would be a better word. The last time we talked about religion— "

She laughed. "I was pretty hard on you." She reached out to stroke the back of his neck softly as he drove. "I hurt you too, didn't I? I'm sorry, Ken. Forgive me?"

"Sure. But tell me what happened after I left."

"I owe this partly to Jay. He helped me see that I needed to judge the church for itself. I wasn't able to do that while you were here—while my feelings about the church were all wrapped up with how I felt about you."

"Maybe I should have gone away sooner."

"Just don't do it again!" She held his arm tightly. "Anyway, I did what you asked me to do. I spent a lot of time reading on the boat and thinking about all the things I had learned from you. I also had some interesting talks with Jack, about religion— and about you. He told me a lot about your past."

Ken grimaced. "I'll bet that was disappointing."

"Not really. I was impressed with the way you changed your life after you found the church. I thought, if reading the Book of Mormon had done that for you, maybe I ought to take it more seriously."

Jean gazed out the window past Ken, seeing nothing in particular, as he drove. "It was the Book of Mormon that did it for me too. When I was somewhere in the middle of the book of Alma, I think I began to understand something you tried to teach me. I always thought I had strong faith; if I only believed, God would bless me. And he did. But my faith was passive. While I was reading, I began to see that I could go out and do something with it, work with it, and it would grow, and I would grow."

"Like you did when you helped Vonnie years ago?"

"Yes, I guess so. I didn't understand it back then. But when I read that in the book, I saw that it could be true for me, or for anyone. After that, I began to pay more attention."

She told him about the joy she felt when she read of the resurrected Savior's appearance among the Nephites. She told him about being so touched that she cried after reading about the Savior's blessing of the Nephite children. And she told him about her struggle to receive an answer to her prayers.

"Then, when I finally needed to know for *myself,* not you, more than I've ever needed anything else in my life—" Her voice broke.

He parked the car in her parents' driveway and turned to look at her. He touched her cheek lightly.

"Anyway," she said, wiping at her eyes, "it happened the way you said—the light inside of me, in my heart, and everywhere else. I was crying, just like today. But I was so happy I didn't know how to say it."

He handed her his handkerchief. She dabbed at her eyes. "Does this happen all the time when you talk about it?"

"No—but sometimes," he answered. "Well, more than sometimes."

"Ken, I felt like the Lord was actually happy that I finally wanted to know the truth for myself. And the knowing was so *strong*. It just came again while I was telling you about it." She looked at him pleadingly. "I know I did the right thing. But I still don't know how to explain it to people—to my mother. And it scares me when I see how much I still have to learn. Please, help me!"

He stroked her cheek lightly. "Of course, Jean, all I can.

But I still have a lot to learn too. Sometimes I think the learning will take more than a lifetime."

"Well, after what I felt, I'll do whatever it takes."

Ken glanced toward her house. "How did your father feel?"

"He sided with Mom—mostly out of loyalty, I think. But he wouldn't try to stop me from being baptized when she wanted him to. Daddy told her I had to be responsible for my own life. They didn't come to my baptism, but Jay and Allie did, so at least there was some family support."

Jean opened her purse and searched for her compact. "I'd better fix my makeup before we go in."

"How bad will it be in there?" he asked, grinning. "If your mother goes for the carving knife, is it the ham on her mind, or something else?"

"Don't worry," she said, squeezing his hand. "I'll protect you."

Jay and Allison greeted him warmly. Richard was cordial. Carol was civil. The only awkward moments came during dinner. Carol had provided a carafe of ice water on the table for Ken and Jean. But Richard was nonplussed and Carol seemed irritated when Jay also declined the wine. Then, Carol mentioned pointedly how unhappy Jean had been because Ken had not called or written. "You must have been *very* busy," she added.

"He was traveling constantly, Mother," Jean replied. "And they had to work early and late." Carol seemed surprised by her daughter's quick defense of Ken after having been ignored by him for a month and a half. But Allison suppressed a smile.

At Richard's invitation, Ken told them about some of his experiences. He had spent one night camping out by the Rio Grande in the Big Bend country in order to get the morning light just right for a photo. He shot photographs from helicopters over Dallas and Houston. There had been an all-night vigil watching for the elusive ghost lights in the Big Thicket area of

East Texas. But he had been glad to be done with it all. "I wanted to get back here as soon as possible," he said, squeezing Jean's hand.

Allison smiled. Jay smiled. Richard smiled. Carol looked down at her plate.

When dinner was over, Carol began to clear the table. She ended up at Ken's place with the stack of plates.

"Carol, can I help with those?" Ken asked.

"All right. If you'll take them to the kitchen, I'll gather up the goblets."

Ken maneuvered through the swinging door to the kitchen with the china, placed the stack of plates on the countertop, and turned to leave as Carol entered.

"Ken—wait a minute, please?"

"Yes?"

Carol put the goblets on the counter carefully one by one. Then she looked up at him. "You won, after all. I just hope that what you've got my daughter into isn't going to hurt her in the long run."

"If there's a winner here, Carol, it's Jean. Watch her. As good as she is now, she'll be a better person in a year."

"I hope you're right. For Jean's sake." Carol turned to go.

"Carol?"

"Yes?"

"I thought the two of us were friends once—before your daughter and I fell in love. You and Richard are two of the finest people I know, and I respect you. Do you think we could be friends again?"

"Yes . . . yes, I'd like that." She smiled slightly. "I have a feeling I'd better get used to it."

Her smile faded, and she stared past Ken, out the window of the dining nook. "I can't pretend I'm happy about what Jean has done. But there are worse things that could have happened to my daughter. I was complaining one night about how wicked you are, pulling her away from the things her parents have taught her. And Jay asked me, 'Carol, of all the men Jean has ever dated, which one do you think has been the best for her?' "

She looked Ken in the eyes. "He had me there. I have to admit you're a good man. And I like you." Then her eyes flashed with the fire he had seen many times before. "But I can't help believing you're wrong. I hope someday you'll see it. In the meantime, I don't want you preaching to me—or to the rest of my family."

"Carol, I'll do what you ask about that, as long as I'm in your house. But I can't promise not to share what I know—with anyone who's interested."

Jean pushed her way through the door, carrying a load of silverware. "It seemed as though the two of you were taking a long time to stack the dishes in here. I thought I could help."

"*Did* you?" Carol asked. She smiled knowingly. "Don't worry, Jean. I'm not being *too* hard on him."

Ken smiled too. "We were just having another of our little chats about you and me, and religion." He looked at Carol. "Your mother and I are friends again—I think."

"We are," Carol replied, "as long as I don't have to listen to you talk about your church." She glanced at Jean. "Either of you."

Jean was surprised by her mother's pointed response. But Ken was equal to its note of challenge. His expression was solemn enough as he replied, "I promise, Carol." But Jean recognized the playful smile teasing at the corners of his mouth as he added, "Of course, I'll be glad to answer your questions about it anytime."

"Don't hold your breath!" Carol slipped past Jean and pushed her way out of the kitchen. Jean watched her mother go. Then she smiled at Ken. "Haven't you learned yet to be careful when you're matching wits with the Bradley women?"

"I hope to have plenty of time to get onto it."

Back in the dining room, Jean said their good-byes. "We're going for a ride," she explained, taking Ken's arm and steering him toward the door.

"Stick around," Richard replied, winking in their direction. "You're about to see what a black belt can do with a dishwasher and a load of dishes."

"Let them go, Daddy," Allison said. "Can't you see they've got a lot to catch up on?"

Ken and Jean had reached the front door when Richard called out, "Ken?" They turned to see him standing in the dining room doorway. "I haven't seen my daughter this happy in weeks. Welcome back."

Ken drove slowly up Ocean Drive toward the T-heads. Jean sat half turned in her seat, studying his profile. She thought of all the times she had wanted to see him and she couldn't. "Tell me about your visit in Houston," she said as they neared the downtown waterfront.

"Well, I would have been back last night, but I didn't feel good about leaving until I had gone to see my father. We made peace—I think." Ken frowned momentarily. "No, that's not true. *I* made peace, with my feelings about him."

"You don't hate him anymore?"

"No. I think I really lost the hate a long time ago. I believe I've been afraid of the feelings he brought out in me. But I found out yesterday that I don't have to let them be there." He thought for a moment. "It was strange; in a way, I felt as if he's proud of me—but he can't tell me that." Ken looked at her. "He showed me your letter and wanted to know about you. He'd like to meet you sometime."

The *Rum Runner* bobbed gently at its moorings as Ken parked on the T-head. Ken and Jean walked down the pier, stepped into the stern of the boat, and stood looking at the city, his arm around her shoulders.

"How did you do at marketing your photos in Houston?" she asked.

"A lot better than I expected. That's something I need to talk to you about." He took a deep breath and let it out slowly. "There's a hot new design-and-illustration group up there that's doing really well. They have their own photo studio, and they offered me a job. I took it. I have to start at the first of the month."

Startled, Jean took a step away from him so she could look him in the face. "October first?"

"They need to take on another photographer right away, and the man in charge of their studio liked my work. He had me shoot with him for a day on a couple of assignments, then he took me to the boss and said, 'Let's hire this man.' They wanted an answer Friday afternoon. After I talked to Allie, and she said maybe I hadn't blown my chance with you, I took the job. I thought it could be important to us."

Jean thought for a moment. "Is this a good opportunity for you?"

"Yes. Their photographer can teach me what I need to know about studio work, and there'll be plenty of chances to do the kind of location shooting I like. They'll even arrange my schedule so I can take design and photography classes at the university. The pay is only fair to start, but there'll be a raise in six months if I work out well for them."

She wrinkled her brow. "I'm afraid I won't see much of you. You'll be terribly tied down there, won't you?"

"Probably. It will be tough to work and take classes at the same time. If I'm careful, the rest of the money my grandfather left me will just about pay for the schooling I need. That way, my paycheck can go for living expenses."

Jean hugged her arms to herself. She was looking down at the deck, watching the toe of her shoe trace the grain pattern in one of the planks. Her lips were a thin line.

Ken raised the subject that had been on both of their minds for most of the day. "I told you once that I couldn't ask anyone to marry me until I had a future to offer. It'll be a while—"

"Sounds like it might be a long while—maybe years. Money will be pretty tight while you're in school, won't it?" Her toe continued its movement on the deck.

"Well, yes . . . sure. But life won't be impossible. The money I'll get from the magazine assignment could help us with some things. And I put a down payment on a two-bedroom mobile home yesterday, before I left Houston." Jean raised her eyes and looked at him intently. "I think two people could make it on my salary," Ken continued, "if we—"

"Yes."

"What?"

"I said yes. You're really asking me, aren't you? I just wanted to let you know how I felt . . . if you were."

"I'm asking," Ken said, reaching out to her.

He was unprepared for her bear hug, pinning his arms to his sides. The two of them almost toppled over the side before he could steady himself on one of the stern seats. "That's one of the things I've always liked about you—enthusiasm," he said, his voice muffled by her hair.

"I just wanted to get a word in before you had a chance to talk yourself out of the idea," she answered, letting him go.

"Hmm. I was trying to say I feel like I have a future to offer you, but it may be a while before we live in the kind of place you're used to. Didn't say it very well, did I?" He knelt on one knee. "Miss Bradley, will you—"

She bent to kiss him on the forehead. "Get up, Mr. Mc-

Arthur. We're already past that part. You know the answer—and I don't care where I live, if it's with you."

As he stood up, Ken reached into his jacket and withdrew an envelope. He opened it, took out a ring, and slipped it on her finger.

She studied the ring. The diamond was large, but the setting was conservative, elegant in its simplicity. "I love it," she said, smiling at him. "You made a good choice."

"I made a good choice of the woman to wear it, but give Jack the credit for the ring. He left it in the safe for me to find last night."

She admired the ring again, turning it so she could see it better in the fading twilight. "I'm sure it's top quality, knowing Jack. But is this a good idea right now, Ken? . . . I mean, on a tight budget?"

"Don't worry about my finances, Jean; everything will work out. I forgot to tell you about the boat. Jack is paying me far more than it's worth. And the ring—"

"You're not selling the boat?" she asked. "You're not selling the boat!" She slipped the ring off her finger and held it out to him in her palm. "You can't sell the *Rum Runner*. I can do without a ring until you can afford it some other way."

"Jean, listen to me before you get your pretty jaw set." He took her hand in his and closed her fingers around the ring. "This is the right time in my life for me to sell—"

"But the boat means so much to you," she protested. "It's your legacy from your grandfather."

"He left me more important legacies—things I can't put my hands on. I think he knew I'd have to outgrow the boat someday. Who else do you think he would want to have it?"

She thought it over. "Well, I know it would mean a lot to Jack." She opened her hand slowly. "But the ring?"

"I started to tell you that there's no need to worry about the cost. It's Jack's gift to you." Ken opened the envelope that had held the ring, took out a piece of embossed stationery, and handed it to Jean. She turned it toward the street light on the jetty so she could read Jack's note:

Kenneth,

In my business, I've learned never to pass up a flawless gem. If you don't give this to your Jean, with my compliments, and ask her to marry you, you'll be making the mistake of a lifetime.

Jack

Jean looked up. "That sweet old man."

Ken took the ring and slipped it back on her finger. She touched the band, then looked up at him. "You've been carrying this around in your pocket all day—even before you knew I had been baptized. Were you going to give it to me anyway?"

His expression was half smile, half puzzlement. "I can't answer that, Jean. I mean, I don't know. I argued with myself all the way home last night. Part of me was saying, 'Remember, eternal family,' and another part was saying, 'You can't live without her. Ask her to marry you and love her into the church.' Then I'd think of our arguments when you were learning about the church. And then I'd think of how hard I'd pushed you to see things my way, and how often I let you know that your ideas were wrong. . . . And I wondered if things would work better if I let you know that I loved you just the way you were.

"I still don't know what I would have done today . . . about the ring. But I decided that I could never give you up, unless you didn't care about me anymore. I was going to find you and tell you that."

She put her hands behind his neck and pulled him down so she could kiss him. When she let him go, he held her at arm's length, his hands on her shoulders. "So—how soon?"

She studied his face as she answered. "September second."

"September second. . . . That was last week!"

"One year from last Friday—or as close to it as we can get. That's the soonest I would be able to go to the temple with you."

"The temple . . . " He sat down heavily on the bench behind him. "Oh—yes . . . *Next* September."

Jean sat down beside him. "Isn't that what you wanted, Ken? The temple?"

The Man in the Iron Mask was there in his face, just for a moment, then disappeared. Ken sighed. "I was so eager to get you into the church that I forgot it would be a year before you could go to the temple. I haven't had any experience with weddings in the church. . . . You know, my family weren't . . . anyway . . . so I just . . . I was thinking maybe a couple of months."

Jean hadn't seen him dejected very often, but he clearly was now. "We don't have to wait, Ken," she said softly, taking his hand. "The bishop told me he would marry us right away if we wanted. Then we could be sealed in a year." She gazed at the distant lights across the bay. "But I know what being married in the temple means to you. And now it's pretty important to me too."

Ken looked at her thoughtfully. "You talked with the bishop? There's more to this, isn't there, Jean?"

"Yes." She glanced down at the ring. "I couldn't explain it all to you . . . before." She recounted her interview with the bishop: his questions about their marriage plans, his counsel, her angry exit, and her wavering about baptism.

"What made you decide to go ahead?"

"I knew in my heart what was right. But I was upset because this seemed like another barrier in our way, and I was afraid of losing you because you had never said anything about waiting. That night I woke up around midnight, and I was just lying there missing you horribly, when this quiet little voice somewhere in my mind said, 'If you had to wait a year for him, would you do it?' " She squeezed his hand. "I knew I'd wait for you as long as it took. And then the little voice asked, 'Do you think he'd wait for you?' And I . . . hoped you would."

"Of course I would." He took her right hand and held it.

"Anyway, I got out of bed and knelt down and said thanks to the Lord for helping me see things that way. I had the strong feeling again that he loves me very much and that if I would go ahead, whatever happened would be the best thing for me. So I called the bishop back the next morning and told him I still wanted to be baptized." She smiled wryly. "You've never heard me so humble."

"Did the bishop tell you anything else?"

"He told me that if we're going to wait a year, we'll have to be very, very careful about temptation." She looked him in the eyes. "Can we do that?"

He was silent for a moment. "Jean, everything about you attracts me. But yes, for you—for us—I can do that."

She sighed. "I can too. To tell the truth, I've been wanting for weeks—for months, I think—to live with you as your wife, not just so we can share our nights, but so we can share all our days. I can wait, though."

He pulled her closer, and they sat silently for several minutes looking out over the bay. Finally Ken spoke. "I was just thinking about your parents. I don't believe they're going to understand why we want to be married in the temple—or why they can't come."

"I know." She blinked back some tears. "Mom wasn't speaking to me yesterday because I went ahead with the baptism; I'm not sure my relationship with her will ever be quite the same again anyway. And Daddy—well, I hope Daddy won't be hurt. He was so proud when Allie got married, walking her down the aisle on his arm . . . " She clutched Ken's arm and said nothing for several seconds. He could feel the tension in her.

"I love Mom and Dad very much, Ken. I don't want to hurt them in any way. But this has to be *our* decision—between you and me—doesn't it?" She looked down at her left hand and spread her fingers apart so the ring stood out. "Now that I understand what temple marriage can mean, I want that with you more than anything else. I just hope Mom and Dad love me enough to try to understand."

"I can see that I didn't give this enough thought, Jean."

"What?"

"The sacrifice that you'd have to make—cutting your family almost completely out of it. I just hadn't realized what you probably thought I was asking you to do for me."

"Not just for you. For us."

"And you're strong enough to do it." He was silent for a time, gazing out at the water. Then: "I can't do that. *We* can't do that."

"Do what?"

"Shut your family out." He looked at her. "I don't want our love for each other to put a wall between you and your parents. I told you once that you're blessed to have a family like yours. We should do everything we can to keep close to them."

"What are you saying, Ken?"

"I think we should get married here and make it a family affair, as much as we can."

"But what about the temple?"

"We'll keep that date—next September second. I'll schedule it as soon as possible. It will be our main goal."

"Ken, I know how long you've planned to be married in the temple. You'd do this for me?"

"For you. And for all of us. We'll be keeping your family ties strong. And we won't be giving up the dream. But I think the two of us can make more progress together in a year than we would apart." He thought for a moment. "Jean, I'm trying to be sure I'm not saying this just because I don't want to wait. Things would probably be different for two different people. But this feels right to me. What do you think?"

"I think . . . " She leaned her head against his chest, and her voice was muffled. "I think I love you more than you could possibly know." He felt wetness on his shirt, and then her body shook with wracking sobs.

"Jean, what's wrong?" Ken held her tightly and stroked her hair.

She couldn't answer. Finally her body stopped heaving, and her sobs subsided into sniffles. "Tension," she murmured. "Too much tension, I think. Don't let go of me, Ken—please!" She put her arms around his chest. "I've been worrying so much . . . first, about whether you'd come back to me. . . . And if you did, would you wait a year to marry me? . . . And then Mom and Dad and Allie and Jay—how was I going to tell them that I was getting married, and they couldn't come?" She let go of him to wipe her eyes with the back of her hand. "Can I have your handkerchief again?"

"No."

She looked up at him questioningly.

"I'd have to let go of you to get it."

He still had his left arm around her. Jean slipped it off her shoulders and intertwined the fingers of her hand with his. "It's okay. I'll hold on to you," she said, managing a smile.

She dabbed at her eyes with the handkerchief he gave her. "I know my makeup's a wreck. And I've got it on your shirt. . . . And—anyway, I was worried about all those things. Thank you for being so understanding."

"I haven't been very good at that at all, Jean. But I'll try harder." He kissed her lightly on the cheek and smiled at her. "So, now—how soon?"

"September twenty-seventh."

"That's only three weeks!"

"And two days. But I'm not letting you move away to Houston without me. Do they allow fancy weddings in the ward building?"

"No, I don't think so. The ones I've seen haven't been like that."

"Well, if it's only a reception, my mother can pull it off. Give her three weeks, and she can organize anything."

Ken chuckled. "All she'd have to do is ask Irene Steiner, and she'd have half the ward ready to help."

"Come on," Jean said, tugging at his arm as she stood.

"Where are we going?"

"Back to my house. I can't wait to share the news. First we'll tell Mom and Dad, and then we'll go see Allie and Jay. And Jack. Do you know where Jack lives? We have to tell him." She waved her left hand airily toward the downtown skyline. "And anyone else in town who wants to know. Maybe we could get a bulletin on the ten o'clock news."

She led him up the pier toward her car. When he stopped to open the door for her, she put her arms around him and hugged him tightly. Then she stepped back. "Ken, there's something else we need to talk about. I've never planned to give up working entirely if I got married; I've invested too much in my profession. And I could help us out right now. Is that all right with you?"

He nodded. "I thought that's what you'd want to do—at least until we have children."

"Right—until we have children. And then we'll decide together how I can be the kind of mommy I want to be." She leaned back against the car and held onto his hands. "So tomorrow I start checking on work in Houston."

"I, ah, know how you hate to have people meddle in your

life," Ken said. He looked serious. "I took a long-shot chance anyway and did some checking up there Friday—just in case this subject came up."

"And you found me a job already?" She put on a mock scowl. "You're in trouble, Mr. McArthur. But tell me about it anyway."

"Not a job, exactly. Two of the television stations expect to have openings in the next three months. And there's a video production company that's looking for a writer who might be able to handle some directing too."

"Mmm. That last one sounds interesting. It might fit in better with family life." She smiled. "I don't suppose you'd happen to have the names of the people to contact?"

Slowly, Ken smiled back. He pulled a piece of paper from his jacket pocket and handed it to her.

As they were driving down Ocean Drive toward her parents' home, he said, "Jean, what was it that made you worry about whether I'd wait to marry you?"

"I was wondering whether I'm really the right woman for you. I love you deeply, Ken. I owe you my life, in more ways than one. But you probably deserve someone better—more of a spiritual equal."

He turned his head quickly to look at her, startled. "What could possibly make you think *that?*"

"Becky Rollins."

"Becky? How do you know Becky?"

"She came to the nursery last week while I was there—something to do with her stake job. Carla introduced us and told her I had been going with you."

Ken frowned. "If Becky said anything to make you feel bad, I don't think she—"

"No, Ken, it was nothing like that. Becky's a wonderful, kind person. It's just that she scares me to death—she and some of those other strong women in the church who come from western pioneer families and quote Joseph Smith by heart. Maybe you ought to be married to someone like that."

Ken turned the car into Cole Park, a narrow strip of green lawn on the bluff overlooking the bay, and parked. He turned to face Jean. She stared down at her hands in her lap.

"Jean, let's put some things in perspective about the two of us." He gently lifted her chin with his fingers and turned her face toward him. "Look at me. Remember, this is the guy who was on probation ten years ago for picking up auto parts by moonlight."

Her eyes widened in surprise.

"Jack didn't tell you that part of the story?"

She shook her head.

"Well, I've come a long way since then. But I've still got a long way to go." He paused. "Do you remember hearing me talk about my years in seminary?"

"No, I don't. Did you?"

"No. I never had a chance to take it. As for *my* pioneer ancestry . . . " He laughed. "You were already better than me in so many ways before I met you. I have a lot to learn from you—if you can handle living with me while I do it." He took both her hands.

A lighted excursion boat traced a white wake on the dark water below the park. Overhead, a passenger jet banked inland toward the airport across the city. Ken watched it go. "This isn't some western valley in the 1840s, Jean, but in a way, we'll be pioneers. In our family, the history of the church begins with the two of us. I wouldn't want to start out with anyone else. Would you?"

Slowly she raised his right hand to her face and brushed it lightly with her lips. Then she smiled. "Roll the wagon, Heber. I'm ready."